Lewis Baxter Monroe

Young Folks' Readings, for Social and Public Entertainment

Lewis Baxter Monroe

Young Folks' Readings, for Social and Public Entertainment

ISBN/EAN: 9783744776899

Printed in Europe, USA, Canada, Australia, Japan

Cover: Foto ©Andreas Hilbeck / pixelio.de

More available books at **www.hansebooks.com**

Young Folks' Readings,

for

Social and Public Entertainment.

edited by

Lewis B. Monroe.

———

BOSTON:

LEE AND SHEPARD, PUBLISHERS.

NEW YORK:

CHARLES T. DILLINGHAM.

1877.

Electrotyped at the Boston Stereotype Foundry,
19 Spring Lane.

PREFACE.

THREE volumes of "Public and Parlor Readings" have already been given to the public, and have met a cordial reception. Now comes the demand for something adapted to younger minds. Accordingly this book has been prepared. The range of pieces it contains will be found suitable for young persons from ten to sixteen years of age. Yet, while there is little or nothing here which may not be fully appreciated by the "Young Folks," we feel confident that adults will derive equal pleasure from the use of the pieces in their public and private entertainments.

We are gratified to see on every hand indications that reading is more and more appreciated as a graceful and elegant accomplishment, and a source of enjoyment in the social circle and public assembly. It only needs that this growing taste should be properly cultivated to make the art of reading a powerful means of moral and esthetic culture, without losing a whit of its value as a delightful amusement. "To read well is to think well, to feel well, and to render well; it is to possess at once intellect, soul, and taste."

We hope that the specimens we have given will act as incentives to the young to go to the original sources, and cultivate a more intimate acquaintance with the gifted authors quoted.

A part of the pieces have been written or adapted especially for this book. Beyond this, our thanks are due to the various writers and publishers by whose kind permission the selections have been used. We are particularly indebted to J. T. Trowbridge, Esq., for valuable assistance. His "Vagabonds" and "Darius Green," given in the other volumes of this series, have enjoyed a popularity with readers and audiences only rivalled by Poe's "Raven" and "Bells." And we doubt not the pieces he has furnished for this volume — some of them prepared by him especially for the purpose — are also destined to become prime favorites.

CONTENTS.

CONTENTS.

CICELY AND THE BEARS.

I.

"O, YES! O, yes! O, yes! ding-dong!"
The bellman's voice is loud and strong,
So is his bell: "O, yes! ding-dong!"

He wears a coat with golden lace;
See how the people of the place
Come running to hear what the bellman says!

"O, yes! Sir Nicholas Hildebrand
Has just returned from the Holy Land,
And freely offers his heart and hand —

"O, yes! O, yes! O, yes! ding-dong!"
All the women hurry along,
Maids and widows, a clattering throng.

"O, sir, you are hard to understand!
To whom does he offer his heart and hand?
Explain your meaning, we do command!"

9

" O, yes ! ding-dong ! you shall understand !
O, yes ! Sir Nicholas Hildebrand
Invites the ladies of this land

" To feast with him, in his castle strong,
This very day at three.   Ding-dong !
O, yes ! O, yes ! O, yes ! ding-dong ! "

Then all the women went off to dress,
Mary, Margaret, Bridget, Bess,
Patty, and more than I can guess.

They powdered their hair with golden dust,
And bought new ribbons — they said they must —
But none of them painted, we will trust.

Long before the time arrives,
All the women that could be wives
Are dressed within an inch of their lives.

Meanwhile Sir Nicholas Hildebrand
Had brought with him from the Holy Land
A couple of bears — O, that was grand !

He tamed the bears, and they loved him true ;
Whatever he told them they would do —
Hark ! 'tis the town clock striking two !

II.

Among the maidens of low degree
The poorest of all was Cicely —
A shabbier girl could hardly be.

" O, I should like to see the feast,
But my frock is old, my shoes are pieced,
My hair is rough ! " — (It never was greased.)

The clock struck three !   She durst not go !
But she heard the band, and, to see the show,
Crept after the people that went in a row.

When Cicely came to the castle gate,
The porter exclaimed, " Miss Shaggypate,
The hall is full, and you come too late ! "

Just then the music made a din,
Flute, and cymbal, and culverin,
And Cicely, with a squeeze, got in.

O, what a sight !   Full fifty score
Of dames that Cicely knew, and more,
Filling the hall from dais to door !

The dresses were like a garden bed,
Green and gold, and blue and red —
Poor Cicely thought of her tossy head !

She heard the singing — she heard the clatter —
Clang of flagon and clink of platter —
But, O, the feast was no such matter !

For she saw Sir Nicholas himself,
Raised on a dais just like a shelf,
And fell in love with him — shabby elf !

Her heart beat quick ; aside she stepped ;
Under the tapestry she crept,
Tousling her tossy hair, and wept !

Her cheeks were wet, her eyes were red.
" Who makes that noise ? " the ladies said ;
" Turn out that girl with the shaggy head ! "

III.

Just then there was heard a double roar,
That shook the place, both wall and floor :
Everybody looked to the door.

It was a roar, it was a growl ;
The ladies set up a little howl,
And flapped and clucked like frightened fowl.

Sir Hildebrand for silence begs —
In walked the bears on their hinder legs,
Wise as owls, and merry as grigs !

The dark girls tore their hair of sable ;
The fair girls hid underneath the table ;
Some fainted ; to move they were not able.

But most of them could scream and screech —
Sir Nicholas Hildebrand made a speech —
" Order ! ladies, I do beseech !"

The bears looked hard at Cicely,
Because her hair hung wild and free —
" Related to us, miss, you must be !"

Then Cicely, filling two plates of gold
As full of cherries as they could hold,
Walked up to the bears, and spoke out bold : —

" Welcome to you ! and to *you*, Mr. Bear !
Will you take a chair ? will *you* take a chair ?
This is an honor, we do declare !" ·

Sir Hildebrand strode up to see,
Saying, " Who may this maiden be ?
Ladies, this is the wife for me !"

Almost before they could understand,
He took up Cicely by the hand,
And danced with her a saraband.

Her hair was rough as a parlor broom ;
It swung, it swirled all round the room —
Those ladies were vexed, we may presume.

Sir Nicholas kissed her on the face,
And set her beside him on the dais,
And made her the lady of the place.

The nuptials soon they did prepare,
With a silver comb for Cicely's hair :
There were bands of music everywhere.

And in that beautiful bridal show
Both the bears were seen to go
Upon their hind legs to and fro !

Now every year on the wedding day
The boys and girls come out to play,
And scramble for cherries as they may.

With a cheer for this and the other bear,
And a cheer for Sir Nicholas, free and fair,
And a cheer for Cis, of the tossy hair —

With one cheer more (if you will wait)
For every girl with a curly pate,
Who keeps her hair in a proper state.

Sing bear's grease ! curling-irons to sell !
Sing combs and brushes ! sing tortoise-shell !
O, yes ! ding-dong ! the crier, the bell !
Isn't this a pretty tale to tell ?

THE TEST OF SIGHT.

A CHINESE STORY.

TWO young, short-sighted fellows, Chang and Ching,
  Over their chop-sticks idly chattering,
Fell to disputing which could see the best.
At last they agreed to put it to the test.
Said Chang, "A marble tablet, so I hear,
Is placed upon the Bo-hee temple near,
With an inscription on it. Let us go
And read it (since you boast your optics so),
Standing together at a certain place
In front, where we the letters just may trace ;
Then he who quickest reads the inscription there,
The palm for keenest eyes henceforth shall bear."
"Agreed," said Ching ; " and let us try it soon :
Suppose we say to-morrow afternoon."
" Nay, not so soon," said Chang ; " I'm bound to go
To-morrow a day's ride from Ilo-hang-ho,
And shan't be ready till the following day.
At ten A. M., on Thursday, let us say."

So 'twas arranged. But Ching was wide awake ;
Time by the forelock he resolved to take,
And to the temple went at once, and read
Upon the tablet, " To the illustrious Dead,
The chief of Mandarins, the great Goh-bang."
Scarce had he gone, when stealthily came Chang,
Who read the same ; but, peering closer, he
Spied in a corner — what Ching failed to see —
The words, " This tablet is erected here
By those to whom the great Goh-bang was dear."

So, on the appointed day — both innocent
As babes, of course — these honest fellows went
And took their distant station.   And Ching said,
" I can read plainly ' To the illustrious Dead,
The chief of Mandarins, the great Goh-bang.' "
"And is that all that you can spell ? " said Chang.
" I see what you have read ; but furthermore,
In smaller letters, toward the temple-door,
Quite plain, ' This tablet is erected here
By those to whom the great Goh-bang was dear.' "

" My sharp-eyed friend, there are no such words," said
          Ching.
" They're there," said Chang, " if I see anything,
As clear as daylight."   " Patent eyes, indeed,
You have !" cried Ching. "Do you think I cannot
          read ? "
" Not at this distance, as I can," Chang said,
" If what you say you saw is all you read."

In fine, they quarrelled, and their wrath increased ;
Till Chang said, " Let us leave it to the priest.
Lo, here he comes to meet us."   " It is well "
Said honest Ching ; " no falsehood he will tell."

The good man heard their artless story through,
And said, " I think, dear sirs, there must be few
Blest with such wondrous eyes as those you wear.
There's no such tablet or inscription there.
There was one, it is true ; 'twas moved away
And placed *within* the temple yesterday."
                              C. P. CRANCH.

THAT TEN DOLLARS.

IT was odd, very odd; reckon it up this way or that way, or in whatever way I might, the result was just the same — I had ten dollars more than I could account for. I went over the whole quarter's receipts again, to see if something had not been omitted; but everything was quite right. " Ha! what's this? It looks like a scratching out; and yet it can't be, for I never use a penknife." So I held the leaf up to the light, and scanned it closely, and then, turning it over, scrutinized it again. " It certainly does look very much like an erasure ; but no, 'tis only a little roughness on the surface of the paper." I was completely puzzled. It was quite possible for me to have too little ; but to have ten dollars too much — I could not understand that at all. " Well," I said to myself, " it's better, at any rate, than having ten dollars too little." Still, the idea of there being a mistake somewhere made me feel very uncomfortable.

I had been busy preparing my accounts in order to present them to my employers in the morning, for the morrow was quarter-day, and I knew that in nothing could a clerk offend so much as by being wrong in his balance. So I thought a little, and then determined to consult Jackson, our managing clerk. I was young at the time — not more than twenty; and, having been in the establishment only a few months, I knew but little of his character. He was exceedingly attentive to business; but there were some vague floating rumors going the round of the place, which accredited him with anything but a steady life.

But he had always been very civil, and even kind, to me; and so, in my dilemma, I sought his advice. He went over my accounts with me, but could detect nothing wrong.

"Well, Watson," he said, "you are on the right side now, and if you take my advice, you will keep there. Just pocket the money, and say nothing about it."

Seeing that I demurred, he continued, —

"Of course you can do as you please; but I know this much, if you were that ten dollars short, you would have to make it up in quick time."

I was again about to make my objections to this mode of procedure, when I was cut short by a salesman, who came to say that Mr. Jackson was wanted in the sale-room. As he strode away, Jackson turned round, and said, —

"I'll see you about it again, Watson; in the mean time, you need not mention it to any one."

I saw no more of him till my labors were done for the day, and I was reaching my hat down from its peg, when he tapped me over the shoulder.

"One word, Watson, before you go: if ever it should be found out where the mistake lies, I will make it all right for you. Good night."

That night the ten dollars were ever before me. The last thing I remember, before falling asleep, was thinking of the ten dollars; I slept, and dreamed of ten dollars. In the morning, whilst at breakfast, I laid the whole affair before my mother, and asked her counsel.

"Give up the money, of course."

"But you see, mother, I am afraid it would offend

2

Jackson, he seems so much to wish me to hush
it up."

"Never mind Jackson; do what is right, and I am
sure it will be better for you in the end. Tell Mr.
Elliot"—the head partner—"how it is, and I am
certain he won't be angry."

I ate the remainder of my meal in silence; for,
whilst I did not wish to make an enemy of Jackson,
who could, if he pleased, make my situation very un-
pleasant, I had strong compunctions about keeping
the money. Breakfast was over, and, as I was leaving home, my mother took hold of my hand, and
said,—

"Promise me, Henry, before you go, that you will
give up the money."

I hesitated.

"Surely, Henry, you would not steal?"

"*Steal?* Never!" And I promised at once.

Jackson found no time to speak to me that morning,
being engaged with Mr. Elliot; but when, in my turn,
I entered the private office, I saw him cast an inquir-
ing glance towards me.

"This seems all right, Watson," said Mr. Elliot,
after looking over my account. "Have you anything
else?"

"Yes, sir; I have still ten dollars, of which I am
unable to give any account."

"Strange! Are you sure that you have missed
nothing?"

"Quite, sir; I have been over everything several
times, and last night Mr. Jackson was kind enough to
assist me."

"It's strange; but you can put the money back into

your safe. I dare say it will be found out before the next quarter is up. And by the by, Watson, I intend to raise your salary. Holloway is going to leave, and I wish you to take his place."

I thanked him, and heartily, too; for a hundred dollars a year was no small increase at our house.

"Let me see. I think, Jackson, he had better begin to-morrow."

"Yes, sir; it will be most convenient."

"You hear, Watson. I believe there's nothing more. Good morning."

There was joy in our house that night, and on the morrow I went forth with a light heart to take possession of Holloway's stool.

And now, dear reader, just take a jump over the next three years. Jackson was still in his place; but I had risen step by step, until I occupied a post inferior only to that held by himself. The mystery attached to my ten dollars had never been unravelled, and they still reposed peacefully in my safe. Jackson and I got on very well together; but there was one thing which I could not understand. For a few nights before quarter-day, Jackson always, under some pretence or other, took the books home with him; but as I did not consider it my place to interfere, I said nothing.

It was the quarter-day at the end of the three years of which I have spoken, and I was assisting Mr. Elliot in examining the account of one of the junior clerks, whose ledger exhibited a glaring deficiency of one hundred and fifty dollars. The youth was not the brightest in the world, and for a time he seemed stunned. But he was sure it must be some mistake

of mine; his cash was all right three days ago; and he
took the book to see for himself. The result was the
same — deficit, one hundred and fifty dollars. Again
he went over it, and I could see the big drops of sweat
roll down his face as he again came to the same horrible conclusion — deficit, one hundred and fifty dollars.
A third time he essayed to reconcile the difference ;
but, suddenly stopping short, he turned to Mr. Elliot,
and cried, —

" These are not my figures, sir."

" Then whose are they ? "

" I don't know, sir ; they are not mine ; look, sir,
something has been scratched out here."

" Umph ! So there has. Has the ledger ever been
out of your care ? "

" No, sir — that is, yes — twice."

" When ? "

" Last night and the night before."

" Who had it ? "

" Mr. Jackson."

" Then call Mr. Jackson up here."

He came.

" Mr. Jackson," said Mr. Elliot, " there's an error
in Brown's account : something appears to have been
scratched out ; and as I understand you have had his
ledger the last two nights, I thought perhaps you
could explain it."

Jackson turned deadly pale, and, bending down to
hide the ghastly hue of his countenance, he pretended
to examine the figures.

Yes ; there had been an erasure ; but he could explain it. He had a private memorandum in his desk ;
he would fetch it.

Ten minutes went by, but Jackson did not return.

"Watson," said Mr. Elliot, "will you go and say that I shall be pleased if Mr. Jackson will come here immediately?"

I went, but could not find him.

"Osborne," I asked of a porter, "have you seen Mr. Jackson?"

"Yes, sir; he went out about ten minutes ago."

"Went out?"

"Yes, sir; he came down stairs looking very white, and, taking his hat, he said he felt rather ill, and would get a little air."

I went back and told Mr. Elliot.

"O!" was all he uttered; and then turning on his heel, he motioned for us to follow. He first went to Osborne, who repeated his story again; and then he crossed to Jackson's desk, which was locked. A smith was sent for, and the lock forced.

"Mr Watson," said Mr. Elliot, taking out Jackson's books,—he had never called me *Mr.* Watson before,— "will you come with me to my private room? I shall want you for a few minutes."

That few minutes expanded into hours; and the discovery of embezzlements by Jackson, to the extent of some thousand dollars, was the result of our labor. These frauds extended over several years; and, by a curious coincidence, the very first of them was connected with my ten dollars — the last, of course, with Brown's hundred and fifty. Need I say that Jackson was never heard of again?

That night I walked home as the managing clerk of the firm of Elliot and Co.; and never since have I forgotten the lesson taught me by my ten dollars.

THE O'LINCOLN FAMILY.

A FLOCK of merry birds were sporting in the grove ;
  Some were warbling cheerily, and some were mak-
    ing love :
These were Bobolincoln, Wadolincoln, Winterseeble, Con-
    queedle ;
A livelier set were never led by tabor, pipe, or fiddle ;
Crying, "Phew, shew, Wadolincoln ! see, see, Bobolincoln,
Down among the tickle tops, hiding in the buttercups !
I know the saucy chap ; I see his shining cap
Bobbing in the clover there : see, see, see !"

Up flies Bobolincoln, perching on an apple tree,
Startled by his rival's song, quickened by his raillery.
Soon he spies the rogue afloat, curveting in the air,
And merrily he turns about, and warns him to beware !
" 'Tis you that would a wooing go, down among the
    rushes, O !
But wait a week, till flowers are cheery ; wait a week,
    and ere you marry
Be sure of a house wherein to tarry !
Wadolink, Whiskodink, Tom Denny, wait, wait, wait !"

Every one's a funny fellow ; every one's a little mellow ;
Follow, follow, follow, o'er the hill and in the hollow !
Merrily, merrily, there they hie ; now they rise, and now
    they fly ;
They cross and turn, and in and out, and down in the
    middle, and wheel about,
With a " Phew, shew, Wadolincoln ! listen to me, Bobo-
    lincoln !
Happy's the wooing that's speedily doing, that's speedily
    doing ;
That's merry and over, with the bloom of the clover !
Bobolincoln, Wadolincoln, Winterseeble, follow, follow
    me !"

O, what a happy life they lead, over the hill and in the
    mead !
How they sing, and how they play !   See, they fly away,
    away !
Now they gambol o'er the clearing ; off again, and then
    appearing ;
Poised aloft on quivering wing, now they soar, and now
    they sing, —
"O, let us be merry and moving !   O, let us be happy
    and loving !
For when midsummer has come, and the grain has ripened
    its ear,
The haymakers scatter our young, and we mourn for the
    rest of the year !
Then Bobolincoln, Wadolincoln, Winterseeble, haste, haste
    away !"

                    WILSON FLAGG.

THE BLACKSMITH OF BOTTLEDELL.

HORNY hands and swarthy face,
   Burliest of a burly race,
The Saxon blacksmith took his place,

Beside his anvil. " Sir," said I,
" They say you've laid a fortune by ;
Why still your hard vocation ply ? "

" Stranger," said he, " I see your plan,
A prying, interviewing man,
Come to find out all you can,

" And put it in the papers.   Well,
You see I *did* quit work a spell,
Till Tom Sparks came to Bottledell ;

"Tom Sparks, the blacksmith over there,
At t'other corner of the square,
And folks said I wa'n't anywhere —

"That this Tom Sparks could beat me blind
At blacksmith work of any kind,
Specially putting on hosses' shoes behind!"

The speaker paused and breathed a spell,
And from his eyes the flash that fell
Lit the bravest face in Bottledell.

"Stranger, I don't care what you say;
I'm rather odd, I've got my way;
I'll get on *top*, and there *I'll stay* —

"That is, I don't care what the loss is,
Learn my trade over, work under bosses,
Or beat Tom Sparks a shoeing hosses!"

There is a lesson, — learn it well, —
Taught in the story that I tell
Of that proud smith of Bottledell.

He had a soul, the type of those
To whom success forever goes,
For whom the victor's laurel grows.

Such wills as his have caught the world,
And held it fast when thrones were hurled
Together, and the red flames curled

Above the wreck.   When Cæsar fell
No grander spirit said farewell
Than had the smith of Bottledell!

                              JAMES MAURICE THOMPSON

THE STONE-CUTTER.

ONCE upon a time there was in Japan a poor stone-cutter — a simple workman in the quarries. His life was rude; he worked much, gained little, and was not at all contented with his fate.

"O, if I could only be rich enough to rest, to sleep on thick matting, wrapped in a kirimon of soft silk!" Such was the sigh which he breathed to Heaven. An angel intercepted it.

"It shall be according to thy desire," said the angel to him. And he at once became rich; and he rested, slept upon thick matting, and wrapped himself in a kirimon of soft silk.

It happened that the emperor passed by. He was preceded by heralds on foot and horseback, followed by a brilliant escort of cavaliers, and surrounded by persons who held over his head an immense parasol, resplendent with gold.

"What good does it do me to be rich," murmured the man, "as long as I have not the right to go out with an escort, and my head protected by a golden parasol? Why am I not the emperor?"

"Thou shalt be," said the angel.

And, indeed, he became the emperor. He had an escort before and behind him, and people who held above his head an immense parasol, resplendent with gold.

However, the sun, with his ardent beams, dried up the country, and the dusty road, quivering with his brightness, fatigued the eyes.

"It is a great advantage to be emperor," cried the

man, "when the heat of the day exhausts you, and the sun never ceases to make you feel his power! But if one could be the sun!"

"Behold! are you satisfied?" the angel asked; for he had become the sun, and he darted his beams up and down, right and left, and all around him. And he scorched the herbage of the earth and the faces of the princes upon the earth.

But now a cloud thrust itself between the earth and him; it held back the rays of the sun, and prevented them from falling upon the earth's surface.

"There is strength," cried the sun; "a cloud capable of resisting my power. It would be better if I were a cloud."

"Very well," said the angel.

And the transformation was at once accomplished. The new cloud placed itself haughtily between the sun and the earth, and so thoroughly intercepted the rays of the sun that it soon saw the earth covered with its shadow. Then it caused big drops of rain, and pouring showers, and waterspouts to fall on the lands, so that the torrents burst their bounds, and the rivers spread over and devastated the fields.

Nothing resisted the force of the inundation; only a rock defied it, perfectly motionless. In vain the bellowing waters beat in their fury; the rock yielded not, but the foaming waves died at its foot.

"A rock, then, is my superior," said the cloud; "I would rather be in its place."

"You shall be," said the angel.

And he was transformed into a steep, unshaken rock, insensible to the rays of the sun, indifferent to the torrents of rain and the shock of the tumultuous waves.

Nevertheless, he distinguished at his feet a man of poor appearance, hardly clothed, but armed with a chisel and a hammer; and the man, with the help of these instruments, struck off pieces of the rock, which he dressed into stones proper for cutting.

"What is that?" cried the rock; "has a man the power of rending pieces of stone from my breast? Shall I be weaker than he? Then it is absolutely necessary that I should be that man."

"Have your will," said the angel; and he became again what he had been — a poor stone-cutter, a simple workman in the quarries. His life was rude, he worked much, and gained little; but he was contented with his lot.

[From "Japan in Our Day," by BAYARD TAYLOR.]

THE TWO CHURCH-BUILDERS.

I.

A FAMOUS king would build a church,
    A temple vast and grand ;
And, that the praise might be his own,
    He gave a strict command
That none should add the smallest gift
    To aid the work he planned.

II.

And when the mighty dome was done,
    Within the noble frame,
Upon a tablet broad and fair,
    In letters all aflame
With burnished gold, the people read
    The royal builder's name.

III.

Now, when the king, elate with pride,
    That night had sought his bed,
He dreamed he saw an angel come
    (A halo round his head),
Erase the royal name, and write
    Another in its stead.

IV.

What could it mean?   Three times that night
    That wondrous vision came ;
Three times he saw that angel hand
    Erase the royal name,
And write a woman's in its stead,
    In letters all aflame.

V.

Whose could it be?   He gave command
    To all about his throne
To seek the owner of the name
    That on the tablet shone ;
And so it was the courtiers found
    A widow poor and lone.

VI.

The king, enraged at what he heard,
    Cried, " Bring the culprit here ! "
And to the woman, trembling sore,
    He said, " 'Tis very clear
That you have broken my command ;
    Now let the truth appear ! "

VII.

" Your majesty," the widow said,
    " I can't deny the truth ;
I love the Lord, — my Lord and yours, —

And so, in simple sooth,
I broke your majesty's command.
(I crave your royal ruth.)

VIII.

" And since I had no money, sire,
    Why, I could only pray
That God would bless your majesty ;
    And when along the way
The horses drew the stones, I gave
    To one a wisp of hay."

IX.

" Ah ! now I see," the king exclaimed,
    " Self-glory was my aim ;
The woman gave for love of God,
    And not for worldly fame ;
'Tis my command the tablet bear
    The pious widow's name."

JOHN G. SAXE.

MY SISTER.

WHO held the tempting cherry nigh,
    And always tried to make me cry,
And stuck the scissors in my eye ?
                My sister.

Who threw my playthings on the floor,
And broke my doll behind the door,
And my best ribbons always wore ?
                My sister.

Who pinched my kitten's ear or tail,
And ducked her in the water pail,
And laughed at her unearthly wail ?
                My sister.

Who spilled her coffee in my lap,
And tore mamma's new breakfast cap,
And blurred with ink my atlas map ?
                    My sister.

Who's glad dear sister's married now,
And not at home to raise a row ?
I know who's happy, any how !
                    Her sister !

AWAKING A BOY.

CALLING a boy up in the morning can hardly be classed under the head of " pastimes," especially if the boy is fond of exercise the day before. And it is a little singular that the next hardest thing to getting a boy out of bed is getting him into it.

There is rarely a mother who is a success at rousing a boy. All mothers know this ; so do their boys. And yet the mother seems to go at it in the right way. She opens the stair-door, and insinuatingly observes, " Johnny !" There is no response. " John-*ny!*" Still no response. Then there is a short, sharp " John !" followed a moment later by a prolonged and emphatic " John Henry !"

A grunt from the upper regions signifies that an impression has been made, and the mother is encouraged to add, " You'd better be getting down here to your breakfast, young man, before I come up there, an' give you something you'll feel." This so startles the young man that he immediately goes to sleep again. And the operation has to be repeated several times.

A father knows nothing about this trouble. He merely opens his mouth as a soda bottle ejects its cork, and the "John Henry" that cleaves the air of that stairway goes into that boy like electricity, and pierces the deepest recesses of his very nature. And he pops out of that bed, and into his clothes, with a promptness that is commendable.

It is rarely a boy allows himself to disregard the paternal summons. About once a year is believed to be as often as is consistent with the rules of health. He saves his father a great many steps by his thoughtfulness.

THE WONDERFUL SACK.

THE apple boughs half hid the house
  Where lived the lonely widow;
Behind it stood the chestnut wood,
  Before it spread the meadow.

She had no money in her till;
  She was too poor to borrow;
With her lame leg she could not beg;
  And no one cheered her sorrow.

She had no wood to cook her food,
  And but one chair to sit in;
Last spring she lost a cow, that cost
  A whole year's steady knitting.

She had worn her fingers to the bone;
  Her back was growing double;
One day the pig tore up her wig, —
  But that's not half her trouble.

Her best black gown was faded brown ;
    Her shoes were all in tatters,
With not a pair for Sunday wear :
    Said she, " It little matters !

" Nobody asks me now to ride ;
    My garments are not fitting ;
And with my crutch I care not much
    To hobble off to meeting.

" I still preserve my Testament,
    And though the *Acts* are missing,
And *Luke* is torn, and *Hebrews* worn,
    On Sunday 'tis a blessing.

" And other days I open it
    Before me on the table,
And there I sit, and read, and knit,
    As long as I am able."

One evening she had closed the book,
    But still she sat there knitting ;
" Meow-meow ! " complained the old black cat ;
    " Mew-mew ! " the spotted kitten.

And on the hearth, with sober mirth,
    " Chirp, chirp ! " replied the cricket.
'Twas dark, — but hark ! " Bow-ow ! " the bark
    Of Ranger at the wicket !

Is Ranger barking at the moon ?
    Or what can be the matter ?
What trouble now ?   " Bow-ow ! bow-ow ! " —
    She hears the old gate clatter.

" It is the wind that bangs the gate,
    And I must knit my stocking ! "
But hush ! — what's that ?   Rat-tat ! rat-tat !
    Alas ! there's some one knocking !

"Dear me! dear me! who can it be?
  Where, where is my crutch-handle?"
She rubs a match with hasty scratch;
  She cannot light the candle!

Rat-tat! scratch, scratch! the worthless match!
  The cat growls in the corner.
Rat-tat! scratch, scratch! Up flies the latch,—
  "Good evening, Mrs. Warner!"

The kitten spits and lifts her back,
  Her eyes glare on the stranger;
The old cat's tail ruffs big and black;
  Loud barks the old dog Ranger!

Blue burns at last the tardy match,
  And dim the candle glimmers;
Along the floor beside the door
  The cold white moonlight shimmers.

"Sit down!"—the widow gives her chair.
  "Get out!" she says to Ranger.
"Alas! I do not know your name."
  "No matter!" quoth the stranger.

His limbs are strong, his beard is long,
  His hair is dark and wavy;
Upon his back he bears a sack;
  His staff is stout and heavy.

"My way is lost, and with the frost
  I feel my fingers tingle."
Then from his back he slips the sack,—
  Ho! did you hear it jingle?

"Nay, keep your chair! while you sit there,
  I'll take the other corner."
"I'm sorry, sir, I have no fire!"
  "No matter, Mrs. Warner!"

3

He shakes his sack, — the magic sack !
  Amazed the widow gazes !
Ho, ho ! the chimney's full of wood !
  Ha, ha ! the wood it blazes !

Ho, ho ! ha, ha ! the merry fire !
  It sputters and it crackles !
Snap, snap ! flash, flash ! old oak and ash
  Send out a million sparkles.

The stranger sits upon his sack
  Beside the chimney-corner,
And rubs his hands before the brands,
  And smiles on Mrs. Warner.

She feels her heart beat fast with fear ;
  But what can be the danger ?
" Can I do aught for you, kind sir ? "
  " I'm hungry ! " quoth the stranger.

" Alas ! " said she, " I have no food
  For boiling or for baking ! "
" I've food, " quoth he, " for you and me ! "
  And gave his sack a shaking.

Out rattled knives, and forks, and spoons !
  Twelve eggs, potatoes plenty !
One large soup dish, two plates of fish,
  And bread enough for twenty !

And Rachel, calming her surprise,
  As well as she was able,
Saw, following these, two roasted geese,
  A tea-urn, and a table !

Strange, was it not ? each dish was hot ;
  Not even a plate was broken ;
The cloth was laid, and all arrayed,
  Before a word was spoken !

"Sit up ! sit up ! and we will sup,
    Dear madam, while we're able !"
Said she, " The room is poor and small
    For such a famous table !"

Again the stranger shakes the sack ;
    The walls begin to rumble !
Another shake ! the rafters quake !
    You'd think the roof would tumble !

Shake, shake ! the room grows high and large,
    The walls are painted over !
Shake, shake ! out fall four chairs, in all,
    A bureau, and a sofa !

The stranger stops to wipe the sweat
    That down his face is streaming.
" Sit up ! sit up ! and we will sup,"
    Quoth he, " while all is steaming !"

The widow hobbled on her crutch ;
    He kindly sprang to aid her.
" All this," said she, " is too much for me !"
    Quoth he, " We'll have a waiter !"

Shake, shake, once more ! and from the sack
    Out popped a little fellow,
With elbows bare, bright eyes, sleek hair,
    And trousers striped with yellow.

His legs were short, his body plump,
    His cheek was like a cherry ;
He turned three times ; he gave a jump ;
    His laugh rang loud and merry !

He placed his hand upon his heart,
    And scraped and bowed so handy !
" Your humble servant, sir," he said,
    Like any little dandy.

The widow laughed a long, loud laugh,
    And up she started, screaming ;
When ho ! and lo ! the room was dark !—
    She'd been asleep and dreaming !

The stranger and his magic sack,
    The dishes and the fishes,
The geese and things, had taken wings,
    Like riches, or like witches !

All, all was gone ! She sat alone ;
    Her hands had dropped their knitting.
" Meow-meow ! " the cat upon the mat ;
    " Mew-mew ! mew-mew ! " the kitten.

The hearth is bleak, — and hark ! the creak,
    " Chirp, chirp ! " the lonesome cricket.
" Bow-ow ! " says Ranger to the moon ;
    The wind is at the wicket.

And still she sits, and as she knits,
    She ponders o'er the vision :
" I saw it written on the sack,
    ' A CHEERFUL DISPOSITION.'

" I know God sent the dream, and meant
    To teach this useful lesson,
That out of peace and pure content
    Springs every earthly blessing ! "

Said she, " I'll make the sack my own !
    I'll shake away all sorrow ! "
She shook the sack for me to-day ;
    She'll shake for you to-morrow.

She shakes out hope ; and joy, and peace,
    And happiness come after ;
She shakes out smiles for all the world ;
    She shakes out love and laughter.

For poor and rich, — no matter which, —
    For young folks or for old folks,
For strong and weak, for proud and meek,
    For warm folks and for cold folks ; —

For children coming home from school,
    And sometimes for the teacher ;
For white and black, she shakes the sack, —
    In short, for every creature.

And everybody who has grief,
    The sufferer and the mourner,
From far and near, come now to hear
    Kind words from Mrs. Warner.

They go to her with heavy hearts,
    They come away with light ones ;
They go to her with cloudy brows,
    They come away with bright ones.

All love her well, and I could tell
    Of many a cheering present
Of fruits and things their friendship brings,
    To make her fireside pleasant.

She always keeps a cheery fire ;
    The house is painted over ;
She has food in store, and chairs for four,
    A bureau, and a sofa.

She says these seem just like her dream,
    And tells again the vision :
" I saw it written on the sack, —
    ' A Cheerful Disposition ! ' "

J. T. TROWBRIDGE.

PETER'S RIDE TO THE WEDDING.

PETER would ride to the wedding — he would ;
  So he mounted his ass ; — and his wife,
She was to ride behind, if she could,
" For," says Peter, " the woman, she should
  Follow, not lead through life.

" He's mighty convenient, the ass, my dear,
  And proper and safe — and now
You hold by the tail, while I hold by the ear,
And we'll ride to the kirk in time, never fear,
  If the wind and the weather allow."

The wind and the weather were not to be blamed,
  But the ass had adopted the whim,
That two at a time was a load never framed
For the back of one ass, and he seemed quite ashamed
  That two should stick fast upon him.

"Come, Dobbin," says Peter, "I'm thinking we'll trot."
  " I'm thinking we won't," says the ass,
In language of conduct, and stuck to the spot
As if he had sworn he would sooner be shot
  Than lift up a toe from the grass.

Says Peter, says he, " I'll whip him a little."
  " Try it, my dear," says she.
But he might just as well have whipped a brass kettle.
The ass was made of such obstinate mettle
  That never a step moved he.

" I'll prick him, my dear, with a needle," said she ;
  " I'm thinking he'll alter his mind."
The ass felt the needle, and up went his heels ;
" I'm thinking," says Peter, " he's beginning to feel
  Some notion of moving — behind.

" Now lend me the needle, and I'll prick his ear,
   And set t'other end, too, agoing."
The ass felt the needle, and upward he reared ;
But kicking and rearing was all, it appeared,
   He'd any intention of doing.

Says Peter, says he, " We get on rather slow ;
   While one end is up, t'other sticks to the ground ;
But I'm thinking a method to move him I know :
Let's prick head and tail together, and so
   Give the creature a start all around."

So said, so done ; all hands were at work,
   And the ass he did alter his mind,
For he started away with so sudden a jerk
That in less than a trice he arrived at the kirk,
   But he left all his lading behind.

LITTLE PAT AND THE PARSON.

HE stands at the door of the church peeping in ;
   No troublesome beadle is near him ;
The preacher is talking of sinners and sin,
   And little Pat trembles to hear him ;
A poor little fellow alone and forlorn,
   Who never knew parent or duty, —
His head is uncovered, his jacket is torn,
   And hunger has withered his beauty.

The white-headed gentleman shut in the box
   Seems growing more angry each minute ;
He doubles his fist, and the cushion he knocks,
   As if anxious to know what is in it.
He scolds at the people who sit in the pews ;
   Pat takes them for kings and princesses.
(With his little bare feet — he delights in their shoes :
   In his rags — he feels proud of their dresses !)

The parson exhorts them to think of their need,
  To turn from the world's dissipation,
The naked to clothe, and the hungry to feed.
  Pat listened with strong approbation !
And when the old clergyman walks down the aisle,
  Pat runs up to meet him right gladly.
" Shure, give me my dinner," says he, with a smile,
  " And a jacket, — I want them quite badly !"

The kings and princesses indignantly stare,
  The beadle gets word of the danger,
And, shaking his silver-tipped stick in the air,
  Looks knives at the poor little stranger.
But Pat's not afraid ; he is sparkling with joy,
  And cries — who so willing to cry it ? —
" You'll give me my dinner — I'm *such* a poor boy :
  You said so — now *don't* you deny it !"

The pompous old beadle may grumble and glare,
  And growl about robbers and arson ;
But the boy who has faith in the sermon stands there,
  And smiles at the white-headed parson !
The kings and princesses may wonder and frown,
  And whisper he wants better teaching ;
But the white-headed parson looks tenderly down
  On the boy who has faith in his preaching.

He takes him away without question or blame,
  As eager as Patsy to press on,
For he thinks a good dinner (and Pat thinks the same)
  Is the moral that lies in the lesson.
And after long years, when Pat, handsomely dressed —
  A smart footman — is asked to determine
Of all earthly things what's the thing he likes best,
  He says, " Och ! shure, the master's ould sermin !"

BOTH SIDES.

" KITTY, Kitty, you mischievous elf,
What have you, pray, to say for yourself ? "

But Kitty was now
Asleep on the mow,
And only drawled dreamily, " Me-a-ow ! "

" Kitty, Kitty, come here to me —
The naughtiest Kitty I ever did see !
I know very well what you've been about ;
Don't try to conceal it ; murder will out.
Why do you lie so lazily there ? "

" O, I have had a breakfast rare ! "

" Why don't you go and hunt for a mouse ? "

" O, there's nothing fit to eat in the house ! "

" Dear me ! Miss Kitty,
This *is* a pity ;
But I guess the cause of your change of ditty.
What has become of the beautiful thrush
That built her nest in the heap of brush ?
A brace of young robins as good as the best ;
A round little, brown little, snug little nest ;
Four little eggs all green and gay,
Four little birds all bare and gray,
And Papa Robin went foraging round,
Aloft on the trees, and alight on the ground.
North wind, or south wind, he cared not a groat,
So he popped a fat worm down each wide-open throat ;
And Mamma Robin through sun and storm
Hugged them up close, and kept them all warm ;
And me, I watched the dear little things
Till the feathers pricked out on their pretty wings,

And their eyes peeped up o'er the rim of the nest.
Kitty, Kitty, you know the rest.
The nest is empty, and silent, and lone ;
Where are the four little robins gone ?
O Puss ! you have done a cruel deed !
Your eyes, do they weep ? your heart, does it bleed ?
Do you not feel your bold cheeks turning pale ?
Not you ! You are chasing your wicked tail,
Or you just cuddle down in the hay and purr,
Curl up in a ball, and refuse to stir.
But you need not try to look good and wise ;
I see little robins, old Puss, in your eyes ;
And this morning, just as the clock struck four,
There was some one opening the kitchen door,
And caught you creeping the wood-pile over.
Make a clean breast of it, Kitty Clover ! "

   Then Kitty arose,
   Rubbed up her nose,
And looked very much as if coming to blows ;
   Rounded her back,
   Leaped from the stack,
On *her* feet, at *my* feet, came down with a whack.
Then, fairly awake, she stretched out her paws,
Smoothed down her whiskers, and unsheathed her claws,
   Winked her green eyes
   With an air of surprise,
And spoke rather plainly for one of her size.

" Killed a few robins ; well, what of that ?
What's virtue in man can't be vice in a cat.
There's a thing or two *I* should like to know :
Who killed the chicken a week ago,
For nothing at all that I could spy,
But to make an overgrown chicken pie ?
   'Twixt you and me,
   'Tis plain to see,
The odds is, you like fricassee,

While my brave maw
Owns no such law,
Content with viands *à-la*-raw.

"Who killed the robins?   O, yes! O, yes!
I *would* get the cat now into a mess!
Who was it put
An old stocking-foot,
Tied up with strings
And such shabby things,
On to the end of a sharp, slender pole,
Dipped it in oil, and set fire to the whole,
And burnt all the way from here to the miller's
The nests of the sweet young caterpillars?
Grilled fowl, indeed!
Why, as I read,
You had not even the plea of need;
For all you boast
Such wholesale roast,
I saw no sign, at tea or toast,
Of even a caterpillar's ghost.

"Who killed the robins?   Well, I *should* think!
Hadn't somebody better wink
At my peccadilloes, if houses of glass
Won't do to throw stones from at those who pass?
I had four little kittens a month ago, —
Black, and Malta, and white as snow;
And not a very long while before
I could have shown you three kittens more.
And so in batches of fours and threes,
Looking back as long as you please,
You would find, if you read my story all,
There were kittens from time immemorial.

"But what am I now?   A cat bereft.
Of all my kittens, but one is left.
I make no charges, but this I ask:
What made such a splurge in the waste-water cask?

You are quite tender-hearted.   O, not a doubt !
But only suppose old Black Pond could speak out.
O, bother ! don't mutter excuses to me :
Qui facit per alium facit per se."

" Well, Kitty, I think full enough has been said,
And the best thing for you is, go straight back to bed.
  A very fine pass
  Things have come to, my lass,
  If men must be meek
  While pussy-cats speak
Grave moral reflections in Latin and Greek !"
         GAIL HAMILTON.

THE WORSTED STOCKING.

"FATHER will have done the great chimney to-night
—won't he, mother ? " said little Tom Howard,
as he stood waiting for his father's breakfast, which he
carried to him at his work every morning.

" He said he hoped all the scaffolding would be down
to-night," answered his mother, " and that'll be a fine
sight ; for I never like the ending of those great chimneys, it's so risky.   Thy father's to be the last up."

" Eh, then, but I'll go and see him, and help 'em to
give a shout afore he comes down," said Tom.

" And then," continued his mother, " if all goes
right, we are to have a frolic to-morrow, and go into
the country, and take our dinners, and spend all the
day amongst the woods."

" Hurrah !" cried Tom, as he ran off to his father's
place of work with a can of milk in one hand and some
bread in the other.   His mother stood at the door as
he went merrily whistling down the street ; and then
she thought of the dear father he was going to, and

the dangerous work he was engaged in ; and then her heart sought its sure refuge, and she prayed to God to protect and bless her treasures.

Tom, with a light heart, pursued his way to his father, and leaving him his breakfast, went to his own work, which was at some distance. In the evening, on his way home, he went round to see how his father was getting on. James Howard, the father, and a number of other workmen had been building one of those lofty chimneys, which, in our great manufacturing towns, almost supply the place of other architectural beauty. This chimney was one of the highest and most tapering that had ever been erected; and as Tom, shading his eyes from the slanting rays of the setting sun, looked up to the top in search of his father, his heart almost sank within him at the appalling height. The scaffolding was almost all down; the men at the bottom were removing the last beams and poles. Tom's father stood alone on the top. He looked all round to see that everything was right, and then, waving his hat in the air, the men below answered him with a long, loud cheer, little Tom shouting as heartily as any of them. As their voices died away, however, they heard a very different sound — a cry of alarm and horror from above : " The rope ! the rope ! "

The men looked round, and coiled upon the ground lay the rope, which, before the scaffolding was removed, should have been passed over the top of the chimney for Tom's father to come down by. The scaffolding had been taken down without their remembering to take the rope up. There was a dead silence. They all knew it was impossible to throw the rope up

high enough or skilfully enough to reach the top of
the chimney ; or if it could, it would hardly have been
safe.   They stood in silent dismay, unable to give any
help, or think of any means of safety.

And Tom's father! He walked round and round
the little circle, the dizzy height seeming every moment to grow more fearful, and the solid earth farther and farther from him.   In the sudden panic he
lost his presence of mind, and his senses almost failed
him.   He shut his eyes ; he felt as if the next moment
he must be dashed to pieces on the ground below.

The day had passed as industriously and swiftly as
usual with Tom's mother at home.   She was always
busily employed for her husband and children in some
way or other, and to-day she had been harder at work
than usual, getting ready for the holiday to-morrow.
She had just finished all her preparations, and her
thoughts were silently thanking God for her happy
home and for all the blessings of life, when Tom ran
in.   His face was as white as ashes, and he could
hardly get his words out: " Mother! mother! he
canna get down !"

" Who, lad?   Thy father?" asked his mother.

"They've forgotten to leave him the rope," answered
Tom, still scarcely able to speak.   His mother started
up horror-struck, and stood for a moment as if para-
lyzed ; then, pressing her hands over her face, as if
to shut out the terrible picture, and breathing a prayer
to God for help, she rushed out of the house.

When she reached the place where her husband
was at work, a crowd had collected round the foot
of the chimney, and stood there quite helpless, gazing up with faces full of horror. " He says he'll

throw himself down," exclaimed they, as Mrs. Howard came up. "He's going to throw himself down."

"Thee munna do that, lad," cried the wife, with clear, hopeful voice. "Thee munna do that. Wait a bit. Tak' off thy stocking, lad, and unravel it, and let down the thread with a bit of mortar. Dost hear me, Jem?"

The man made a sign of assent, for it seemed as if he could not speak; and, taking off his stocking, unravelled the worsted thread, row after row. The people stood round in breathless silence and suspense, wondering what Tom's mother could be thinking of, and why she sent in such haste for the carpenter's ball of twine.

"Let down one end of the thread with a bit of stone, and keep fast hold of the other," cried she to her husband. The little thread came waving down the tall chimney, blown hither and thither by the wind; but at last it reached the outstretched hands that were waiting for it. Tom held the ball of string while his mother tied one end of it to the worsted thread. "Now, pull it up slowly," cried she to her husband. And she gradually unwound the string as the worsted drew it gently up. It stopped — the string had reached her husband. "Now, hold the string fast and pull it up," cried she. And the string grew heavy and hard to pull, for Tom and his mother had fastened the thick rope to it. They watched it gradually and slowly uncoiling from the ground, as the string was drawn higher.

There was but one coil left. It had reached the top. "Thank God! Thank God!" exclaimed the wife. She hid her face in her hands — in silent

prayer, and tremblingly rejoiced.   The rope was up.
The iron to which it should be fastened was there
all right; but would her husband be able to make use
of them?   Would not the terror of the last hour have
so unnerved him as to prevent him from taking the
necessary measures for his safety?   She did not know
the magic influence which her few words had exer-
cised over him.   She did not know the strength that
the sound of her voice, so calm and steadfast, had filled
him with; as if the little thread that carried him the
hope of life once more had conveyed to him some por-
tion of that faith which nothing ever destroyed or
shook in her true heart.   She did not know that, as
he waited there, the words came over him, "Why art
thou cast down, O my soul? and why art thou dis-
quieted within me?   Hope thou in God."

There was a great shout.   "He's safe, mother; he's
safe!" cried little Tom.

" Thou'st saved me, Mary!" said her husband, folding her in his arms.   "But what ails thee?   Thou
seem'st more sorry than glad about it!"

But Mary could not speak, and if the strong arm
of her husband had not held her up, she would have
fallen to the ground.   The sudden joy, after such great
fear, had overcome her.

"Tom," said his father, "let thy mother lean on thy
shoulder, and we will take her home."   And in their
happy home they poured forth their thanks to God for
his great goodness; and their happy life together felt
dearer and holier for the peril it had been in, and for
the nearness that the danger had brought them unto
God.   And the holiday, next day — was it not a
thanksgiving day?

THE STORY OF THE LITTLE RID HIN.

THERE was once't upon a time
    A little small rid hin
Off in the good ould country
    Where yees ha' nivir bin.

Nice and quiet shure she was,
    And nivir did any harrum ;
She lived alane all be herself,
    And worked upon her farrum.

There lived out-o'er the hill,
    In a great din o' rocks,
A crafty, shly, and wicked
    Ould folly iv a fox.

This rashkill iv a fox,
    He tuk it in his head
He'd have the little rid hin ;
    So, whin he wint to bed,

He laid awake and thaught,
    What a foine thing 'twad be
To fetch her home, and bile her up
    For his ould marm and he.

And so he thaught and thaught,
    Until he grew so thin
That there was nothin' left of him
    But jist his bones and shkin.

But the small rid hin was wise ;
    She always locked her door,
And in her pocket pit the key,
    To keep the fox out, shure.

4

But at last there came a schame
  Into his wicked head ;
And so he tuk a great big bag,
  And to his mither said, —

" Now have the pot all bilin'
  Agin the time I come ;
We'll ate the small rid hin to-night,
  For shure I'll bring her home."

And so away he wint
  Wid the bag upon his back,
An' up the hill and through the woods
  Softly he made his thrack.

And thin he came alang,
  Craping as shtill's a mouse,
To where the little small rid hin
  Lived in her shnug ould house.

An' out she comes hersel',
  Jist as he got in sight,
To pick up shticks to make her fire.
  " Aha ! " says fox, " all right.

" Begorra, now, I'll have yees
  Widout much throuble more ; "
An' in he shlips quite unbeknownst,
  An' hides be'ind the door.

An' thin a minute afther,
  In comes the small rid hin,
An' shuts the door, an' locks it, too,
  An' thinks, " I'm safely in."

An' thin she tarns around,
  An' looks behind the door ;
Thare shtands the fox wid his big tail
  Shpread out upon the floor.

Dear me ! she was so schared
  Wid such a wondrous sight,
She dropped her apronful of shticks,
  An' flew up in a fright,

An' lighted on the bame
  Across on top the room ;
" Aha !" says she, " ye don't have me ;
  Ye may as well go home."

" Aha ! " says fox, " we'll see ;
  I'll bring yees down from that."
So out he marched upon the floor
  Right under where she sat.

An' thin he whiruled around,
  An' round, an' round, an' round,
Fashter, an' fashter, an' fashter,
  Afther his tail on the ground.

Until the small rid hin
  She got so dizzy, shure,
Wid lookin' at the fox's tail,
  She jist dropped on the floor.

An' fox, he whipped her up,
  An' pit her in his bag,
An' off he started all alone,
  Him and his little dag.

All day he tracked the wood,
  Up hill an' down again ;
And wid him, schmothrin' in the bag,
  The little small rid hin.

Sorra a know she knowed
  Awhere she was that day ;
Says she, " I'm biled an' ate up, shure,
  An' what'll be to pay ? "

Thin she betho't hersel',
    An' tuk her schissors out,
An' schnipped a big hole in the bag,
    So she could look about.

An' 'fore ould fox could think
    She lept right out — she did,
An' thin picked up a great big shtone
    An' popped it in instid ;

An' thin she rins off home ;
    Her outside door she locks ;
Thinks she, " You see you don't have me,
    You crafty, shly ould fox."

An' fox, he tugged away
    Wid the great big hivy shtone
Thimpin' his shoulders very bad
    As he wint in alone.

An' whin he came in sight
    O' his great din o' rocks,
Jist watchin' for him at the door
    He shpied ould mither fox.

" Have ye the pot a-bilin' ? "
    Says he to ould fox thin ;
" Shure an' it is, me child," says she ;
    " Have ye the small rid hin ? "

" Yes, jist here in me bag,
    As shure as I shtand here ;
Open the lid till I pit her in :
    Open it — niver fear."

So the rashkill cut the shtring,
    An' hild the big bag over ;
" Now when I shake it in," says he,
    Do ye pit on the cover."

" Yis, that I will ; " an' thin
 The shtone wint in wid a dash,
An' the pot o' boilin' wather
 Came over them ker-splash.

An' schalted 'em both to death,
 So they couldn't brathe no more ;
An' the little small rid hin lived safe,
 Jist where she lived before.

THE KING AND THE LOCUSTS.

A STORY WITHOUT AN END.

THERE was a certain king, who, like many other
 kings, was very fond of hearing stories told. To
this amusement he gave up all his time ; but yet he
was never satisfied. All the exertions of all his courtiers were in vain. The more he heard, the more he
wanted to hear. At last he made a proclamation, that
if any man would tell him a story that should last forever, he would make him his heir, and give him the
princess, his daughter, in marriage ; but if any one
should pretend that he had such a story, but should
fail, — that is, if the story did come to an end, — he
was to have his head chopped off.

For such a rich prize as a beautiful princess and a
kingdom many candidates appeared ; and dreadfully
long stories some of them told. Some lasted a week,
some a month, some six months : poor fellows ! they all
spun them out as long as they possibly could, you may
be sure ; but all in vain ; sooner or later they all came
to an end ; and, one after another, the unlucky story-
tellers had their heads chopped off.

At last came a man who said that he had a story which would last forever, if his majesty would be pleased to give him a trial.

He was warned of his danger: they told him how many others had tried, and lost their heads; but he said he was not afraid, and so he was brought before the king. He was a man of a very composed and deliberate manner of speaking; and, after making all requisite stipulations for time for his eating, drinking, and sleeping, he thus began his story: —

"O king! there was once a king who was a great tyrant. And, desiring to increase his riches, he seized upon all the corn and grain in his kingdom, and put it into an immense granary, which he built on purpose, as high as a mountain.

"This he did for several years, till the granary was quite full up to the top. He then stopped up doors and windows, and closed it up fast on all sides.

"But the bricklayers had, by accident, left a *very* small hole near the top of the granary. And there came a flight of locusts, and tried to get at the corn; but the hole was so small that only one locust could pass through it at a time. So *one* locust went in and carried off *one* grain of corn; and then *another* locust went in and carried off *another* grain of corn; and then *another* locust went in and carried off *another* grain of corn; and then *another* locust went in and carried off *another* grain of corn; and then *another* locust went in and carried off *another* grain of corn; and then *another* locust went in and carried off *another* grain of corn; and then *another* locust went in and carried off *another* grain of corn —"

He had gone on thus from morning to night (ex-

cept while he was engaged at his meals) for about a
month; when the king, though a very patient king,
began to be *rather* tired of the locusts, and interrupted his story with: "Well, well, we have had
enough of the locusts; we will suppose that they
have helped themselves to all the corn they wanted;
tell us what happened afterwards." To which the
story-teller answered, very deliberately, " If it please
your majesty, it is impossible to tell you what happened afterwards before I have told you what happened first." And so he went on again: " And then
another locust went in and carried off *another* grain
of corn; and then *another* locust went in and carried
off *another* grain of corn; and then *another* locust went
in and carried off *another* grain of corn." The king
listened with admirable patience six months more,
when he again interrupted him with: "O friend, I
am weary of your locusts! How soon do you think
they will have done?" To which the story-teller
made answer: "O king, who can tell? At the time
to which my story has come, the locusts have cleared
away a small space, it may be a cubit, each way round
the inside of the hole; and the air is still dark with
locusts on all sides; but let the king have patience,
and, no doubt, we shall come to the end of them in
time."

Thus encouraged, the king listened on for another
full year, the story-teller still going on as before:
" And then *another* locust went in and carried off
another grain of corn; and then *another* locust went
in and carried off *another* grain of corn; and then
another locust went in and carried off *another* grain
of corn," till at last the poor king could bear it no

longer, and cried out, " O man, that is enough ! Take
my daughter ! take my kingdom ! take anything —
take everything ! only let us hear no more of those
abominable locusts ! "

And so the story-teller was married to the king's
daughter, and was declared heir to the throne ; and
nobody ever expressed a wish to hear the rest of his
story, for he said it was impossible to come to the
other part of it till he had done with the locusts.
The unreasonable caprice of the foolish king was
thus overmatched by the ingenious device of the
wise man.

GRIPER GREG.

GRIPER GREG, of the village of Willoughby Waterless,
A miserly hunks who was sonless and daughterless,
Nieceless and nephewless, why did he haste to lay
Gold in queer corners for strangers to waste away ?

Were there no claimants upon his cold charity —
Poor fellow-creatures heart-void of hilarity —
         Fatherless, motherless,
         Sisterless, brotherless,
         Husbandless, wifeless,
         Forkless and knifeless,
Dinnerless, supperless wretches, to pray or beg ?
None in his neighborhood, loudly to say to Greg :
" Stone-hearted miser, behold you, we perish !
Give us some victuals, our faint frames to cherish " ?

Yes, there were orphans, Tom, Jack, Dick, and Ned,
Lean, tiny creatures, ill clothed and worse fed ;
Widows there were, Dinah, Ruth, Prue, and Kate,
Bearers alike of the hard blows of Fate ;

Old pauper Will, too, who travelled on crutches,
With mouth pulled aside by neuralgical clutches,
And limbs drawn awry by rheumatical twitches,
Bewrapped in old blankets, without coat or breeches, —
No sister, no daughter, no wife, to take care of him ;
The very dogs barked, " Bow-wow ! Beggar ! beware
      of him !"

And many more hunger-bit, tatter-clad sorrowers,
Fain would have been relieved, beggars or borrowers,
At Griper Greg's door, where they often cried piteously ;
But Greg — he grinned fiercely, and frowned on them
      viciously.

        One day, the snow fell thick and fast,
            One drear midwinter's day ;
        And Greg was out upon the waste
            That round his cottage lay.

        No sight was there, except the snow,
            Upon the wild, wide moor ;
        And in Greg's heart began to grow
        Stern, deadly self-accusings, how
            He'd used the houseless poor.
        " If I die here," Greg wildly cried,
            " My soul's forever lost !
        Had I my gold here by my side,
            It would not pay the cost
        To ransom me from endless pain !
        O ! could I reach my home again,
        I'd give to every suffering fellow
        Whiskey enough to make him mellow."

" They are good words ye've said !" cried beggarman
      Pat,
Who wandered, all weathers, without coat or hat,
Upon the wide waste, and now chanced to be near
Enough to the miser, his heart-grief to bear ;

"They are good words ye've said; and no better by
          preacher
Were ever delivered about the dear crayture;
Make me mellow with him, and no ill shall betide ye,
For to Willoughby Waterless safely I'll guide ye!"

"O, joy!" shouted Greg, "guide me home from the
          waste,
And the sweetest of mutton this night ye shall taste!"
"Bad luck to your mutton! be't sweeter than candy,
'Tis wormwood compared with strong whiskey or brandy!"
"Then I'll fill ye with brandy," cried Greg, in grim fear
That if he refused he would perish, left here.
So home sped the miser by beggar Pat guided,
And home safely reached — but, there, ill Greg betided.

Griper Greg, all a-cold, shared the brandy with Pat
Till discretion and safety he wholly forgat,
And joked of his gold huddled up in sly corners,
To hide it from burglars by night, and day's corners.
Sleep seized him so nimbly, he stopped in his story,
And Pat — wide awake then — was quite in his glory,
And soon picked the locks, and was off with the plunder.
Greg waked the next morning with sore grief and wonder
To find the noon passed while he had been sleeping;
Then looked for his gold, and forthwith fell to weeping.
"O, it's gone — it's all gone! and the curses it's
          brought me
Might all have been saved, if I'd only bethought me
Of sweet love and kindness, and had friends about me;
For then on the heath they would surely have sought me.
But to scrape and to save has been always my plan,
And so nobody loves me — a wretched old man!"
Meanwhile the thief-beggarman far off was drinking
With horrid companions, and, cunningly winking,
Said, "Look here, my boys! when yer handle yer tools,
Always try 'em on misers, for *misers is fools!*"

THE CHILDREN.

WHEN the lessons and tasks are all ended,
   And the school for the day is dismissed,
And the little ones gather around me
   To bid me good night and be kissed ;
O, the little white arms that encircle
   My neck in a tender embrace !
O, the smiles that are halos of heaven,
   Shedding sunshine of love on my face !

And when they are gone, I sit dreaming
   Of my childhood, too lovely to last ;
Of love that my heart will remember,
   When it wakes to the pulse of the past,
Ere the world and its wickedness made me
   A partner of sorrow and sin ;
When the glory of God was about me,
   And the glory of gladness within.

O, my heart grows weak as a woman's,
   And the fountains of feeling will flow,
When I think of the paths steep and stony,
   Where the feet of the dear ones must go ;
Of the mountains of sin hanging o'er them,
   Of the tempest of Fate blowing wild ;
O, there is nothing on earth half so holy
   As the innocent heart of a child !

They are idols of hearts and of households ;
   They are angels of God in disguise ;
His sunlight still sleeps in their tresses,
   His glory still gleams in their eyes.
O, those truants from home and from heaven,
   They have made me more manly and mild !
And I know how Jesus could liken
   The kingdom of God to a child.

I ask not a life for the dear ones,
　All radiant, as others have done,
But that life may have just enough shadow
　To temper the glare of the sun ;
I would pray God to guard them from evil,
　But my prayer would bound back to myself;
Ah ! a seraph may pray for a sinner,
　But a sinner must pray for himself.

The twig is so easily bended,
　I have banished the rule and the rod ;
I have taught them the goodness of knowledge,
　They have taught me the goodness of God.
My heart is a dungeon of darkness,
　Where I shut them from breaking a rule ;
My frown is sufficient correction ;
　My love is the law of the school.

I shall leave the old house in the autumn,
　To traverse its threshold no more ;
Ah ! how I shall sigh for the dear ones
　That meet me each morn at the door !
I shall miss the "good nights" and the kisses,
　And the gush of their innocent glee,
The group on the green, and the flowers
　That are brought every morning to me.

I shall miss them at morn and at eve,
　Their song in the school and the street;
I shall miss the low hum of their voices,
　And the tramp of their delicate feet.
When the lessons and tasks are all ended,
　And Death says, "The school is dismissed !"
May the little ones gather around me,
　To bid me good night and be kissed.

DICKINSON.

THE EAGLE AND THE SPIDER.

AN eagle had soared above the clouds to the loftiest peak of the Caucasus. There, on an ancient cedar, it settled, and admired the landscape visible at its feet. It seemed as if the borders of the world could be seen from thence. Here flowed rivers, winding across the plains; there stood woods and meadows, adorned with the full garb of spring; and, beyond, frowned the angry Caspian Sea, black as a raven's wing.

"Praise be to thee, O Jove, that, as ruler of the world, thou hast bestowed on me such powers of flight that I know of no heights to me inaccessible," — thus the eagle addressed Jupiter, — "insomuch that I now look upon the beauties of the world from a point whither no other being has flown."

"What a boaster you are!" replies a spider to it from a twig. "As I sit here, am I lower than you, comrade?"

The eagle looks up. Truly enough, the spider is busy spinning its web about a twig overhead, just as if it wanted to shut out the sunlight from the eagle.

"How did you get up to this height?" asked the eagle. "Even among the strongest of wing there are some who would not dare to trust themselves here. But you, weak and wingless, is it possible you can have crawled here?"

"No, I didn't use that means of rising aloft."

"Well, then, how did you get here?"

"Why, I just fastened myself on to you, and you brought me yourself from down below on your tail-feathers. But I know how to maintain my position here without your help, so I beg you will not assume such airs in my presence ; for know that I — "

At this moment a gust of wind comes suddenly flying by, and whirls away the spider again into the lowest depths.

KRILOF.

NEVER GIVE UP.

NEVER give up ! It is wiser and better
   Always to hope, than once to despair ;
Fling off the load of doubt's cankering fetter,
   And break the dark spell of tyrannical care.
Never give up ! or the burden may sink you ;
   Providence kindly has mingled the cup ;
And in all trials and troubles, bethink you,
   The watchword of life must be, " Never give up !"

Never give up ! There are chances and changes,
   Helping the hopeful, a hundred to one ;
And, through the chaos, high Wisdom arranges
   Every success, if you'll only hope on.
Never give up ! for the wisest is boldest,
   Knowing that Providence mingles the cup ;
And of all maxims, the best, as the oldest,
   Is the true watchword of, " Never give up !"

Never give up ! Though the grape-shot may rattle,
   Or the full thunder-cloud over you burst ;
Stand like a rock, and the storm and the battle
   Little shall harm you, though doing their worst.
Never give up ! If adversity presses,
   Providence wisely has mingled the cup ;
And the best counsel, in all your distresses,
   Is the stout watchword of, " Never give up !"

TUPPER.

KITTEN GOSSIP.

KITTEN, kitten, two months old,
 Woolly snowball, lying snug,
Curled up in the warmest fold
 Of the warm hearth-rug,
Turn your drowsy head this way.
What is Life? O, kitten, say!

" Life?" said the kitten, winking her eyes,
And twitching her tail in a droll surprise —
" Life? O, it's racing over the floor,
Out at the window and in at the door;
 Now on the chair-back, now on the table,
'Mid balls of cotton and skeins of silk,
And crumbs of sugar and jugs of milk,
 All so cosy and comfortable.
It's patting the little dog's ears, and leaping
Round him and over him while he's sleeping —
Waking him up in a sore affright,
Then off and away like a flash of light,
Scouring and scampering out of sight.
Life? O, it's rolling over and over
On the summer-green turf and budding clover;
Chasing the shadows, as fast as they run,
Down the garden paths in the midday sun,
Prancing and gambolling, brave and bold,
Climbing the tree-stems, scratching the mould.
That's life!" said the kitten two months old.

Kitten, kitten, come sit on my knee,
And lithe and listen, kitten, to me;
One by one, O, one by one,
The sly, swift shadows sweep over the sun —
Daylight dieth, and kittenhood's done.
And, kitten, O, the rain and the wind!

For cathood cometh, with careful mind,
And grave cat-duties follow behind.
Hark! there's a sound you cannot hear;
I'll whisper its meaning in your ear:
>   *Mice!*
(The kitten stared with her great green eyes,
And twitched her tail in a queer surprise) —
>   *Mice!*
No more titbits dainty and nice;
No more mischief and no more play;
But watching by night and sleeping by day,
Prowling wherever the foe doth lurk —
Very short commons and very sharp work.
And, kitten, O, the hail and the thunder —
That's a blackish cloud, but a blacker's under.
Hark! but you'll fall from my knee I fear,
When I whisper that awful word in your ear —
>   *R-r-r-rats!*
(The kitten's heart beat with great pit-pats,
But her whiskers quivered, and from their sheath
Flashed out the sharp, white, pearly teeth.)
>   *R-r-r-rats!*
The scorn of dogs, but the terror of cats;
The cruelest foes and the fiercest fighters;
The sauciest thieves and the sharpest biters.
But, kitten, I see you've a stoutish heart;
So, courage! and play an honest part ·
>   Use well your paws,
>   And strengthen your claws,
And sharpen your teeth, and stretch your jaws —
Then woe to the tribes of pickers and stealers,
Nibblers and gnawers, and evil dealers!
But now that you know life's not precisely
The thing your fancy pictured so nicely,
Off and away! race over the floor,
Out of the window, and in at the door;
Roll in the turf, and bask in the sun,
Ere night-time cometh, and kittenhood's done.
>   T. WESTWOOD.

JOHN BURNS OF GETTYSBURG.

HAVE you heard the story that gossips tell
  Of Burns of Gettysburg? No? Ah, well:
Brief is the glory that hero earns,
Briefer the story of poor John Burns:
He was the fellow who won renown, —
The only man who didn't back down
When the rebels rode through his native town;
But held his own in the fight next day,
When all his townsfolk ran away.
That was in July, sixty-three,
The very day that General Lee,
Flower of Southern chivalry,
Baffled and beaten, backward reeled
From a stubborn Meade and a barren field.

I might tell how, but the day before,
John Burns stood at his cottage door,
Looking down the village street,
Where, in the shade of his peaceful vine,
He heard the low of his gathered kine,
And felt their breath with incense sweet;
Or, I might say, when the sunset burned
The old farm gable, he thought it turned
The milk that fell, in a babbling flood
Into the milk-pail, red as blood!
Or how he fancied the hum of bees
Were bullets buzzing among the trees.
But all such fanciful thoughts as these
Were strange to a practical man like Burns,
Who minded only his own concerns,
Troubled no more by fancies fine
Than one of his calm-eyed, long-tailed kine, —
Quite old-fashioned and matter-of-fact,
Slow to argue, but quick to act.

5

That was the reason, as some folks say,
He fought so well on that terrible day.

And it was terrible.   On the right
Raged for hours the heady fight,
Thundered the battery's double bass, —
Difficult music for men to face ;
While on the left — where now the graves
Undulate like the living waves
That all that day unceasing swept
Up to the pits the rebels kept —
Round shot ploughed the upland glades ;
Sown with bullets, reaped with blades ;
Shattered fences here and there
Tossed their splinters in the air ;
The very trees were stripped and bare ;
The barns that once held yellow grain
Were heaped with harvests of the slain ;
The cattle bellowed on the plain,
The turkeys screamed with might and main,
And brooding barn-fowl left their rest
With strange shells bursting in each nest.

Just where the tide of battle turns,
Erect and lonely stood old John Burns.
How do you think the man was dressed ?
He wore an ancient long buff vest,
Yellow as saffron, — but his best ;
And, buttoned over his manly breast,
Was a bright blue coat, with a rolling collar,
And large gilt buttons, — size of a dollar, —
With tails that the country-folk called " swaller."
He wore a broad-brimmed, bell-crowned hat,
White as the locks on which it sat.
Never had such a sight been seen
For forty years on the village green,
Since old John Burns was a country beau,
And went to the " quiltings " long ago.

Close at his elbows all that day,
Veterans of the Peninsula,
Sunburnt and bearded, charged away ;
And striplings, downy of lip and chin, —
Clerks that the Home Guard mustered in, —
Glanced, as they passed, at the hat he wore,
Then at the rifle his right hand bore ;
And hailed him, from out their youthful lore,
With scraps of a slangy *répertoire:*
" How are you, White Hat!" " Put her through !"
" Your head's level ! " and " Bully for you ! "
Called him " Daddy," — begged he'd disclose
The name of the tailor who made his clothes,
And what was the value he set on those ;
While Burns, unmindful of jeer and scoff,
Stood there picking the rebels off, —
With his long brown rifle, and bell-crowned hat,
And the swallow-tails they were laughing at.

'Twas but a moment, for that respect
Which clothes all courage their voices checked ;
And something the wildest could understand
Spake in the old man's strong right hand ;
And his corded throat, and the lurking frown
Of his eyebrows under his old bell-crown ;
Until, as they gazed, there crept an awe
Through the ranks in whispers, and some men saw,
In the antique vestments and long white hair,
The Past of the Nation in battle there ;
And some of the soldiers since declare
That the gleam of his old white hat afar,
Like the crested plume of the brave Navarre,
That day was their oriflamme of war.

So raged the battle.   You know the rest :
How the rebels, beaten and backward pressed,
Broke at the final charge, and ran,
At which John Burns — a practical man —

Shouldered his rifle, unbent his brows,
And then went back to his bees and cows.

That is the story of old John Burns;
This is the moral the reader learns :
In fighting the battle, the question's whether
You'll show a hat that's white, or a feather !
                                        BRET HARTE.

LILLIPUT LEVEE.

WHERE does Pinafore Palace stand ?
    Right in the middle of Lilliput-land !
There the queen eats bread and honey,
There the king counts up his money !

O, the glorious revolution !
O, the provisional constitution !
Now the children, clever, bold folks,
Have turned the tables upon the old folks !

Easily the thing was done,
For the children were more than two to one ;
Brave as lions, quick as foxes,
With hoards of wealth in their money-boxes !

They seized the keys ; they patrolled the street ;
They drove the policeman off his beat ;
They built barricades ; they stationed sentries —
You must give the word when you come to the entries.

They dressed themselves in the riflemen's clothes ;
They had pea-shooters ; they had arrows and bows,
So as to put resistance down —
Order reigns in Lilliput-town !

They made the baker bake hot rolls ;
They made the wharfinger send in coals ;
They made the butcher kill the calf ;
They cut the telegraph-wires in half ;

They went to the chemist's, and with their feet
They kicked the physic all down the street ;
They went to the school-room and tore the books ;
They munched the puffs at the pastry-cook's ;

They sucked the jam ; they lost the spoons ;
They sent up several fire-balloons ;
They let off crackers ; they burnt a guy ;
They piled a bonfire ever so high ;

They offered a prize for the laziest boy,
And one for the most magnificent toy ;
They split or burnt the canes off-hand ;
They made new laws in Lilliput-land.

" Never do to-day what you can
Put off till to-morrow," one of them ran ;
" Late to bed and late to rise,"
Was another law which they did devise.

They passed a law to have always plenty
Of beautiful things : we shall mention twenty :
A magic lantern for all to see,
Rabbits to keep, and a Christmas-tree,

A boat, a house that went on wheels,
An organ to grind, and honey at meals,
Drums and wheelbarrows, Roman candles,
Whips with whistles let into the handles,

A real live giant, a roc to fly,
A goat to tease, a copper to shy,
A garret of apples, a box of paints,
A saw and a hammer, and no complaints.

Nail up the door, slide down the stairs,
Saw off the legs of the parlor chairs —
That was the way in Lilliput-land,
The children having the upper hand.

They made the old folks come to school,
All in pinafores — that was the rule —
Saying, Eener-deener-diner-duss,
Kattler-wheeler-whiler-wuss;

They made them learn all sorts of things
That nobody liked.   They had catechizings;
They kept them in ! they sent them down
In class, in school, in Lilliput-town.

O, but they gave them tit-for-tat !
Thick bread and butter, and all that;
Stick-jaw pudding that tires your chin,
With the marmalade spread ever so thin !

They governed the clock in Lilliput-land;
They altered the hour or the minute-hand;
They made the day fast; they made the day slow;
Just as they wished the time to go;

They never waited for king or for cat;
They never wiped their shoes on the mat;
Their joy was great; their joy was greater;
They rode in the baby's perambulator !

There was a levee in Lilliput-town,
At Pinafore Palace.   Smith and Brown,
Jones and Robinson, had to attend —
All to whom they cards did send.

Every one rode in a cab to the door;
Every one came in a pinafore;
Lady and gentleman, rat-tat-tat,
Loud knock, proud knock, opera-hat !

The place was covered with silver and gold ;
The place was full as it ever could hold ;
The ladies kissed her Majesty's hand ;
Such was the custom in Lilliput-land.

His Majesty knighted eight or ten,
Perhaps a score, of the gentlemen,
Some of them short, and some of them tall —
Arise, Sir What's-a-name What do-you-call !

Nuts and nutmeg (that's in the negus) ;
The bill of fare would perhaps fatigue us ;
Forty-five fiddlers to play the fiddle ;
Right foot, left foot, down the middle.

Conjuring tricks with the poker and tongs,
Riddles and forfeits, singing of songs ;
One fat man, too fat by far,
Tried, " Twinkle, twinkle, little star ! "

His voice was gruff, his pinafore tight ;
His wife said, " Mind, dear ; sing it right ; "
But he forgot, and said, Fa-la-la !
The queen of Lilliput's own papa !

She frowned, and ordered him up to bed ;
He said he was sorry ; she shook her head ;
His clean shirt-front with his tears was stained ;
But discipline had to be maintained.

The constitution ! The law ! The crown !
Order reigns in Lilliput-town !
The queen is Jill, and the king is John ;
I trust the government will get on.

THE SOLDIER BIRD.

IN the spring of 1861, Chief Sky, a Chippewa Indian, living in the northern wilds of Wisconsin, found an eagle's nest. To make sure of his prize, he cut the tree down, and caught the eaglets as they were sliding from the nest to run and hide in the grass. One died. He carried the other home, and built a nest in a tree close by his wigwam. The eaglet was as large as a hen, and covered with soft down. The red children were delighted with their new pet; and as soon as he became acquainted, he would sit down in the grass, and see them play with the dogs.

But Chief Sky was poor, and he was obliged to sell the noble bird to a white man for a bushel of corn. The white man brought him to Eau Claire, a small village where the enlisted soldiers were busy in preparing to go to the war. "Here's a recruit," said the man. "An eagle! an eagle!" shouted the soldiers; "let him enlist!" and sure enough, he was sworn into the service, with ribbons around his neck — red, white, and blue.

On a perch surmounted by stars and stripes the company took him to Madison, the capital of the state. As they marched into Camp Randall, with colors flying, drums beating, and the people cheering, the eagle seized the flag in his beak, and spread his wings, his bright eye kindling with the spirit of the scene. Shouts rent the air, — "The Bird of Columbia! the Eagle of Freedom forever!"

The state made him a new perch, and the boys named him "Old Abe;" and the Eighth Wisconsin

Regiment was henceforth called "The Eagle Regiment." On the march he was carried at the head of the company, and everywhere was greeted with delight.

At St. Louis a gentleman offered five hundred dollars for him, and another his farm. No, no; the boys had no notion of parting with their bird. He was above all price, — an emblem of battle and of victory. Besides, he interested their minds, and made them think less of hardships and of home.

It was really amusing to witness the strange freaks and droll adventures of this bird during his three years' service, — his flights in the air, his fights with the guinea-hens, and his races with the boys. When the regiment was in summer quarters at Clear Creek, the eagle was allowed to run at large, and every morning went to the river, half a mile off, where he splashed and played in the water to his heart's content, faithfully returning to camp when he was satisfied.

Old Abe's favorite place of resort was the sutler's tent, where a live chicken found " no quarter " in his presence. But rations became scarce, and for two days Abe had nothing to eat. Hard-tack he objected to; fasting was disagreeable; and Thomas, his bearer, could not get beyond the pickets to a farm-yard. At last, pushing his way to the colonel's tent, he pleaded for poor Abe. The colonel gave him a pass, and Thomas procured for him an excellent dinner.

One day a farmer asked Thomas to come and show the eagle to his children. Satisfying the curiosity of the family, Thomas set him down in the barn-yard. O, what a screeching and scattering among the fowls!

for Abe pounced upon one and gobbled up another, to
the great amazement of the farmer, who declared that
such wanton behavior was not in the bargain. Abe,
however, thought there was no harm in "confiscating"
in time of war.

Abe was in twenty battles, besides thirty skirmishes.
He was at the siege of Vicksburg, the storming of
Corinth, and marched with Sherman in his grand
campaign. The whiz of bullets and scream of shells
were his delight. As the battle grew hotter and
hotter, he would flap his wings, and mingle his wildest
notes with the thundering din around him.

He was, very fond of music, especially Yankee
Doodle and John Brown. Upon parade he always
gave heed to the word, "Attention!" With his eye
on the commander, he would listen and obey orders,
noting time accurately. After parade he would put
off his soldierly air, flap his wings, and make himself
at home.

The enemy called him "Yankee Buzzard," "Old
Owl," and other hard names; but his eagle nature
was quite above noticing it. One general gave
orders to his men to be sure and capture the eagle
of the Eighth Wisconsin; saying he "would rather
have him than a dozen battle-flags." But for all that,
he scarcely lost a feather, — only one from his right
wing.

At last the war was over, and the brave Wisconsin
Eighth, with their live eagle and torn and riddled
flags, were welcomed back to Madison. They went
out a thousand strong, and returned a little band,
scarred and toilworn, having fought and won.

And what of the Soldier Bird? In the name of the

gallant veterans, Captain Wolf presented him to the state. Governor Lewis accepted the illustrious gift, and ample quarters are provided for him in the beautiful State-House grounds, where may he long live to tell us

"What heroes from the woodland sprang,
   When, through the fresh-awakened land,
   The thrilling cry of Freedom rang."

BEAUTIFUL GRANDMAMMA.

GRANDMAMMA sits in her quaint arm-chair ;
   Never was lady more sweet and fair ;
Her gray locks ripple like silver shells,
And her own brow its story tells
Of a gentle life and peaceful even,
A trust in God and a hope in heaven.

Little girl Mary sits rocking away
In her own low seat, like some winsome fay ;
Two doll babies her kisses share,
And another one lies by the side of her chair ;
May is fair as the morning dew,
Cheeks of roses and ribbons of blue.

"Say, grandmamma," says the pretty elf,
"Tell me a story about yourself :
When you were little, what did you play ?
Were you good or naughty, the whole long day ?
Was it hundreds and hundreds of years ago ?
And what makes your soft hair as white as snow ?

"Did you have a mamma to hug and kiss ?
And a dolly like this, and this, and this ?

Did you have a pussy like my little Kate ?
Did you go to bed when the clock struck eight ?
Did you have long curls and beads like mine ?
And a new silk apron, with ribbons fine ? ''

Grandmamma smiled at the little maid,
And, laying aside her knitting, she said,
" Go to my desk, and a red box you'll see ;
Carefully lift it and bring it to me."
So May put her dollies away, and ran,
Saying, " I'll be careful as ever I can."

Then grandmamma opened the box, and lo !
A beautiful child, with throat like snow,
Lips just tinted like pink shells rare,
Eyes of hazel, and golden hair,
Hand all dimpled, and teeth like pearls,
Fairest and sweetest of little girls.

" O, who is it ? '' cried winsome May.
" How I wish she were here to-day !
Wouldn't I love her like everything ;
Say, dear grandmamma, who can she be ? ''
" Darling," said grandma, " that child was me."

May looked long at the dimpled grace,
And then at the saint-like, fair old face ;
" How funny," she cried. with a smile and a kiss,
" To have such a dear little grandma as this !
Still," she added, with smiling zest,
" I think, dear grandma, I like *you* best."

So May climbed on the silken knee,
And grandmamma told her history ;
What plays she played, what toys she had,
How at times she was naughty, or good, or sad.
" But the best thing you did," said May, "don't you see?
Was to grow a beautiful grandma for me."

Standard of the Cross.

THE BOYS.

" THE boys are coming home to-morrow : "
  This our rural hostess said,
Whilst Lou and I shot flitting glances,
  Full of vague unspoken dread.

Had we hither come for quiet,
  Hither fled the city's noise,
But to change it for the tumult
  Of those horrid country boys ;

Waking one with wild hallooing
  Early every summer day,
Shooting robins, teasing kittens,
  Frightening wrens away ;

Tumbling over trailing flounces,
  Tumbling volumes gold and blue ;
Clamoring for sugared dainties,
  Tracking earth the passage through ?

These, and other kindred trials,
  Fancied we with woful sigh ;
" Those boys, those horrid boys, to-morrow ! "
  Sadly whispered Lou and I.

I wrote those lines one happy summer ;
  To-day I smile to read them o'er,
Remembering how full of terror
  We watched all day the opening door.

They came, the boys, six feet in stature,
  Graceful, easy, polished men ;
I vowed to Lou, behind my knitting,
  To trust no mother's word again.

For boyhood is a thing immortal
   To every mother's heart and eye,
And sons are boys to her forever,
   Change as they may to you or I.

To her no line comes sharply marking
   Whither or when their childhood went,
Nor when the eye-glance upward turning,
   Levelled at last their downward bent!

Now, by the window still and sunny,
   Warmed by the rich October glow,
The dear old lady waits and watches,
   Just as she waited years ago.

For Lou and I are now her daughters;
   We married those two country boys,
In spite of all our sad forebodings
   About their awkward ways and noise.

Lou springs up to meet a footfall;
   I list no more for coming feet;
Mother and I are waiting longer
   For steps on Beulah's golden street.

But when she blesses Lou's beloved,
   And seals it with a tender kiss,
I know that loving thoughts go upward —
   Words to another world than this.

Always she speaks in gentle fashion
   About "my boys," — she always will,
Though one is gray, and one has vanished
   Beyond the touch of time or ill.

POLITICS.

BILL MORE and I, in days gone by,
　　Were friends the long year through,
Save when, above the melting snow,
　　Wild March his trumpet blew.

Outspoken foes, we then arose ;
　　Each chose a different way ;
For March, to our New Hampshire hills,
　　Brings back town-meeting day.

Its gingerbread and oranges,
　　Alike on Bill and me,
That day bestowed, but only one
　　Could share its victory.

For what was victory ?　We had
　　Opposing views of that,
For Billy was an old line Whig,
　　And I a Democrat.

The tide of politics ran high
　　Among the village boys,
And those were truest patriots
　　Who made the greatest noise.

And who could higher toss his cap,
　　Or louder shout than I ?
Till all the mountain echoes learnt
　　My party battle-cry !

One time, — it was election morn, —
　　Beside the town-house door,
Among a troop of cheering boys,
　　I came on Billy More.

" Cheer on ! " I called ; " I would not give,
  For your hurrahs, a fig ;
But say, what do the Whigs believe ?
  Speak, Billy ! you're a Whig."

And Bill said, " I don't know nor care ;
  You needn't ask me that ;
You'd better tell me, if you can,
  Why you're a Democrat."

And I commenced, in bold disdain, —
  " What ? tell you, if I can ?
I ?   Why, my father 's candidate
  For second selectman.

" And he knows — I know — he knows — he —
  I think — I feel — I — I —
I — I — I am a Democrat, —
  And *that's* the reason why."

" Ha! ha!" the mocking shout that rose, —
  I seem to hear it now,
And feel the hot tumultuous blood
  That crimsoned cheek and brow !

I might have spared my blushes then,
  I should have kept my shame
For men, grown men, who fight to-day
  For just a party name !

This side or that, they cast their votes,
  And pledge their faith, and why ?
Go ask, and you will find them wise
  As Billy More and I !

                              MARION DOUGLASS.

LITTLE BENNY.

I HAD told him Christmas morning,
  As he sat upon my knee,
Holding fast his little stockings,
  Stuffed as full as full could be,
And attentive listening to me,
  With a face demure and mild,
That old Santa Claus, who filled them,
  Did not love a naughty child.

" But we'll be good — won't we, moder ? "
  And from off my lap he slid,
Digging deep among the goodies
  In the crimson stockings hid ;
While I turned me to my table,
  Where a tempting goblet stood,
Brimming high with dainty custard,
  Sent me by a neighbor good.

But the kitten, there before me,
  With his white paw, nothing loath,
Sat, by way of entertainment,
  Slapping off the shining froth ;
And, in not the gentlest humor
  At the loss of such a treat,
I confess I rather rudely
  Thrust him out into the street.

Then how Benny's blue eyes kindled !
  Gathering up the precious store
He had busily been pouring
  In his tiny pinafore,
With a generous look that shamed me,
  Sprang he from the carpet bright,
Showing by his mien indignant,
  All a baby's sense of right.

6

"Come back, Harney," called he loudly,
     As he held his apron white,
" You shall have my candy wabbit ! "
     But the door was fastened tight;
So he stood, abashed and silent,
     In the centre of the floor,
With defeated look alternate
     Bent on me and on the door.

Then as by some sudden impulse
     Quickly ran he to the fire,
And while eagerly his bright eyes
     Watched the flames go higher and higher,
In a brave, clear key, he shouted,
     Like some lordly little elf,
" Santa Kaus, come down de chimney,
     Make my moder 'have herself ! "

" I will be a good girl, Benny,"
     Said I, feeling the reproof;
And straightway recalled poor Harney,
     Mewing on the gallery roof.
Soon the anger was forgotten,
     Laughter chased away the frown,
And they gambolled 'neath the live-oaks
     Till the dusky night came down.

In my dim, fire-lighted chamber,
     Harney purred beneath my chair,
And my play-worn boy beside me,
     Knelt to say his evening prayer:
" God bess fader, God bess moder,
     God bess sister " — then a pause,
And the sweet young lips devoutly
     Murmured, " God bess Santa Kaus."

He is sleeping : brown and silken
     Lie the lashes, long and meek,

Like caressing, clinging shadows
 On his plump and peachy cheek ;
And I bend above him weeping
 Thankful tears, O Undefiled !
For a woman's crown of glory,
 For the blessing of a child.

THE ETERNAL BURDEN.

A PRINCE in the East had taken a widow's field away from her, though she would not sell it to him. The widow went to a wise judge, and complained of her misfortune. The judge arose, took a sack, and laid it on his mule.

So he came to the prince, who was just then in his garden adjoining the widow's field. The judge asked permission of the prince to fill the sack with earth from the poor woman's field, as a keepsake for her. The prince granted it, and said, —

" Why has the woman been so foolish as not to sell me the field? Now she is punished for her folly."

When the judge had filled the sack, he asked the prince to help him lift it upon the mule's back. The prince tried it, but said at once, —

" The sack is too heavy for me."

Then said the judge, with great earnestness, —

" If this sack full of earth is so heavy even now, how heavily will the whole field weigh upon you throughout eternity?"

This thought made the prince afraid, and he gave the widow back her field.

LETTING THE OLD CAT DIE.

NOT long ago I wandered near
   A playground in the wood,
And there heard words from a youngster's lips
   That I've never quite understood.

" Now let the old cat die," he laughed ;
   I saw him give a push,
Then gayly scamper away, as he espied
   A face peep over the bush.

But what he pushed, or where he went,
   I could not well make out,
On account of the thicket of bending boughs
   That bordered the place about.

" The little villain has stoned a cat,
   Or hung it upon a limb,
And left it to die all alone," I said,
   " But I'll play the mischief with him."

I forced my way through the boughs
   The poor old cat to seek,
And what did I find but a swinging child
   With her bright hair brushing her cheek.

Her bright hair floated to and fro,
   Her little red dress flashed by ;
But the loveliest thing of all, I thought,
   Was the gleam of her laughing eye.

Swinging and swinging back and forth,
   With the rose-light in her face,
She seemed like a bird and flower in one,
   And the forest her native place.

" Steady ! I'll send you up, my child ; "
   But she stopped me with a cry :
" Go 'way ! go 'way ! don't touch me, please ;
   I'm letting the old cat die."

" You're letting him die !" I cried, aghast ;
   " Why, where's the cat, my dear ? "
And lo ! the laugh that filled the wood
   Was a thing for the birds to hear.

" Why, don't you know," said the little maid,
   The sparkling, beautiful elf,
" That we call letting the old cat die
   When the swing stops all itself ? "

Then swinging and swinging, and looking back,
   With the merriest look in her eye,
She bade me good by, and I left her alone
   Letting the old cat die.

THE WIVES OF BRIXHAM.

YOU see the gentle water,
   How silently it floats ;
How cautiously, how steadily,
   It moves the sleepy boats ;
And all the little loops of pearl
   It strews along the sand,
Steal out as leisurely as leaves
   When summer is at hand.

But you know it can be angry,
   And thunder from its rest,
When the stormy taunts of winter
   Are flying at its breast ;

And if you like to listen,
　　And draw your chairs around,
I'll tell you what it did one night
　　When you were sleeping sound.

The merry boats of Brixham
　　Go out to search the seas ;
A stanch and sturdy fleet are they,
　　That like a swinging breeze ;
And before the woods of Devon,
　　And the silver cliffs of Wales,
You may see, when summer evenings fall,
　　The light upon their sails.

But when the year grows darker,
　　And gray winds hunt the foam,
They go back to Little Brixham,
　　And ply their toil at home.
And thus it chanced one winter's night,
　　When a storm began to roar,
That all the men were out at sea,
　　And all the wives on shore.

Then as the wind grew fiercer,
　　The women's cheeks grew white, —
It was fiercer in the twilight,
　　And fiercest in the night.
The strong clouds set themselves like ice
　　Without a star to melt,
The blackness of the darkness
　　Was darkness to be felt.

The storm, like an assassin,
　　Went on its wicked way,
And struck a hundred boats adrift,
　　To reel about the bay.
They meet, they crash! — God keep the men
　　God give a moment's light !

There is nothing but the tumult,
  And the tempest, and the night.

The men on shore were anxious, —
  They dreaded what they knew ;
What do you think the women did ?
  Love taught them what to do !
Outspoke a wife : " We've beds at home,
  We'll burn them for a light, —
Give us the men and the bare ground !
  We want no more to-night."

They took the grandame's blanket,
  Who shivered and bade them go ;
They took the baby's pillow,
  Who could not say them no ;
And they heaped a great fire on the pier,
  And knew not all the while
If they were heaping a bonfire,
  Or only a funeral pile.

And, fed with precious food, the flame
  Shone bravely on the black,
Till a cry rang through the people,
  " A boat is coming back ! "
Staggering dimly through the fog,
  Come shapes of fear and doubt ;
But when the first prow strikes the pier,
  Cannot you hear them shout ?

Then all along the breadth of flame
  Dark figures shrieked and ran,
With, " Child, here comes your father ! "
  Or, " Wife, is this your man ? "
And faint feet touch the welcome stone,
  And wait a little while ;
And kisses drop from frozen lips,
  Too tired to speak or smile.

So, one by one, they struggled in,
   All that the sea would spare ;
We will not reckon through our tears
   The names that were not there ;
But some went home without a bed,
   When all the tale was told,
Who were too cold with sorrow
   To know the night was cold.

And this is what the men must do
   Who work in wind and foam ;
And this is what the women bear
   Who watch for them at home.
So when you see a Brixham boat
   Go out to face the gales,
Think of the love that travels
   Like light upon her sails.

CHRISTOPHER COLUMBUS.

THE MAN WHO DISCOVERED AMERICA TWO POINTS OFF THE PORT BOW.

ONE day, in his garden, he observed an apple falling from its tree, whereupon a conviction flashed suddenly through his mind that the earth was round.

By breaking the shell of an egg, and making it stand on end at the dinner-table, he demonstrated that he could sail due west, and in course of time arrive at another hemisphere.

He started a line of emigrant packets from Palos, Spain, and landed at Philadelphia, where he walked up Market Street with a loaf of bread under each arm. The simple-hearted natives took him out to see their new park.

On his second voyage, Columbus was barbarously murdered at the Sandwich Islands, or, rather, would have been but for the intervention of Pocahontas, a lovely maiden, romantically fond of distressed travellers.

After this little incident he went west, where his intrepidity and masterly financial talent displayed itself in the success with which he acquired land and tobacco without paying for them.

As the savages had no railroad of which they could make him president, they ostracized him — sent him to the Island of St. Helena.

But the spirit of discovery refused to be quenched; and the next year we find him landing at Plymouth Rock in a blinding snow-storm. It was here that he shot an apple from his son's head.

To this universal genius are we indebted also for the exploration of the sources of the Nile, and for an unintelligible, but correspondingly valuable, scientific report of a visit to the valley of the Yellowstone.

He took no side in our late unhappy war; but during the Revolution, he penetrated with a handful of the Garde Mobile into the mountain fastnesses of Minnesota, where he won that splendid series of victories, which, beginning with Guilford Court House, terminated in the glorious storming of Chapultepec.

Ferdinand and Isabella rewarded him with chains. Genoa, his native city, gave him a statue, and Boston has named in his honor one of her proudest avenues.

One day he rushed from the bath, exclaiming, "Eureka!" and the presumption is, that he was right.

THE PUZZLED CENSUS-TAKER.

"GOT any boys?" the marshal said
　　To a lady from over the Rhine;
And the lady shook her flaxen head,
　　And civilly answered, "*Nine!*" *

"Got any girls?" the marshal said
　　To the lady from over the Rhine;
And again the lady shook her head,
　　And civilly answered, "*Nine!*"

"But some are dead?" the marshal said
　　To the lady from over the Rhine;
And again the lady shook her head,
　　And civilly answered, "*Nine!*"

"Husband, of course?" the marshal said
　　To the lady from over the Rhine;
And again she shook her flaxen head,
　　And civilly answered, "*Nine!*"

"The d—l you have!" the marshal said
　　To the lady from over the Rhine;
And again she shook her flaxen head,
　　And civilly answered, "*Nine!*"

"Now what do you mean by shaking your head,
　　And always answering '*Nine?*'"
"*Ich kann nicht Englich!*" civilly said
　　The lady from over the Rhine.
JOHN G. SAXE.

* *Nein,* pronounced *Nine,* is the German for "*No!*"

TRUTH.

BE true, be true ! whate'er beside,
  Of wit or wealth, or rank be thine,
Unless with simple truth allied,
  The gold that glitters in thy mine
Is only dross, the brass of pride,
  Or vainer tinsel, made to shine.

Be true, be true ! to nerve your arm
  For any good ye wish to do ;
To save yourselves from sin and harm,
  And win all honors old and new ;
To work on hearts as with a charm, —
  The maxim is, Be true, be true !

Be true, be true ! that easy prize
  So lovable to human view,
So laudable beyond the skies,
  Alas ! is reached by very few —
The simple ones, though more than wise, —
  Whose motto is, Be true, be true !

M. F. TUPPER.

LINGERING LATIMER.

LINGERING LATIMER lived up a tree,
    Just like a sloth !
Slackest and slowest of slow boys was he,
    Lazy and loth !

He kept a pet tortoise, and *that* had the gout, —
    A very poor goer ;
And Lingering Latimer, when they went out
    For a walk, was the slower !

There was nothing about him would run — not his nose,
    We are told !
But the secret of *that* was (it's under the rose),
    He could not catch — cold !

In his prospects we cannot but own there is hope
    Of a sort :
He may live by performing upon the slack rope,
    And can never run — short !

ODE TO SPRING.

WRITTEN IN A LAWYER'S OFFICE.

WHEREAS, on sundry boughs and sprays,
    Now divers birds are heard to sing,
And sundry flowers their heads upraise, —
    Hail to the coming on of Spring !

The birds aforesaid, happy pairs !
    Love midst the aforesaid boughs enshrines,
In household nests, themselves, their heirs,
    Administrators, and assigns.

The songs of the said birds arouse
    The memory of our youthful hours,
As young and green as the said boughs,
    As fresh and fair as the said flowers.

O, busiest term of Cupid's court !
    When tender plaintiffs actions bring ;
Season of frolic and of sport,
    Hail, as aforesaid, coming Spring !

ROBERT OF LINCOLN.

MERRILY swinging on brier and weed,
    Near to the nest of his little dame,
Over the mountain-side or mead,
    Robert of Lincoln is telling his name —
        "Bob-o-link, bob-o-link, spink, spank, spink.
        Snug and safe is that nest of ours,
        Hidden among the summer flowers :
            Chee, chee, chee."

Robert of Lincoln is gayly dressed,
    Wearing a bright black wedding coat ;
White are his shoulders and white his crest,
    Hear him call in his merry note —
        "Bob-o-link, bob-o-link, spink, spank, spink.
        Look what a nice new coat is mine,
        Sure there was never a bird so fine.
            Chee, chee, chee."

Robert of Lincoln's Quaker wife,
    Pretty and quiet, with plain brown wings,
Passing at home a patient life,
    Broods in the grass while her husband sings —
        "Bob-o-link, bob-o-link, spink, spank, spink.
        Brood, kind creature, you need not fear
        Thieves and robbers while I am here.
            Chee, chee, chee."

Modest and shy as a nun is she,
    One weak chirp her only note ;
Braggart and prince of braggarts is he,
    Pouring boasts from his little throat —
        "Bob-o-link, bob-o-link, spink, spank, spink.
        Never was I afraid of man ;
        Catch me, cowardly knaves, if you can.
            Chee, chee, chee."

Six white eggs on a bed of hay,
   Flecked with purple, a pretty sight !
There, as the mother sits all day,
   Robert is singing with all his might —
      " Bob-o-link, bob-o-link, spink, spank, spink,
      Nice good wife, that never goes out,
      Keeping house while I frolic about.
        Chee, chee, chee."

Soon as the little ones chip the shell,
   Six wide mouths are open for food ;
Robert of Lincoln bestirs him well,
   Gathering seeds for the hungry brood —
      " Bob-o-link, bob-o-link, spink, spank, spink ;
      This new life is likely to be
      Hard for a gay young fellow like me.
        Chee, chee, chee."

Robert of Lincoln at length is made
   Sober with work, and silent with care ;
Off is his holiday garment laid,
   Half forgotten that merry air —
      " Bob-o-link, bob-o-link, spink, spank, spink ;
      Nobody knows but my mate and I
      Where our nest and nestlings lie.
        Chee, chee, chee."

Summer wanes ; the children are grown ;
   Fun and frolic no more he knows ;
Robert of Lincoln's a humdrum crone ;
   Off he flies, and we sing as he goes —
      " Bob-o-link, bob-o-link, spink, spank, spink ;
      When you can pipe that merry old strain,
      Robert of Lincoln, come back again :
        Chee, chee, chee."   BRYANT.

AT SEA.

THE night is made for cooling shade,
  For silence, and for sleep ;
And when I was a child, I laid
My hands upon my breast, and prayed,
  And sank to slumbers deep.
Childlike as then, I lie to-night,
And watch my lonely cabin light.

Each movement of the swaying lamp
  Shows how the vessel reels ;
As o'er her deck the billows tramp,
And all her timbers strain and cramp
  With every shock she feels,
It starts and shudders, while it burns,
And in its hingèd socket turns.

Now swinging slow, and slanting low,
  It almost level lies ;
And yet I know, while to and fro
I watch the seeming pendule go
  With restless fall and rise,
The steady shaft is still upright,
Poising its little globe of light.

O, hand of God ! O, lamp of peace !
  O, promise of my soul !—
Though weak, and tossed, and ill at ease,
Amid the roar of smiting seas,
  The ship's convulsive roll,
I own, with love and tender awe,
You perfect type of faith and law !

A heavenly trust my spirit calms,
　　My soul is filled with light :
The ocean sings his solemn psalms,
The wild winds chant : I cross my palms,
　　Happy as if, to-night,
Under the cottage-roof, again
I heard the soothing summer-rain.

J. T. TROWBRIDGE.

THE SHADOW ON THE BLIND.

MR. FERDINAND PLUM was a grocer by trade ;
　　By attention and tact he a fortune had made ;
No tattler, nor maker of mischief, was he,
But as honest a man as you'd e'er wish to see.
Of a chapel, close by, he was deacon, they say,
And his minister lived just over the way.

Mr. Plum was retiring to rest one night,
He had just undressed and put out the light,
　　　And pulled back the blind
　　　As he peeped from behind
('Tis a custom with many to do so you'll find),
　　　When, glancing his eye,
　　　He happened to spy
On the blinds on the opposite side — O, fie !
Two shadows ; each movement of course he could see,
And the people were quarrelling evidently.
" Well, I never ! " said Plum, as he witnessed the strife,
" I declare, 'tis the minister beating his wife ! "
The minister held a thick stick in his hand,
And his wife ran away as he shook the brand,
While her shrieks and cries were quite shocking to hear,
And the sounds came across most remarkably clear.

" Well, things are deceiving,
    But — ' seeing's believing,' "
Said Plum to himself, as he turned into bed ;
    " Now, who would have thought
    That man would have fought
And beaten his wife on her shoulders and head
    With a great big stick,
    At least three inches thick ?
I am sure her shrieks quite filled me with dread.
    I've a great mind to bring
    The whole of the thing
Before the church members ; but, no, I have read
A proverb, which says, ' Least said soonest mended.' "
And thus Mr. Plum's mild soliloquy ended.

But, alas ! Mr. Plum's eldest daughter, Miss Jane,
Saw the whole of the scene, and could not refrain
From telling Miss Spot, and Miss Spot told again
(Though of course in strict confidence) *every* one
Whom she happened to know, what the parson had done.
So the news spread abroad, and soon reached the ear
Of the parson himself, and he traced it, I hear,
To the author, Miss Jane. Jane could not deny,
But at the same time she begged leave to defy
The parson to prove she had uttered a lie.

A church meeting was called : Mr. Plum made a speech.
He said, " Friends, pray listen a while, I beseech.
What my daughter has said is most certainly true,
For I saw the whole scene on the same evening, too ;
But, not wishing to make an unpleasantness rife,
I did not tell either my daughter or wife.
But, of course, as Miss Jane saw the whole of the act,
I think it but right to attest to the fact."
" 'Tis remarkably strange !" the parson replied :
" It is plain Mr. Plum must *something* have spied ;

Though the wife-beating story, of course, is denied :
And in *that* I can say I am grossly belied."
While he ransacks his brain, and ponders, and tries
To recall any scene that could ever give rise
To so monstrous a charge, just then his wife cries,
" I have it, my love ; you remember that night
When I had such a horrible, terrible fright.
We both were retiring that evening to rest —
I was seated, my dear, and but partly undressed —
When a horrid old rat jumped close to my feet ;
My shrieking was heard, I suppose, in the street ;
You caught up the poker, and ran round the room,
And at last knocked the rat, and so sealed its doom.
Our *shadows*, my love, must have played on the blind ;
And this is the mystery solved you will find."

Moral.

Don't believe every tale that is handed about ;
We have all enough faults and *real* failings, without
Being burdened with those of which there's a doubt.

THE PORTRAITS.

A PAINTER, who wanted a picture of Innocence,
drew the likeness of a child at prayer. The
little suppliant was kneeling by the side of his mother,
who regarded him with tenderness. The palms of his
lifted hands were reverently pressed together; his
rosy cheeks spoke of health, and his mild, blue eye
was upturned with an expression of devotion and
peace.

This portrait of young Rupert was highly prized by
the painter; for he had bestowed on it great pains: he
hung it up in his study, and called it Innocence.

Years rolled along, and the painter became an aged man; but the picture of Innocence still adorned his study walls. Often had he thought of painting a contrast to his favorite portrait; but opportunity had not served. He had sought for a striking model of guilt; but had failed to find one. At last he effected his purpose by paying a visit to a neighboring jail.

On the damp floor of his dungeon lay a wretched culprit, named Randal, heavily ironed. Wasted was his body, worn was his cheek, and anguish unutterable was seen in his hollow eye; but this was not all. Vice was visible in his face, guilt was branded, as with a hot iron, and horrid imprecations burst from his blaspheming tongue.

The painter executed the task to the life, and bore away the successful effort of his pencil. The portraits of young Rupert and old Randal were hung, side by side, in his study; the one representing Innocence and the other Guilt.

But who was young Rupert, who kneeled in prayer by the side of his mother in meek devotion? And who was old Randal, who lay manacled on the dungeon floor, cursing and blaspheming? Alas, the two were one! Young Rupert and old Randal were the same. Led by bad companions into the paths of sin, no wonder that young Rupert found bitterness and sorrow.

Well may youth and age walk humbly before God, putting up the prayer, " Keep me as the apple of the eye, hide me under the shadow of thy wings."

THE THREE WARNINGS.

THE tree of deepest root is found
 Least willing still to quit the ground;
'Twas therefore said by ancient sages
 That love of life increased with years,
So much, that in our latter stages,
When pains grow sharp, and sickness rages,
 The greatest love of life appears.
This great affection to believe,
Which all confess, but few perceive,
If old assertions can't prevail,
Be pleased to hear a modern tale.

When sports went round, and all were gay,
On neighbor Dobson's wedding day, .
Death called aside the jocund groom
With him into another room,
And looking grave, " You must," says he,
" Quit your sweet bride, and come with me."
" With you! and quit my Susan's side?
With you?" the hapless husband cried;
" Young as I am, 'tis monstrous hard!
Besides, in truth, I'm not prepared;
My thoughts on other matters go;
This is my wedding day, you know."
What more he urged I have not heard,
 His reasons could not well be stronger;
So Death the poor delinquent spared,
 And left to live a little longer.
Yet, calling up a serious look, —
His hour-glass trembled while he spoke, —
" Neighbor," he said, " farewell; no more
Shall Death disturb your mirthful hour;
And, farther, to avoid all blame
Of cruelty upon my name,

To give you time for preparation,
And fit you for your future station,
Three several warnings you shall have
Before you're summoned to the grave :
Willing, for once, I'll quit my prey,
   And grant a kind reprieve,
In hopes you'll have no more to say,
But, when I call again this way,
   Well pleased the world will leave."
To these conditions both consented,
And parted perfectly contented.

What next the hero of our tale befell,
How long he lived, how wise, how well,
How roundly he pursued his course,
And smoked his pipe, and stroked his horse,
   The willing Muse shall tell :
He chaffered then, he bought, he sold,
Nor once perceived his growing old,
   Nor thought of Death as near ;
His friends not false, his wife no shrew,
Many his gains, his children few,
   He passed his hours in peace.
But while he viewed his wealth increase,
While thus along life's dusty road
The beaten track content he trode,
Old Time, whose haste no mortal spares,
Uncalled, unheeded, unawares,
   Brought on his eightieth year.
And now one night, in musing mood,
   As all alone he sate,
   The unwelcome messenger of fate
Once more before him stood.
Half killed with anger and surprise,
" So soon returned ? " old Dobson cries.
" So soon, d'ye call it ? " Death replies ;
" Surely, my friend, you're but in jest !
   Since I was here before

'Tis six and forty years at least,
    And you are now fourscore ! "
" So much the worse," the clown rejoined ;
" To spare the aged would be kind ;
Besides, you promised me Three Warnings,
Which I have looked for nights and mornings ! "
" I know," cries Death, " that at the best,
I seldom am a welcome guest ;
But don't be captious, friend, at least :
I little thought you'd still be able
To stump about your farm and stable ;
Your years have run to a great length :
I wish you joy, though, of your strength ! "
" Hold," says the farmer, " not so fast !
I have been lame these four years past."
" And no great wonder," Death replies :
" However, you still keep your eyes,
And sure, to see one's loves and friends,
For legs and arms must make amends."
" Perhaps," says Dobson, " so it might,
But latterly I've lost my sight."
" This is a shocking story, faith :
But there's some comfort still," says Death.
" Each strives your sadness to amuse ;
I warrant you hear all the news."
" There's none," cried he : and if there were
I'm grown so deaf, I could not hear."
" Nay, then," the spectre stern rejoined,
    " Cease, prythee, cease these foolish yearnings;
If you are deaf, and lame, and blind,
    You've had your three sufficient warnings ;
So come along ! no more we'll part,"
He said, and touched him with his dart.
And now old Dobson, turning pale,
Yields to his fate.   So ends my tale.
                                    MRS. THRALE.

DER BABY.

SO help me gracious, efery day
  I laugh me wild to see der vay
My schmall young baby drie to play —
    Dot funny leetle baby.

Vhen 1 look on dhem leetle toes,
Und saw dot funny leetle nose,
Und heard der vay dot rooster crows,
    I schmile like 1 was grazy.

Und vhen I heard der real nice vay
Dhem beoples to my wife dhey say,
"More like his fater every day,"
    1 vas so proud like blazes.

Sometimes dhere comes a leetle schquall,
Dot's vhen der vindy vind vill crawl
Righd in its leetle schtomach schmall, —
    Dot's too bad for der baby.

Dot makes him sing at night so schveet,
Und gorrybarric he must eat,
Und I must chump shpry on my feet,
    To help dot leetle baby.

He bulls my nose and kicks my hair,
Und grawls me ofer everywhere,
Und shlobbers me — but vat I care?
    Dot vas my schmall young baby.

Around my head dot leetle arm
Vas schqueezin me so nice and varm —
O! may dhere never coom some harm
    To dot schmall leetle baby.

"GUILTY OR NOT GUILTY?"

SHE stood at the bar of justice,
    A creature wan and wild,
In form too small for a woman,
    In feature too old for a child ;
For a look so worn and pathetic
    Was stamped on her pale young face,
It seemed long years of suffering
    Must have left that silent trace.

"Your name," said the judge, as he eyed her,
    With kindly look, yet keen,
"Is —"   "Mary Maguire, if you please, sir."
    "And your age?"   "I am turned fifteen."
"Well, Mary," — and then from a paper
    He slowly and gravely read, —
"You are charged here — I am sorry to say it —
    With stealing three loaves of bread.

"You look not like an offender,
    And I hope that you can show
The charge to be false. Now, tell me,
    Are you guilty of this, or no?"
A passionate burst of weeping
    Was at first her sole reply ;
But she dried her tears in a moment,
    And looked in the judge's eye.

"I will tell you just how it was, sir ;
    My father and mother are dead,
And my little brothers and sisters
    Were hungry, and asked me for bread.
At first I earned it for them,
    By working hard all day,
But somehow the times were hard, sir,
    And the work all fell away.

" I could get no more employment ;
    The weather was bitter cold :
The young ones cried and shivered
    (Little Johnnie's but four years old) ; —
So what was I to do, sir ?
    I am guilty, but do not condemn ;
I *look* — O ! was it *stealing?*
    The bread to give to them."

Every man in the court-room —
    Graybeard and thoughtless youth —
Knew, as he looked upon her,
    That the prisoner spake the truth.
Out from their pockets came kerchiefs,
    Out from their eyes sprung tears,
And out from old, faded wallets
    Treasures hoarded for years.

The judge's face was a study,
    The strangest you ever saw,
As he cleared his throat and murmured
    Something about the *law.*
For one so learned in such matters,
    So wise in dealing with men,
He seemed, on a simple question,
    Sorely puzzled just then.

But no one blamed him, or wondered
    When at last these words they heard :
" The sentence of this young prisoner
    Is for the present deferred."
And no one blamed him or wondered
    When he went to her and smiled,
And tenderly led from the court-room,
    Himself, the " guilty " child !

MY BALLOON ASCENT.

IT was in one of my balloon ascents, and a gentleman named Smith had engaged himself to be my
companion : but when the time came his nerve failed,
and I looked round in vain for the person who was to
occupy the vacant seat in the car. Having waited till
the last possible moment, and the crowd becoming
impatient, I prepared to ascend alone. The last cord
that attached me to the earth was about to be cast
off, when suddenly a gentleman pushed forward and
volunteered to go with me. He pressed the request
with so much earnestness, that, having received his
promise to submit in every point to my directions, I
consented to receive him in lieu of the absentee ;
whereupon he sprang with alacrity into the car. In
another minute we were rising above the trees ; and,
in justice to my companion, I must say I never saw
any one exhibit greater coolness and self-possession.
The stranger was as composed as if he had been
sitting at home in his easy arm-chair. A bird could
not have seemed more in its element ; and yet he
solemnly assured me that he had never been in a
balloon before. Instead of evincing any alarm at our
great height from the earth, he expressed the liveliest
pleasure whenever I emptied one or two bags of sand,
and he even urged me to part with more of the ballast. In the mean while the wind carried us quietly
along, and the day being particularly clear, we enjoyed
a delightful bird's-eye view of the great metropolis
and the surrounding country. My companion listened
with great interest, while I pointed out to him the

various objects over which we passed, till I happened
casually to observe that the balloon must be directly
over Hoxton. My fellow-traveller then, for the first
time, betrayed some uneasiness, and anxiously asked
whether I thought he could be recognized by any one
at our then distance from the earth. I told him it was
quite impossible. Nevertheless, he continued very
uneasy, frequently saying, "I hope they don't see
me," and entreating me earnestly to let go more ballast. I said, "Do you live at Hoxton?" He said,
"Yes, yes," and urged me again, and with great
vehemence, to empty the remaining sand-bags. This,
however, was out of the question, considering the
height of the balloon, the course of the wind, and the
proximity of the sea-coast. But my comrade was deaf
to these reasons; he insisted on going higher; and on
my firmly refusing to let go more ballast, he deliberately pulled off, and threw his hat, coat, and waistcoat
overboard. "Huzza! that lightened her!" he shouted.
"But it's not enough yet;" and he began to untie his
cravat. "Nonsense," said I, "my good fellow; nobody
can recognize you at this distance, even with a tel-
escope." "Don't be too sure of that," he sharply
retorted; "they have sharp eyes at Miles's." "At
where?" said I. "At Miles's Madhouse," shouted he.
Then the truth flashed upon me in an instant: I was
sitting in the frail car of a balloon, literally in the
clouds, with a lunatic! The horrors of the situation
for a moment seemed to deprive me of my senses. A
sudden freak, a transient fury, a single struggle, would
send both of us into eternity! In the mean while the
maniac, having divested himself successively of shoes,
stockings, trousers, and everything, threw each to the

winds, repeating his insane cry, "Higher! higher!
higher!" I remained perfectly silent. But judge
of my terror when, having thrown his shirt overboard, he solemnly said, "We are not yet high enough
by a thousand miles: one of us must throw out the
other." To describe my feelings at this speech would
be simply impossible. Cold as the atmosphere felt,
intensely cold, yet great beads of perspiration rolled
off from me. It was horrible! horrible! Words,
remonstrances, prayers, were useless. I had better
have been unarmed in the wilderness, surrounded by
wild Indians. I saw the lunatic deliberately heave
the one, and then the other, bag of ballast from the
car, the balloon, of course, rising with proportionate
rapidity. Up, up, up it soared, to an altitude I dared
not contemplate. Earth was lost to my eyes, and huge
clouds rolled beneath us. I felt the world was gone
forever.

"Have you a wife and children?" he asked, abruptly.

I replied that I had a dear wife and six little ones
depending on me for their bread.

"Ha! ha!" laughed the maniac, with a thrill that
chilled the very marrow in my bones. "I have three
hundred and sixty-five wives, and five thousand and
eighty children, and if you did not make this balloon
so heavy I should have been home with them long
ago."

"And where do they live?" I asked, anxious to gain
time by any question that first occurred to me.

"In the moon!" replied the maniac. "And when
I have lightened this car once more I shall be there in
no time!"

I heard no more — he suddenly sprang upon me,
and throwing his arms round me, grasped me round
the body, when — I awoke, and found it was a night-
mare! And hoping that none of you may have such
a one, we wish you "Good night, and pleasant
dreams."

MRS. JUNE'S PROSPECTUS.

MRS. JUNE is ready for school,
 Presents her kind regard,
And for measures and rule
 Refers to the following

CARD.

To Parents and Friends :
Mrs. June,
Of the firm of Summer and Sun,
Announces the opening of her school
 (Established in the year One).

An unlimited number is received ;
 There is nothing at all to pay ;
All that is asked is a merry heart,
 And time enough to be gay.

The Junior class will bring,
 In lieu of all supplies,
Eight little fingers and two thumbs
 For the making of pretty sand pies.

The Senior class, a mouth
 For strawberries and cream ;
A nose apiece for a rose apiece,
 And a tendency to dream.

8

The lectures are thus arranged :
  Professor Cherry Tree
Will lecture to the climbing class ;
  Terms of instruction — free.

Professor De Forrest Spring
  Will take the class in drink,
And the class in titillation
  Sage Mr. Bobolink.

Young Mr. Oxeye Daisy
  Will demonstrate each day
On " botany," on " native plants,"
  And " the properties of hay."

Miss Nature the class in fun
  (A charming class to teach) ;
And the swinging class and the bird's-nest class
  Miss Hickory and Miss Beech.

And the sleepy class at night,
  And the dinner class at noon,
And the fat, and laugh, and roses class,
  They fall to Mrs. June.

And she hopes her little friends
  Will be punctual as the sun,
For the term, alas ! is very short,
  And she wants them every one.

                      SUSAN COOLIDGE.

THE KING OF DENMARK'S RIDE.

WORD was brought to the Danish king,
          (Hurry !)
That the love of his heart lay suffering,
And pined for the comfort his voice would bring ;
    (O, ride as if you were flying !)
Better he loves each golden curl,
On the brow of that Scandinavian girl,
Than his rich crown-jewels of ruby and pearl ;
    And his Rose of the Isles is dying.

Thirty nobles saddled with speed ;
          (Hurry !)
Each one mounted a gallant steed,
Which he kept for battle and days of need ;
    (O, ride as though you were flying !)
Spurs were stuck in the foaming flank,
Worn-out chargers staggered and sank ;
Bridles were slackened, and girths were burst ;
But, ride as they would, the king rode first,
    For his Rose of the Isles lay dying.

His nobles are beaten, one by one ;
          (Hurry !)
They have fainted, and faltered, and homeward gone ;
The little fair page now follows alone,
    For strength and for courage trying.
The king looked back at that faithful child ;
Wan was the face that answering smiled.
They passed the drawbridge with clattering din,
Then he dropped, and only the king rode in
    Where his Rose of the Isles lay dying.

The king blew a blast on his bugle-horn :
           (Silence !)
No answer came, but faint and forlorn
An echo returned on the cold, gray morn,
    Like the breath of a spirit sighing.
The castle portal stood grimly wide ;
None welcomed the king from that weary ride !
For, dead in the light of the dawning day,
The pale, sweet form of the welcomer lay,
    Who had yearned for his voice in dying.

The panting steed, with a drooping crest,
        Stood weary ;
The king returned from the chamber of rest,
The thick sobs choking in his breast, —
    And that dumb companion eyeing ;
The tears gushed forth, which he strove to check ;
He bowed his head on the charger's neck, —
" O steed, that every nerve didst strain, —
Dear steed ! our ride hath been in vain
    To the halls where my love lay dying.
CAROLINE E. NORTON.

THE FORGET-ME-NOT.

WHEN God had created all the flowers, and had
given them roots, stems, and leaves, he also
painted them very beautifully in many colors, and
gave each of them a name. One flower that was very
fragrant, and had many pink leaves, he called a Rose.
Another little flower, with five purple leaves, he called
a Violet. Another, with little snow-white bells, he
called Lily of the Valley, and a large flower, with

many yellow leaves, like sun-rays, he called Sunflower.

Each flower went away to its own home, and was very happy, and each one spoke its name slowly as it went, so that it might not forget it. Only one tiny flower, with a dress as clear and blue as the sky overhead, stood close by the brook, and was very sorrowful. Many, many tears dropped out of its eyes because it had forgotten its name.

But God had seen the little flower's sorrow, and he knew why it wept. So he lovingly dried its tears, and said, "Weep no more, little flower. I will forgive you that you have forgotten your name, and I will give you a new name which you can easily remember. You might forget your own name sometimes, but you must never forget *my* name; and so, to remind you of this, I will call you 'Forget-me-not.'"

Then the little blue flower was very glad. It looked so cheerful and trusting that everybody who saw it loved it. And so it is to this very day. And to every one its tiny voice says, —

"The Lord above, who made my dress,
  So beautiful and blue,
Who sends the blessèd sunshine down,
  And the refreshing dew,
Through me speaks to each little one,
  'Be thankful for your lot;
Think who sends down each perfect gift,
  And O, "forget-me-not!"'"

THE LITTLE READER.

A HARD, stern man upon a sick bed lay,
    More and more feeble with each passing day ;
No hallowing gleam of heavenly peace was there —
No ray of love divine — no breath of prayer.

Kind Christian friends, on holiest mission bent,
Came bright and hopeful, — sad and anxious went.
Harder and sterner still the Atheist grew ;
The flinty heart no answering softness knew.

Angry, at last, at each persistent call,
With firm refusal he defied them all ;
The Saviour's sacred name he would not hear,
His loving words could find no listening ear.

" Wife ! fetch the blackboard — and a bit of chalk !
One way remains to stop this senseless talk ;
I will *write something*, which is *truth indeed*,
And have it placed where *every one* may read."

The thin, weak hand, that scarce the chalk could hold,
Wrote "GOD IS NOWHERE ;" large, and clear, and bold.
That fearful sentence met his waking sight,
In wretched mockery, by day and night.

Time crept along — hour after hour passed o'er,
While the death-angel still his touch forbore ;
Lower and lower burned the flickering flame,
And, slower yet, the fitful pulses came.

Then, *happier* change repaid the anxious view,
And hope, so long denied, sprang forth anew ;
Through every vein a fuller current flowed,
And Heaven once more the gift of *life* bestowed.

Soon the fond father sought his banished child,
Who erst, with prattle sweet, his heart beguiled;
Charmed to come back, she told her little news,
And showed her "nice new gown and pretty shoes."

"And that's not all," — the tones grew eager now, —
"For I can *read* — my *aunty* taught me how."
"Nonsense, my dear!" the father quick replied,
"*You* cannot read, my child, I'm satisfied."

"Yes, father, dear! O, yes! I *truly* can,
For aunty taught me," — and the child began
To look around, perchance to find some way
Of proving what her words had failed to say.

The father smiled — and, pointing to the wall,
Said, "Well, read *that*, if you can read at all."
She hesitated — and the father spoke —
"I told you so — I knew it was a joke."

But still she kept her deep and earnest eyes
Fixed on the board; and soon, in glad surprise,
Exclaimed, "I know it now! O, yes! I see!
GOD — IS — NOW — HERE. That last word puzzled
    me."

The conscience-stricken man, in mute amaze,
Covered his face, to hide her startled gaze,
While, from the rocky fount, untouched for years,
Burst forth a flood of pure and holy tears.

"My God! my child! — and has my darling learned,
What *I*, with death so near, denied and spurned?
Father! forgive — and fill, with love divine,
That life thy mercy spared, *now wholly thine*."
                                            Olive Leaf.

THE CARRIAGE AND COUPLE.

A MAN in his carriage was riding along,
    A gayly-dressed wife by his side ;
In satin and lace she looked like a queen,
    And he, like a king in his pride.

A wood-sawyer stood on the street as they passed ;
    The carriage and couple he eyed,
And said, as he worked with his saw on a log,
    " I wish I was rich and could ride."

The man in the carriage remarked to his wife,
    " One thing I would do if I could —
I'd give all my wealth for the strength and the health
    Of the man who is sawing the wood."

A pretty young maid with a bundle of work,
    Whose face as the morning was fair,
Went tripping along with a smile of delight,
    While humming a love-breathing air.

She looked in the carriage, the lady she saw,
    Arrayed in apparel so fine,
And said, in a whisper, " I wish from my heart
    Those satins and laces were mine."

The lady looked out on the maid with her work,
    So fair in her calico dress,
And said, " I'd relinquish position and wealth
    Her beauty and youth to possess."

Thus it is in this world ; whatever our lot,
    Our minds and our time we employ
In longing and sighing for what we have not,
    Ungrateful for what we enjoy.

We welcome the pleasure for which we have sighed ;
  The heart has a void in it still,
Growing deeper and wider the longer we live,
  That nought but Religion can fill.

———◦◇◦———

LITTLE DIAMOND AND THE DRUNKEN CABMAN.

ONE night little Diamond woke up suddenly, believing he heard the North Wind thundering along. But it was something quite different. South Wind was moaning round the chimneys, but it was not her voice that had wakened Diamond. Her voice would only have lulled him the deeper asleep. It was a loud, angry voice, now growling like that of a beast, now raving like that of a madman : and when Diamond came a little wider awake, he knew that it was the voice of the drunken cabman, the wall of whose room was at the head of his bed. It was anything but pleasant to hear, but he could not help hearing it. At length there came a cry from the woman, and then a scream from the baby. Thereupon Diamond thought it time that somebody did something ; and as himself was the only somebody at hand, he must go and see whether he could not do the something.

So he got up and put on part of his clothes, and went down the stair, out into the yard, and in at the next door. This, fortunately, the cabman, being drunk, had left open.

By the time he reached the stair all was still, except the voice of the crying baby, which guided him to the right door. He opened it softly, and peeped in.

There, leaning back in a chair, with his arms hanging
down by his side, and his legs stretched out before
him and supported on his heels, sat the drunken cabman. His wife lay in her clothes upon the bed, sobbing, and the baby was wailing in the cradle. It was
very miserable altogether.

Now the way most people do when they see anything very miserable, is to turn away from the sight,
and try to forget it. But Diamond began, as usual, to
try to destroy the misery. The little boy, Diamond,
was just as much one of God's messengers as if he had
been an angel with a flaming sword, going out to fight
the devil. The devil he had to fight just then was
Misery. And the way he fought him was the very
best. Like a wise soldier, he attacked him first in his
weakest point — that was the baby; for Misery can
never get such a hold of a baby as of a grown person.
Diamond was knowing in babies, and he knew he could
do something to make the baby happy. I have known
people who would have begun to fight the devil in a
very different and a very stupid way. They would
have begun by scolding the idiotic cabman; and next
they would make his wife angry by saying it must be
her fault as well as his, and by leaving ill-bred, though
well-meant, shabby little books for them to read, which
they were sure to hate the sight of; while all the time
they would not have put out a finger to touch the
wailing baby. But Diamond had him out of the cradle
in a moment, set him up on his knee, and told him to
look at the light.

Now all the light there was came only from a lamp
in the yard, and it was a very dingy and yellow light,
for the glass of the lamp was dirty, and the gas was

bad; but the light that came from it was, notwithstanding, as certainly light as if it had come from the
sun itself, and the baby knew that, and smiled to it;
and although it was, indeed, a wretched room which
that lamp lighted, — so dreary, and dirty, and empty,
and hopeless! — there in the middle of it sat Diamond
on a stool, smiling to the baby, and the baby on his
knees smiling to the lamp.

The father of him sat staring at nothing, neither
asleep nor awake, not quite lost in stupidity either,
for through it all he was dimly angry with himself, he
did not know why. It was that he had struck his
wife. He had forgotten it, but was miserable about
it notwithstanding. And this misery was the voice
of the great Love that had made him and his wife and
the baby and Diamond speaking in his heart, and telling him to be good. For that great Love speaks in
the most wretched and dirty hearts; only the tone of
its voice depends on the echoes of the place in which
it sounds. On Mount Sinai it was thunder: in the
cabman's heart it was *misery;* in the soul of St. John
it was perfect blessedness.

By and by he became aware that there was a voice
of singing in the room. This, of course, was the voice
of Diamond singing to the baby — song after song,
every one as foolish as another to the cabman, for he
was too tipsy to part one word from another; all the
words mixed up in his ear in a gurgle, without division
or stop; for such was the way he spoke himself, when
he was in this horrid condition. But the baby was
more than content with Diamond's songs, and Diamond
himself was so contented with what the songs were all
about, that he did not care a bit about the songs them-

selves, if only baby liked them. But they did the
cabman good as well as the baby and Diamond, for
they put him to sleep, and the sleep was busy all
the time it lasted, smoothing the wrinkles out of his
temper.

At length Diamond grew tired of singing, and began
to talk to the baby instead. And as soon as he stopped
singing, the cabman began to wake up. His brain was
a little clearer now, his temper a little smoother, and
his heart not quite so dirty. He began to listen, and
he went on listening, and heard Diamond saying to
the baby something like this, for he thought the cabman was asleep : —

"Poor daddy! Baby's daddy takes too much beer
and gin, and that makes him somebody else, and not
his own self at all. Baby's daddy would never hit
baby's mammy if he didn't take too much beer. He's
very fond of baby's mammy, and works from morning
to night to get her breakfast and dinner and supper,
only at night he forgets, and pays the money away for
beer. And they put nasty stuff in the beer, I've heard
my daddy say, that drives all the good out, and lets all
the bad in. Daddy says when a man takes to drink,
there's a thirsty devil creeps into his inside, because
he knows he will always get enough there. And the
devil is always crying out for more drink, and that
makes the man thirsty, and so he drinks more and
more, till he kills himself with it. And then the ugly
devil creeps out of him, and crawls about on his belly,
looking for some other cabman to get into, that he may
drink, drink, drink.

"That's what *my* daddy says, baby. And he says,
too, the only way to make the devil come out, is to

give him plenty of cold water and tea and coffee, and nothing at all that comes from the public-house; for the devil can't abide that kind of stuff, and creeps out pretty soon, for fear of being drowned in it. But your daddy *will* drink the nasty stuff, poor man! I wish he wouldn't, for it makes mammy cross with him, and no wonder! and then when mammy's cross, he's crosser, and there's nobody in the house to take care of them but baby; and you *do* take care of them, baby — don't you, baby? I know you do. Babies always take care of their fathers and mothers — don't they, baby? That's what they come for — isn't it, baby? And when daddy stops drinking beer, and nasty gin with turpentine in it, father says, then mammy *will* be so happy, and look so pretty! and daddy will be so good to baby! and baby will be as happy as a swallow, which is the merriest fellow! And Diamond will be so happy, too! And when Diamond's a man, he'll take baby out with him on the box, and teach him to drive a cab."

He went on with chatter like this till baby was asleep, by which time he was tired, and father and mother were both wide awake, — only rather confused — the one from beer, the other from the blow, — and staring, the one from his chair, the other from her bed, at Diamond. But he was quite unaware of their notice, for he sat half asleep, with his eyes wide open, staring in his turn, though without knowing it, at the cabman, while the cabman could not withdraw his gaze from Diamond's white face and big eyes. For Diamond's face was always rather pale, and now it was paler than usual with sleeplessness, and the light of the street lamp upon it. At length he found himself nodding, and he knew then it was time to put the baby down, lest he should let him fall. So he rose from the little three-legged stool, and laid the baby in the cradle, and covered him up, and then he all but staggered out of the door, he was so tipsy himself with sleep.

"Wife," said the cabman, turning towards the bed, "I do somehow believe that wur a angel just gone. Did you see him, wife? He warn't wery big, and he hadn't got none o' them wingses, you know. It wur one o' them baby-angels you sees on the gravestones, you know."

"Nonsense, hubby!" said his wife; "but it's just as good. I might say better, for you can ketch hold of *him* when you like. That's little Diamond, as everybody knows, and a duck o' diamonds he is! No woman could wish for a better child than he be."

"I ha' heard on him in the stable, but I never see the brat afore. Come, old girl, let bygones be bygones, and gie us a kiss, and make up."

She was a good-natured woman. And her husband was not an ill-natured man, either; and when in the morning he recalled not only Diamond's visit, but how he himself had behaved to his wife, he was very vexed with himself, and gladdened his poor wife's heart by telling her how sorry he was. And for a whole week after he did not go near the public-house, hard as it was to avoid it, seeing a certain rich brewer had built one, like a trap to catch souls and bodies in, at almost every corner he had to pass on his way home. Indeed, he was never quite so bad after that, though it was some time before he began really to reform.

GEORGE MACDONALD.

SANTA CLAUS AND THE MOTHERLESS CHILDREN.

A CHRISTMAS POEM.

'TWAS the eve before Christmas ; " Good night " had
    been said,
And Annie and Willie had crept into bed ;
There were tears on their pillows and tears in their eyes,
And each little bosom was heavy with sighs ;
For to-night their stern father's command had been given
That they should retire precisely at seven,
Instead of eight ; for they troubled him more
With questions unheard of than ever before.
He had told them he thought this delusion a sin,
No such being as " Santa Claus " ever had been,
And he hoped, after this, he should never more hear
How he scrambled down chimneys with presents each
    year.
And this was the reason that two little heads
So restlessly tossed on their soft, downy beds.

Eight, nine, and the clock on the steeple tolled ten ;
Not a word had been spoken by either till then,
When Willie's sad face from the blanket did peep,
And whispered, " Dear Annie, is you fast asleep ? "
" Why, no, brother Willie," a sweet voice replies ;
" I've tried it in vain, but can't shut my eyes ;
For somehow it makes me so sorry because
Dear papa has said there is no ' Santa Claus.'
Now we know there is, and it can't be denied,
For he came every year before mamma died ;
But, then, I've been thinking that she used to pray,
And God would hear everything mamma would say,
And perhaps she asked him to send Santa Claus here,
With the sacks full of presents he brought every year."

" Well, why tan't we pay dest as mamma did then,
And ask Him to send him with presents aden ? "
" I've been thinking so, too."   And without a word more,
Four little bare feet bounded out on the floor,
And four little knees the soft carpet pressed,
And two tiny hands were clasped close to each breast.

" Now, Willie, you know we must firmly believe
That the present we ask for we're sure to receive ;
You must wait just as still till I say the ' Amen,'
And by that you will know that your turn has come then."

" Dear Jesus, look down on my brother and me,
And grant us the favor we're asking of thee ;
I want a wax dolly, a tea-set and ring,
And an ebony work-box that shuts with a spring.
Bless papa, dear Jesus, and cause him to see
That Santa Claus loves us far better than he.
Don't let him get fretful and angry again
At dear brother Willie and Annie.   Amen."

" Please, Desus, 'et Santa Taus tum down to-night,
And bring us some presents before it is 'ight.
I want he should dive me a nice little sed,
With bright, shiny runners, and all painted yed ;
A box full of tandy, a book and a toy,
Amen, and then, Desus, I'll be a good boy."

Their prayers being ended, they raised up their heads,
And with hearts light and cheerful again sought their beds;
They were soon lost in slumber, both peaceful and deep,
And with fairies in dreamland were roaming in sleep.

Eight, nine, and the little French clock had struck ten,
Ere the father had thought of his children again ;
He seems now to hear Annie's half-suppressed sighs,
And to see the big tears stand in Willie's blue eyes.
" I was harsh with my darlings," he mentally said,
" And should not have sent them so early to bed.

But then I was troubled ; my feelings found vent,
For bank stock to-day has gone down ten per cent.
But of course they've forgot their troubles ere this,
And that I denied them the thrice-asked-for kiss ;
But just to make sure, I'll steal up to their door,
For I never spoke harsh to my darlings before."

So saying, he softly ascended the stairs,
And arrived at the door to hear both of their prayers.
His Annie's "bless papa" draws forth the big tears,
And Willie's grave promise falls sweet on his ears.
"Strange, strange I'd forgotten," said he, with a sigh,
"How I longed when a child to have Christmas draw nigh.
I'll atone for my harshness," he inwardly said,
"By answering their prayers ere I sleep in my bed."

Then he turned to the stairs, and softly went down,
Threw off velvet slippers and silk dressing gown,
Donned hat, coat, and boots, and was out in the street,
A millionnaire facing the cold, driving sleet.
Nor stopped he until he had bought everything,
From the box full of candy to the tiny gold ring ;
Indeed, he kept adding so much to his store
That the various presents outnumbered a score.
Then homeward he turned with his holiday load,
And with Aunt Mary's aid in the nursery 'twas stowed.

Miss Dolly was seated beneath a pine tree,
By the side of a table spread out for her tea ;
A work-box well filled in the centre was laid,
And on it a ring, for which Annie had prayed.
A soldier in uniform stood by a sled,
"With bright shining runners, and all painted red."
There were balls, dogs, and horses, books pleasing to see,
And birds of all colors were perched in the tree ;
While Santa Claus, laughing, stood up in the top,
As if getting ready more presents to drop.

And as the fond father the picture surveyed,
He thought for his trouble he had amply been paid,

And he said to himself, as he brushed off a tear,
" I'm happier to-night than ever before.
What care I if bank stock falls ten per cent. more !
Hereafter I'll make it a rule, I believe,
To have Santa Claus visit us each Christmas Eve."
So thinking, he gently extinguished the light,
And tripped down the stairs to retire for the night.

As soon as the beams of the bright morning sun
Put the darkness to flight, and the stars, one by one,
Four little blue eyes out of sleep opened wide,
And at the same moment the presents espied.
Then out of their beds they sprang with a bound,
And the very gifts prayed for were all of them found.
They laughed and they cried in their innocent glee,
And shouted for " papa " to come quick and see
What presents old Santa Claus brought in the night
(Just the things that they wanted), and left before light.

" And now," added Annie, in a voice soft and low,
" You'll believe there's a Santa Claus, papa, I know ; "
While dear little Willie climbed up on his knee,
Determined no secret between them should be,
And told, in soft whispers, how Annie had said
That their dear, blessed mamma, so long ago dead,
Used to kneel down and pray by the side of her chair,
And that God up in heaven had answered her prayer !
" Then we dot up and payed dust as well as we tould,
And Dod answered our payers : now wasn't He dood ? "

" I should say that He was, if He sent you all these,
And knew just what presents my children would please. —
Well, well, let him think so, the dear little elf ;
'Twould be cruel to tell him I did it myself."

Blind father ! who caused your stern heart to relent,
And the hasty word spoken so soon to repent ?
'Twas the Being who bade you steal softly up stairs,
And made you His agent to answer their prayers.

ONLY A SHAVING.

A CHILD, as from school he was bounding by,
  Near the wall of a carpenter's workshop found
A lustrous shaving that lured his eye ;
  And this treasure he timidly picked from the ground.
The thing was tender, transparent, light,
  Silk-soft, odorous, veined so fine
With rosy waves in the richest white, —
  Rare damask of dainty design !

With awe he touched it, and turned it o'er ;
He had never seen such a wonder before ;
And, gay as a ringlet of golden hair,
  It had floated and fallen down at his feet,
Where, fluttering faint in each breath of bright air,
  It lay bathed by the sunshine sweet.

The boy was a widow's sireless son ;
  A poor dame, pious and frugal, she.
Brothers and sisters he had none ;
  Playmates and playthings.few : and he
Was gentle, and dreamy, and pure, as one
  To whom most pleasures privations be
Ere childhood's playing is done.

He would like to have taken his treasure away ;
" But what," he thought, " would my mother say ? "
As he wistfully eyed the windowed wall,
  Whence down from the casement of some ground floor
He thought he had seen the fair thing fall.
  Then he knocked at the half-shut door.

Near it the sturdy head-workman stood ;
He was busily planing a plank of wood ;
His arms were up to the elbows bare,
  Brawny and brown as the branch of an oak,

And heavy with muscle and dusky with hair,
   Down over his forehead and face in a soak
(For the heat of his labor had left them wet),
Fell mane-like, matted, and black as jet,
   A huge, unkempt, and cumbrous coil
Of stubborn curls, that to forehead and face
   Gave a savage look as he stooped at his toil.
With many a sullen and sooty trace
   Of the glue-pot's grease and the work-shop's soil,
His shirt, — last Sunday, though coarse, as clean
   As the parson's own, — this Friday noon
Had the hue of the shift of that famous queen
   Who took Granada, but not so soon
As her oath was taken.
            This man had seen
The gentle child at the door, and thought,
   "'Tis the child of a customer come with a message. —
" Pray what has my little master brought?
   Or what may he want?"
             With no cheerful presage
At the sight of his grim-faced questioner,
   A few faint words the poor child stammers, —
Words unheard 'mid the noisy stir
   Of the hissing saws and the beating hammers.
Then, abashed and blushing, he stands deterred,
With a fluttering heart like a frightened bird,
As he holds the shaving out in his hand,
   Timidly gazing at the strange prize.

The workman was puzzled to understand
This gracious vision. He rubbed his eyes.
   Is it vainly such visions come and go
In flashes across life's laboring way?
   We uplift the forehead, and fain would know
What to think of them. Whence come they?
   For they burst upon us, and brighten the air
For a moment round us, and melt away,
   Lost as we longingly look at them.

" Hi !
Silence, all of you hands down there ! "
And you might have heard the hum of a fly
In the hush of the suddenly silenced place.
" What is it, my child ? "   With a glowing face, —
" Sir," said the child, " I was passing by,
And I saw it fall, as I passed below,
From the window, I think.   So, as it fell near,
I have picked it up, and I bring it you now."
" Bring what ? "   " This beautiful ringlet here.
Have you not missed it ?   It must, I know,
Have been hard to make.   I have taken care.
The wind was blowing it round the wall,
And I never saw anything half so fair.
But it is not broken, I think, at all."

A 'prentice brat, whose cheek was puffed
With a burst of laughter ready to split,
Turned pale, by a single glance rebuffed
Of that workman's eye which had noticed it.
And the man there, shaggy and black as a bear,
Nor any the sweeter for sweat and glue,
Laid a horny hand on the child's bright hair,
With a gentle womanly gesture drew
The child up softly on to his knees,
And gazed in its eyes till his own eyes grew
Humid and red at the rims by degrees.

" What is thine age, fair child ? " he said.
" Five, next June."   " And it pleases thee,
This . . . ringlet-thing ? "   The small bright head
Nodded.   He put the child from his knee,
Swept from the bench a whole curly clan
Of such shavings, and, " Hold up thy pinafore.
There, they are thine.   Run away, little man ! "
" Mine ? "   " All thine."   Then he opened the door,
Stooped, and . . . was it a sigh or a prayer
That, as into the sunshine the sweet child ran,
Away with it passed in its golden hair ?

Anon, when the hubbub again began
Of hammer and saw in the workshop there,
This workman paused from his work, and stood
Looking a while (as though vexed by the view)
At the shape which his work had bequeathed to the wood.

Then he turned him about, and abruptly drew
His pipe from his pocket, and stuffed it, and lit,
   And sat down on the bench by the open door,
And smoked, and smoked.   And in circles blue
   As the faint smoke wandered the warm air o'er,
Still he sat dreamily watching it
   Rise like a ghost from the grimy clay,
   And hover, and linger, and fade away.

I know not what were his thoughts.   But I know
   There be shavings that down from a man's work fall,
Which the man himself, as they drop below,
   Haply accounts of no worth at all ;
And I know there be children that prize them more
   Than the man's true work, be its worth what it may.

OWEN MEREDITH.

ROMANCE AT HOME.

WELL, I think I'll finish that story for the editor
of the "Dutchman." Let me see ; where did I
leave off? — The setting sun was just gilding with his
last ray —

" Ma, I want some bread and molasses !"

" Yes, dear." — gilding with his last ray the church
spire —

" Wife, where's my Sunday pants ?"

" Under the bed, dear." — the church spire of Inver-
ness, when a —

" There's nothing under the bed, dear, but your lace cap — "

" Perhaps they are in the coal-hod in the closet." — when a horseman was seen approaching —

" Ma'am, the *pertators* is out; not one for dinner — "

" Take some turnips ! " — approaching, covered with dust, and —

" Wife, the baby has swallowed a button ! "

" *Reverse him,* dear ! . Take him by the heels." — and waving in his hand a banner, on which was written —

" Ma ! I've torn my pantaloons ! "

— " Liberty or death ! " The inhabitants rushed *en masse* —

" Wife ! *will* you leave off scribbling ? "

" Don't be disagreeable, Smith ; I'm just getting inspired."— to the public square, where De Begnis, who had been secretly —

" Butcher wants to see you, ma'am."

— secretly informed of the traitors' —

" Forgot *which* you said, ma'am, sausages or mutton chop."

— movements, gave orders to fire ! Not less than twenty — " My gracious ! Smith, you haven't been *reversing* that child all this time ! He's as black as your coat ! And that boy of *yours* has torn up the first sheet of my manuscript. There ! it's no use for a married woman to cultivate her intellect. Smith, hand me those twins."

FANNY FERN.

HOW HE SAVED ST. MICHAEL'S.

SO you beg for a story, my darling, my brown-eyed
     Leopold, —
And you, Alice, with face like morning, and curling locks
     of gold ;
Then come, if you will, and listen — stand close beside
     my knee —
To a tale of the southern city — proud Charleston by the
     sea.

It was long ago, my children, ere ever the signal gun
That blazed above Fort Sumter, had wakened the North
     as one ;
Long ere the wondrous pillar of battle-cloud and fire
Had marked where the unchained millions marched on to
     their hearts' desire.

On roofs and the glittering turrets, that night as the sun
     went down,
The mellow glow of the twilight shone like a jewelled
     crown,
And, bathed in the living glory, as the people lifted their
     eyes,
They saw the pride of the city — the spire of St. Michael's
     rise

High over the lesser steeples, tipped with a golden ball,
That hung like a radiant planet caught in its earthward
     fall —
First glimpse of home to the sailor who made the harbor
     round,
And last slow-fading vision dear to the outward bound.

The gently gathering shadows shut out the waning light ;
The children prayed at their bedsides, as you will pray
     to-night ;

The noise of buyer and seller from the busy mart was
  gone,
And in dreams of a peaceful morrow the city slumbered on.

But another light than sunrise aroused the sleeping street,
For a cry was heard at midnight, and the rush of tram-
  pling feet;
Men stared in each other's faces through mingled fire and
  smoke,
While the frantic bells went clashing clamorous stroke on
  stroke!

By the glare of her blazing roof-tree the houseless mother
  fled,
With the babe she pressed to her bosom shrieking in
  nameless dread;
While the fire-king's wild battalions scaled wall and cap-
  stone high,
And planted their flaring banners against an inky sky.

From the death that raged behind them, and the crash of
  ruin loud,
To the great square of the city were driven the surging
  crowd,
Where yet, firm in all the tumult, unscathed by the fiery
  flood,
With its heavenward-pointing finger the church of St.
  Michael stood.

But e'en as they gazed upon it, there rose a sudden wail,
A cry of horror blended with the roaring of the gale,
On whose scorching wings, up-driven, a single flaming
  brand,
Aloft on the towering steeple, clung like a bloody hand.

"Will it fade?" The whisper trembled from a thousand
  whitening lips, —
Far out on the lurid harbor they watched it from the
  ships —

A baleful gleam that brighter and ever brighter shone,
Like a flickering, trembling will-o'-wisp to a steady beacon
    grown.

" Uncounted gold shall be given to the man whose brave
    right hand,
For the love of the perilled city, plucks down yon burn-
    ing brand ! "
So cried the mayor of Charleston that all the people heard,
But they looked each one at his fellow, no man spoke a
    word.

Who is it leans from the belfry, with face upturned to the
    sky ?
Clings to a column, and measures the dizzy spire with his
    eye ?
Will he dare it, the hero undaunted, that terrible, sicken-
    ing height ?
Or will the hot blood of his courage freeze in his veins at
    the sight ?

But see ! he has stepped on the railing, he climbs with
    his feet and his hands !
And firm on a narrow projection, with the belfry beneath
    him, he stands !
Now once, and once only, they cheer him — a single,
    tempestuous breath —
And there falls on the multitude gazing a hush-like still-
    ness of death.

Slow, steadily mounting, unheeding aught save the goal
    of the fire,
Still higher and higher, an atom, he moves on the face of
    the spire.
He stops ! Will he fall ? Lo ! for answer, a gleam like
    a meteor's track,
And, hurled on the stones of the pavement, the red brand
    lies shattered and black !

Once more the shouts of the people have rent the quivering air !
At the church door mayor and council wait with their feet
on the stair ;
And the eager throng behind them press for a touch of
his hand —
The unknown savior whose daring could compass a deed
so grand.

But why does a sudden tremor seize on them while they
gaze ?
And what meaneth that stifled murmur of wonder and
amaze ?
He stood in the gate of the temple he had perilled his life
to save,
And the face of the hero, my children, was the sable face
of a slave !

With folded arms he was speaking, in tones that were
clear, not loud,
And his eyes ablaze in their sockets burnt into the eyes
of the crowd :
" You may keep your gold — I scorn it ! But answer me,
ye who can,
If the deed I have done before you be not the deed of
a man ? "

He stepped but a short space backward, and from all the
women and men
There were only sobs for an answer, and the mayor called
for a pen,
And the great seal of the city, that he might read who
ran ; —
And the slave who saved St. Michael's went out from the
door, — a MAN.

SNYDER'S NOSE.

SNYDER kept a beer saloon, some years ago, "over the Rhine." Snyder was a ponderous Teuton, of very irascible temper, — "sudden and quick in quarrel," — get mad in a minute. Nevertheless his saloon was a great resort for "the boys," — partly because of the excellence of his beer, and partly because they liked to chafe "old Snyder," as they called him; for, although his bark was terrific, experience had taught them that he wouldn't bite.

One day Snyder was missing; and it was explained by his "frau," that he had "gone out fishing mit der poys." The next day one of the boys, who was particularly fond of "roasting" old Snyder, dropped in to get a glass of beer, and discovered Snyder's nose, which was a big one at any time, swollen and blistered by the sun, until it looked like a dead-ripe tomato.

"Why, Snyder, what's the matter with your nose?" said the caller.

"I peen out fishing mit der poys," replied Snyder, laying his finger tenderly against his proboscis; "the sun it pose hot like ash never vas, und I purns my nose. Nice nose — don't it?"

And Snyder viewed it with a look of comical sadness in the little mirror back of his bar. It entered at once into the head of the mischievous fellow in front of the bar to play a joke upon Snyder; so he went out and collected half a dozen of his comrades, with whom he arranged that they should drop in at the saloon one after another, and ask Snyder, "What's the matter with that nose?" to see how long he would stand it. The man who put up the job went in first with a companion, and seating themselves at a table, called for beer. Snyder brought it to them; and the new-comer exclaimed, as he saw him, —

"Snyder, what's the matter with your nose?"

"I yust dell your frient here I peen out fishin' mit der poys, unt de sun he purnt 'em — zwi lager — den cents — all right."

Another boy rushes in.

"Halloo, boys, you're ahead of me this time; s'pose I'm in, though. Here, Snyder, bring me a glass of lager and a pret" — (appears to catch a sudden glimpse of Snyder's nose, looks wonderingly a moment, and then bursts out laughing) — "Ha! ha! ha! Why, Snyder, — ha! ha! — what's the matter with that nose?"

Snyder, of course, can't see any fun in having a burnt nose, or having it laughed at; and he says, in a tone sternly emphatic, —

"I peen out fishin' mit der poys, unt de sun it yust ash hot ash blazes, unt I purnt my nose; dat ish all right."

Another tormentor comes in, and insists on "setting 'em up" for the whole house.

"Snyder," says he, "fill up the boys' glasses, and take a drink yourse— Ho! ho! ho! ho! ha! ha! ha! Snyder, wha— ha! ha!— what's the matter with that nose?"

Snyder's brow darkens with wrath by this time, and his voice grows deeper and sterner, —

"I peen out fishin' mit der poys on the Leedle Miami. De sun pose hot like ash — vel, I purn my pugle. Now,

that is more vot I don't got to say.   Vot gind o' pose-
ness?   Dat ish all right; I purn my *own* nose —
don't it?"

"Burn your nose, — burn all the hair off your head,
for what I care ; you needn't get mad about it."

It was evident that Snyder wouldn't stand more
than one more tweak at that nose ; for he was tramp-
ing about behind his bar, and growling like an exas-
perated old bear in his cage.   Another one of his tor-
mentors walks in.   Some one sings out to him, —

"Have a glass of beer, Billy?"

"Don't care about any beer," says Billy ; "but, Snyder, you may give me one of your best ciga— Ha-a-a!
ha! ha! ha! ho! ho! ho! he! he! he! ah-h-h-ha! ha!
ha! ha!   Why — why — Snyder — who — who — ha-
ha! ha! what's the matter with that nose?"

Snyder was absolutely fearful to behold by this
time ; his face was purple with rage, all except his
nose, which glowed like a ball of fire.   Leaning his
ponderous figure far over the bar, and raising his arm
aloft to emphasize his words with it, he fairly roared, —

"I peen out fishin' mit ter poys.   The sun it pese
hot like ash never vas.   I purnt my nose.   Now you
no like dose nose, you yust take dose nose unt wr-wr-
wr-wring your mean American finger mit 'em!   That's
the kind of man vot I am!"

"FAT CONTRIBUTOR."

THE HIGH TIDE.

MOTHER, dear, what is the water saying?
 Mother, dear, why does the wild sea roar?"
Cry the children, on the white sand playing,
 On the white sand, half a mile from shore.
"Little ones, I fear a storm is growing.
 Come away! O, let us hasten home!"
Calls the mother; and the wind is blowing,
 Flashing up a million eyes of foam.

"Mother, see our footprints as we follow!
 Mother, dear, what crawls along before?"
Creeping round and round, through creek and hollow,
 Runs the tide between them and the shore.
"Hasten!" cries the mother, forward flying.
 "Hasten, or we perish; 'tis the tide!"
Led by her, affrighted now and crying,
 Fly the children, barefoot, at her side.

"Mother, dear, the sea is coming after!
 Mother, 'tis between us and the land."
Looking back, they see the waves with laughter
 Wash their little shoes from off the sand.
"Quicker!" screams the mother, "quicker! quicker!"
 Fast they fly before the sullen sound.
Step by step the mother's heart grows sicker;
 Inch by inch the sea creeps round and round.

"Mother, in the water we are wading;
 Mother, it grows deeper as we go!"
"Hasten, children, hasten! — day is fading —
 Higher creeps the tide so black and slow."
Nay, but at each step the waves grow deeper;
 "Turn this way!" but there 'tis deeper still —
Still the sea breathes like a drunken sleeper —
 Still the foam crawls, and the wind blows shrill.

" Mother, there is land, all green and dry land,
   Grass upon it growing, and a tree ! "
A promontory turned into an island,
   Upsprings there in the ever-rising sea.
" Mother, 'tis so deep, and we are dripping !
   Mother, we are sinking !   Haste, O, haste ! "
In her arms uplifting them, and gripping,
   On she plunges, wading to the waist.

" Mother, set us down among the grasses !
   Mother, we are hungry ! " they now cry ;
Watching the bright water as it passes,
   There they sit, between the sea and sky.
Higher crawls the sea with deep intoning,
   Passing every flood-mark far or near —
" 'Tis the high tide ! " cries the mother, moaning,
   " Coming only once in many a year ! "

Higher ! higher ! lapping round the island
   Flows the water with a sound forlorn.
Those are flowers 'tis snatching from the dry land—
   Pale primroses sweet and newly born.
Smaller grows the isle where they sit sobbing,
   Darker grows the day on every side —
Whiter grows the mother, with heart throbbing
   Madly, as she marks the fatal tide.

" Children, cling around me ! hold me faster !
   Kiss me ! God is going to take all three !
Say the prayer I taught you — He is Master !
   He is Lord, and in His hands lie we ! "
Flowers the tide is snatching while it calls so,
   Flowers its lean hands never snatched before ;
Will it snatch these human flowers also ?
   Where they cling, sad creatures of the shore ?

Nay, for o'er the tide a boat is stealing —
   On their names a man's strong voice doth cry.

"God be praised!" the mother crieth, kneeling,
 "He hath heard our prayer, and help is nigh."
"Father!" cry the children; "this way, father!
 Here we are!" aloud cry girl and boy.
Comes the boat — the children round it gather —
 But the mother smiles and faints for joy.

THE MOTHERLESS TURKEYS.

THE white turkey was dead! The white turkey was
 dead!
How the news through the barn-yard went flying!
Of a mother bereft, four small turkeys were left,
 And their case for assistance was crying.
E'en the peacock respectfully folded his tail,
 As a suitable symbol of sorrow,
And his plainer wife said, "Now the old bird is dead,
 Who will tend her poor chicks on the morrow?
And when evening around them comes dreary and chill,
 Who above them will watchfully hover?"
"Two, each night, *I* will tuck 'neath my wings," said
 the duck,
 "Though I've eight of my own I must cover!"
"I have *so much* to do! For the bugs and the worms,
 In the garden, 'tis tiresome pickin';
I have nothing to spare, — for my own I must care,"
 Said the hen with one chicken.

"How I wish," said the goose, "I could be of some use,
 For my heart is with love over-brimming;
The next morning that's fine, they shall go with my nine.
 Little yellow-backed goslings, out swimming!"
"I will do what I can," the old Dorking put in,
 "And for help they may call upon me, too;
Though I've ten of my own that are only half grown,
 And a great deal of trouble to see to.

But those poor little things, they are all heads and wings,
   And their bones through their feathers are stickin'!"
"Very hard it may be, but, O, don't come to me!"
   Said the hen with one chicken.

"Half my care, I suppose, there is nobody knows, —
   I'm the most overburdened of mothers!
They must learn, little elves, how to scratch for them-
     selves,
   And not seek to depend upon others."
She went by with a cluck, and the goose to the duck
   Exclaimed, in surprise, "Well, I never!"
Said the duck, "I declare, those who have the least care,
   You will find, are complaining forever!
And when all things appear to look threatening and drear,
   And when troubles your pathway are thick in,
For some aid in your woe, O, beware how you go
   To a hen with one chicken!"

                         MARIAN DOUGLASS.

A BIRD'S-EYE VIEW.

QUOTH the boy, "I'll climb that tree,
   And bring down a nest, I know."
Quoth the girl, "I will not see
   Little birds defrauded so.
Cowardly their nests to take,
And their little hearts to break,
   And their little eggs to steal.
Leave them happy for my sake, — .
   Surely little birds can feel!"

Quoth the boy, "My senses whirl;
   Until now I never heard
Of the wisdom of a girl,
   Or the feelings of a bird!
Pretty Mrs. Solomon,

Tell me what you reckon on
    When you prate in such a strain ;
If I wring their necks anon,
    Certainly they *might* feel — pain ! "

Quoth the girl, " I watch them talk,
    Making love and making fun,
In the pretty ash-tree walk,
    When my daily task is done.
In their little eyes I find
They are very fond and kind.
    Every change of song or voice,
Plainly proveth to my mind,
    They can suffer and rejoice."

And the little robin-bird
    (Nice brown back and crimson breast)
All the conversation heard,
    Sitting trembling in his nest.
" What a world," he cried, " of bliss,
Full of birds and girls, were this !
    Blithe we'd answer to their call ;
But a great mistake it is
    Boys were ever made at all."

THE FOX IN THE WELL.

SIR REYNARD once, as I've heard tell,
Had fallen into a farmer's well,
When wolf, his cousin, passing by,
Heard from the depths his dismal cry.

Over the wheel a well-chain hung,
From which two empty buckets swung ;
At one, drawn up beside the brink,
The fox had paused, no doubt, to drink,

And putting in his head, had tipped
The bucket; fox and bucket slipped,
And, hampered by the ball, he fell,
As I have said, into the well.
As down the laden bucket went,
The other made its swift ascent.

His cousin, wolf, beguiled to stop,
Listened astonished at the top;
Looked down, and, by the uncertain light,
Saw Reynard in a curious plight —
There in his bucket at the bottom,
Calling as if the hounds had got him !

" What do you there ? " his cousin cried.
" Dear cousin wolf," the fox replied,
" In coming to the well to draw
Some water, what d'ye think I saw ?
It glimmered bright and still below ;
You've seen it ; you did not know
It was a treasure !   Now, behold !
I've got my bucket filled with gold,
Enough to buy ourselves and wives
Poultry to last us all our lives ! "

The wolf made answer with a grin :
" Dear me ! I thought you tumbled in !
What then is all this noise about ? "
" Because I could not draw it out ;
I called to you," the fox replied :
" First help me ; then we will divide."

" How ? "   " Get into the bucket there."
The wolf, too eager for a share,
Did not one moment pause to think ;
There hung the bucket by the brink,
And in he stepped.   As down he went,
The cunning fox made his ascent,

Being the lighter of the two.
" That's right ! ha ! ha ! how well you do !
How glad I am you came to help !"
Wolf struck the water with a yelp ;
The fox leaped out.   " Dear wolf !" said he,
" You've been so very kind to me,
I'll leave the treasure all to you ;
I hope 'twill do you good !   Adieu !
There comes the farmer."   Off he shot,
And disappeared across the lot,
Leaving the wolf to meditate
Upon his miserable fate —
To flattering craft a victim made,
By his own greediness betrayed !

J. T. TROWBRIDGE.

A LITTLE CHILD'S TRIALS.

MY father had a farm-hand who took a great fancy to me, and when I was not more than two years old, or, at the most, two and a half, he made me a kitten-yoke, and gave me a pair of the prettiest kittens I ever saw.   How long I played with them I do not remember, nor do I know what became of them ; but they disappeared quite suddenly one day, and I have heard nothing of them since.

Undoubtedly they went the way of all kittens, after they begin to overstock the market ; but to me it was a great mystery : and if the poor little things had been caught up while I was playing with them, and whisked off out of sight by hawk or buzzard, or if they had vanished into thin air while I was watching them, yoke and all, I should not have been more puzzled nor astonished.

10

Only one other case of perplexity do I remember that will compare with this; and I must acknowledge that, for a long while, I had no faith in the explanations that were offered me. There came up, one bright summer afternoon, towards nightfall, a prodigious hail-storm — the first I had ever seen, or heard of. Being always inquisitive, and much in earnest, I gathered a wooden dish full of the little white beads, before they missed me from the porch, and hid it away where nobody would be likely to stumble over it.

But, alas! when I went for my little treasure, instead of the white beads, or seed-pearl, I had gathered by handfuls, I found nothing but a little dirty water.

It was in vain they told me that my hailstones had melted; I did not believe them, and I could not. And as I grew older, and came to hear about hailstones and coals of fire mingled together, it seemed still more unlikely; for I had seen nothing that resembled coals of fire, and if there was any lightning, I do not remember it.

To me it was like the manna gathered by the children of Israel without permission — a little round thing that wouldn't keep.

Trivial though such incidents may be in themselves, yet, if they are remembered to the last by the aged man, they must have had their influence upon the child — at an age, too, when the lightest touch may outlast both engraving and sculpture.

If I may trust my memory, the loss of my sled, the loss of my kitten-yoke and little steers, and the loss of my seed-pearl, were the sorest of my trials up to the age of twelve.

JOHN NEAL.

CURFEW MUST NOT RING TO-NIGHT.

ENGLAND'S sun was setting
   O'er the hills so far away,
Filled the land with misty beauty
   At the close of one sad day:
And the last rays kissed the forehead
   Of a man and maiden fair; ''
He with step so slow and weary,
   She with sunny, floating hair;
He with bowed head, sad and thoughtful,
   She with lips so cold and white,
Struggling to keep back the murmur,
   " Curfew shall not ring to-night."

" Sexton," Bessie's white lips faltered,
   Pointing to the prison old,
With its walls so tall and gloomy,
   Walls so dark, and damp, and cold, —
" I've a lover in that prison,
   Doomed this very night to die
At the ringing of the Curfew,
   And no earthly help is nigh :
Cromwell will not come till sunset,"
   And her face grew strangely white,
As she spoke in husky whispers, —
   " Curfew shall not ring to-night."

" Bessie," calmly spoke the sexton, —
   Every word pierced her young heart
Like a thousand gleaming arrows,
   Like a deadly poisoned dart, —
" Long, long years I've rung the Curfew
   From that gloomy shadowed tower;
Every evening, just at sunset,
   It has told the twilight hour.
I have done my duty ever,
   Tried to do it just and right;

Now I'm old, I will not miss it,
   Girl, the Curfew rings to-night."

Wild her eyes, and pale her features,
   Stern and white her thoughtful brow,
And within her heart's deep centre
   Bessie made a solemn vow ;
She had listened while the judges
   Read, without a tear or sigh :
" At the ringing of the Curfew —
   Basil Underwood *must die.*"
And her breath came fast and faster,
   And her eyes grew large and bright —
One low murmur, scarcely spoken,
   " Curfew *must not* ring to-night!"

She with light step bounded forward,
   Sprung within the old church-door,
Left the old man coming slowly
   Paths he'd trod so oft before ;
Not one moment paused the maiden,
   But, with cheek and brow aglow,
Staggered up the gloomy tower,
   Where the bell swung to and fro ;
Then she climbed the slimy ladder,
   Dark, without one ray of light,
Upward still, her pale lips saying,
   " Curfew *shall not* ring to-night."

She has reached the topmost ladder,
   O'er her hangs the great dark bell,
And the awful gloom beneath her,
   Like the pathway down to hell !
See, the ponderous tongue is swinging,
   'Tis the hour of Curfew now —
And the sight has chilled her bosom,
   Stopped her breath and paled her brow.
Shall she let it ring ?   No, never.
   Her eyes flash with sudden light,
And she springs and grasps it firmly —
   " Curfew *shall not* ring to-night ! "

Out she swung, far out ; — the city
　　Seemed a tiny speck below,
There, 'twixt heaven and earth suspended,
　　As the bell swung to and fro ;
And the half-deaf sexton ringing,
　　(Years he had not heard the bell,)
And he thought the twilight Curfew
　　Rung young Basil's funeral knell ;
Still the maiden, clinging firmly,
　　Cheek and brow so pale and white,
Stilled her frightened heart's wild beating —
　　" *Curfew shall not ring to-night!* "

It was o'er — the bell ceased swaying,
　　And the maiden stepped once more
Firmly on the damp old ladder,
　　Where for hundred years before
Human foot had not been planted :
　　And what she this night had done
Should be told long ages after —
　　As the rays of setting sun
Light the sky with mellow beauty,
　　Aged sires with heads of white
Tell the children why the Curfew
　　Did not ring that one sad night.

O'er the distant hills came Cromwell ;
　　Bessie saw him, and her brow,
Lately white with sickening horror,
　　Glows with sudden beauty now.
At his feet she told the story,
　　Showed her hands all bruised and torn ;
And her sweet young face so haggard,
　　With a look so sad and worn,
Touched his heart with sudden pity,
　　Lit his eyes with misty light.
" Go, your lover lives," cried Cromwell ;
　　" Curfew shall not ring to-night!"

MY FATHER'S HALF-BUSHEL.

MY father's half-bushel comes oft to my mind,
　　And wakens deep feelings of various sorts ;
'Twas an honest half-bushel — a noble half-bushel,
　　It held a half-bushel of thirty-two quarts !

When I think of that bushel — my father's half-bushel,
　　That dear old half-bushel, so honest and true !
Then look at the bushels, our city half-bushels,
　　Little dandy half-bushels, it makes one feel blue !

O, my father's half-bushel — that country half-bushel,
　　It's like, or my father's — O, when shall I see ?
'Twas a blessèd half-bushel, and he is a blest man,
　　For he filled his half-bushel, and something threw free !

Alas ! I've long searched for their likeness in vain !
Scarce a man, or half-bushel, but what gives me pain,
So unlike to my father's their measures, and measure,
My life is nigh robbed of all peace and all pleasure !

Yet all the half-bushels, if mean, are not small ;
I'm vexed with the great ones most, after all.
O, mark out that ash-man's next time he shall call,
'Tis a monstrous half-bushel — holds quarts sixty-four :
Do send the base rascal away from your door !

'Tis a fact I am stating, no slanders I utter,
But who can forbear, when cheated, to mutter ?
In New York, a barrel (I pray you, don't laugh)
Won't hold so much ashes as 'taters by half !

Zounds ! what are the lawyers, and what are the laws,
But bugbears and phantoms, mere feathers or straws ?
Unless our half-bushels are all made as one,
Like father's half-bushel, I say we're undone.

THE FRUITS OF LIBERTY.

ARIOSTO tells a pretty story of a fairy, who, by some mysterious law of her nature, was condemned to appear at certain seasons in the form of a foul and poisonous snake. Those who injured her during the period of her disguise were forever excluded from participation in the blessings which she bestowed. But to those who, in spite of her loathsome aspect, pitied and protected her, she afterwards revealed herself in the beautiful and celestial form which was natural to her, accompanied their steps, granted all their wishes, filled their houses with wealth, made them happy in love, and victorious in war.

Such a spirit is Liberty. At times she takes the form of a hateful reptile. She grovels, she hisses, she stings. But woe to those who in disgust shall venture to crush her! And happy are those who, having dared to receive her in her degraded and frightful shape, shall at length be rewarded by her in the time of her beauty and glory!

There is only one cure for the evils which newly acquired freedom produces, and that cure is freedom. When a prisoner first leaves his cell he cannot bear the light of day: he is unable to discriminate colors, or recognize faces. But the remedy is, not to remand him into his dungeon, but to accustom him to the rays of the sun.

The blaze of truth and liberty may at first dazzle and bewilder nations which have become half blind in the house of bondage. But let them gaze on, and they will soon be able to bear it. In a few years men learn to reason. The extreme violence of opinions subsides. Hostile theories correct each other. The scattered elements of truth cease to contend, and begin to coalesce. And at length a system of justice and order is educed out of the chaos.

Many politicians of our time are in the habit of laying it down as a self-evident proposition, that no people ought to be free till they are fit to use their freedom. The maxim is worthy of the fool in the old story, who resolved not to go into the water till he had learned to swim. If men are to wait for liberty till they become wise and good in slavery, they may indeed wait forever.   MACAULAY.

WINK.

I HAVE a kitty, and, what do you think?
  Her name is Puss, but I call her " Wink ; "
And the reason why I call her so
Is this : O, ever so long ago,
My mother brought her home one day
In a little basket, all the way
From — dear me ! where was it ? — I can't remember,
  It was so long — the name of the town,
But the month, I'm sure, was June — or December ;
  And when mother set the basket down
On the kitchen floor, she said, " Little Grace,
Just peep in here, but take care of your face,
For it's something 'live, and it may jump up."
I thought, much as could be, it must be a pup,
For brother Jem had been teasing hard
  For a black one, all fuzzy, and full of his fun,
Like the one that lives in Joe Cassidy's yard ;
  He rolls over and over — he's too fat to run.

But, no ! when I looked in, there lay a kitty,
All cuddled up close, so silky and pretty,
A blue cat — Aunt Eleanor says she's Maltese ;
I don't know what that is, it may be her fleece,
'Cause it shines so ; but soon as my new kitty saw
That the basket was open, she stretched out her paw
To shake hands with her mistress, and just seemed to know
    She had come to a good home where people would
      treat her
Like one of God's creatures, and nobody throw
    Stones and brickbats to hurt her, or cruelly beat her.
So she looked up at me, and said, softly, " You ? you ? "
And winked just as hard as ever she knew.
" Yes, it's I, little Gracie," I answered her then,
And, O, don't you think, *she began winking again!*
Jemmy laughed — so did I — but she didn't get cross
At our fun, like May Fisher and Lilian Morse,
But was just as good-natured as could be, and lay
As still as a mouse, with nothing to say.
I caught her up, then, and hugged her and kissed her —
    They were little soft hugs, and she liked them, I guess —
But Jemmy screamed out, " You are choking her, sister!"
    And frightened her so she hid in my dress.
She's got used to him now, and don't care for his noise,
For she's found out he's just like the rest of the boys.
Jem says she's a stupid, and can't tell a rat
From a rose-bush ; but I know better than that.
And she isn't afraid of them, either, but thinks
    It isn't quite right to kill them for sport,
So she lies on the mat in the wood-shed and winks
    At their pranks, and they never get caught.
I don't care, I am sure, for rats like to live
Just as well as we do, and if people would give
Them their food every day in a little tin dish,
They'd learn to be honest, perhaps, and eat fish,
And pick bones, like the cats, and behave very well,
As poor Wink does. That's all. I've no more to tell.

Mrs. E. D. Kendall.

THE STUBBORN BOOT.

"BOTHER!" was all John Clatterby said.
   His breath came quick, and his cheek was red,
He flourished his elbows, and looked absurd,
While over and over his "Bother!" I heard.

Harder and harder the fellow worked,
Vainly and savagely still he jerked;
The boot, half on, would dangle and flap —
"Bother!" and then he bursted the strap.

Redder than ever his hot cheek flamed;
Harder than ever he fumed and blamed;
He wriggled his heel, and tugged at the leather
Till knees and chin came bumping together.

"My boy," said I, in a voice like a flute,
"Why not — ahem! — try the mate of that boot?
Or the other foot?" — "I'm a goose!" laughed John,
As he stood, in a flash, with his two boots on.

In half the affairs
   Of this busy life
(As that same day
   I said to my wife),
Our troubles come
   From trying to put
The left-hand shoe
   On the right-hand foot;
Or *vice versa*
   (Meaning, reverse, sir),
To try to force,
   As quite of course,
Any wrong foot
   In the right shoe,
Is the silliest thing
   A man can do.

Hearth and Home.

MARSTON MOOR.

To horse ! to horse ! Sir Nicholas, the clarion's note is
    high !
To horse ! to horse ! Sir Nicholas, the big drum makes
    reply !
Ere this hath Lucas marched, with his gallant cavaliers,
And the bray of Rupert's trumpets grows fainter in our
    ears.
To horse ! to horse ! Sir Nicholas ! White Guy is at the
    door,
And the raven whets his beak o'er the field of Marston
    Moor.

Up rose the Lady Alice from her brief and broken prayer,
And she brought a silken banner down the narrow turret-
    stair.
O ! many were the tears that those radiant eyes had shed,
As she traced the bright word "Glory" in the gay and
    glancing thread ;
And mournful was the smile which o'er those lovely fea-
    tures ran,
As she said, "It is your lady's gift ; unfurl it in the
    van !"

"It shall flutter, noble wench, where the best and boldest
    ride,
'Midst the steel-clad files of Skippon, the black dragoons
    of Pride ;
The recreant heart of Fairfax shall feel a sicklier qualm,
And the rebel lips of Oliver give out a louder psalm,
When they see my lady's gewgaw flaunt proudly on their
    wing,
And hear her loyal children shout, "For God, and for the
    King !"

'Tis soon. The ranks are broken, along the royal line
They fly, the braggarts of the court! the bullies of the
    Rhine !
Stout Langdale's cheer is heard no more, and Astley's
    helm is down,
And Rupert sheathes his rapier, with a curse and with a
    frown,
And cold Newcastle mutters, as he follows in their flight,
" The German boar had better far have supped in York
    to-night."

The knight is left alone, his steel-cap cleft in twain,
His good buff jerkin crimsoned o'er with many a gory
    stain ;
Yet still he waves his banner, and cries amid the rout,
" For Church and King, fair gentlemen! spur on, and fight
    it out ! "
And now he wards a Roundhead's pike, and now he hums
    a stave,
And now he quotes a stage-play, and now he fells a
    knave.

God aid thee now, Sir Nicholas ! thou hast no thought
    of fear ;
God aid thee now, Sir Nicholas ! for fearful odds are
    here !
The rebels hem thee in, and at every cut and thrust,
" Down, down," they cry, " with Belial ! down with him
    to the dust ! "
" I would," quoth grim old Oliver, " that Belial's trusty
    sword
This day were doing battle for the saints and for the
    Lord ! "

The Lady Alice sits with her maidens in her bower,
The gray-haired warder watches from the castle's top-
    most tower :

" What news ? what news, old Hubert ? " — " The bat-
    tle's lost and won :
The royal troops are melting, like mists before the sun !
And a wounded man approaches — I'm blind and cannot
    see,
Yet sure I am that sturdy step my master's step must
    be ! "

" I've brought thee back thy banner, wench, from as rude
    and red a fray
As e'er was proof of soldier's thew, or theme for min-
    strel's lay !
Here, Hubert, bring the silver bowl, and liquor *quantum*
    suff.
I'll make a shift to drain it yet, ere I part with boots and
    buff —
Though Guy through many a gaping wound is breathing
    forth his life,
And I come to thee a landless man, my fond and faithful
    wife !

" Sweet, we will fill our money-bags, and freight a ship
    for France,
And mourn in merry Paris for this poor land's mischance;
For if the worst befall me, why, better axe and rope,
Than life with Lenthal for a king, and Peters for a pope !
Alas ! alas ! my gallant Guy ! — curse on the crop-eared
    boor
Who sent me, with my standard, on foot from Marston
    Moor ! "

W. M. PRAED.

CALDWELL OF SPRINGFIELD.

HERE'S the spot. Look around you. Above on the
  height
Lay the Hessians encamped. By that church on the
  right
Stood the gaunt Jersey farmers. And here ran a wall —
You may dig anywhere and you'll turn up a ball.
Nothing more. Grasses spring, waters run, flowers blow
Pretty much as they did ninety-three years ago.

Nothing more, did I say? Stay, one moment; you've
  heard
Of Caldwell, the parson, who once preached the word
Down at Springfield? What, no? Come — that's bad,
  why, he had
All the Jerseys aflame! And they gave him the name
Of the " rebel high priest." He stuck in their gorge,
For he loved the Lord God — and he hated King George!

He had cause, you might say! When the Hessians that
  day,
Marched up with Knyphausen, they stopped on their way
At the " Farms," where his wife, with a child in her arms,
Sat alone in the house. How it happened, none knew
But God — and that one of the hireling crew
Who fired the shot. Enough! — there she lay,
And Caldwell, the chaplain, her husband, away!

Did he preach — did he pray? Think of him, as you
  stand
By the old church to-day; think of him, and that band
Of militant ploughboys! See the smoke and the heat
Of that reckless advance — of that straggling retreat!
Keep the ghost of that wife, foully slain, in your view —
And what could you — what should you — what would
  you do?

Why, just what he did ! They were left in the lurch
For the want of more wadding. He ran to the church,
Broke the door, stripped the pews, and dashed out in the
    road
With his arms full of hymn-books, and threw down his
    load
At their feet ! Then, above all the shouting and shots,
Rang his voice, " Put Watts into 'em — boys, give 'em
    Watts ! "

And they did. That is all. Grasses spring, flowers blow
Pretty much as they did ninety-three years ago.
You may dig anywhere and you'll turn up a ball —
But not always a hero like this — and that's all.

BRET HARTE.

WASHINGTON.

ROME had its Cæsar, great and brave ; but stain was
    on his wreath ;
He lived the heartless conqueror, and died the tyrant's
    death.
France had its eagle ; but his wings, though lofty they
    might soar,
Were spread in false ambition's flight, and dipped in
    murder's gore.

Those hero-gods, whose mighty sway would fain have
    chained the waves —
Who fleshed their blades with tiger zeal to make a world
    of slaves —
Who, though their kindred barred the path, still fiercely
    waded on —
O ! where shall be *their* " glory " by the side of Washing-
    ton ?

He fought, but not with love of strife — he struck but
    to defend ;
And ere he turned a people's foe, he sought to be a friend.
He strove to keep his country's right, by reason's gentle
    word,
And sighed when fell injustice threw the challenge —
    sword to sword.

He stood, the firm, the calm, the wise, the patriot and
    sage ;
He showed no deep, avenging hate — no burst of despot
    rage.
He stood for liberty and truth, and dauntlessly led on,
Till shouts of victory gave forth the name of Washington.

He saved his land, but did not lay his soldier trappings
    down
To change them for the regal vest, and don a kingly
    crown.
Fame was too earnest in her joy — too proud of such a
    son —
To let a robe and title mask a noble Washington.

ELIZA COOKE.

———◆◇◆———

A HUNDRED YEARS AGO.

A HUNDRED years have rolled away,
    Since that high, heroic day
When our fathers, in the fray,
    Struck the conquering blow !
Praise to them — the bold who spoke,
Praise to them — the brave who broke
Stern oppression's galling yoke,
    A hundred years ago.

Pour the wine of sacrifice,
Let the grateful anthem rise,
Shall we e'er resign the prize?
 Never — never — no !
Hearts and hands shall guard those rights,
Bought on Freedom's battle heights,
Where he fixed his signal lights,
 A hundred years ago.

Swear it, by the mighty dead,
Them who counselled, them who led,
By the blood your fathers shed,
 By your mothers' woe ;
Swear it, by the living few,
Them whose breasts were scarred for you,
When to freedom's ranks they flew,
 A hundred years ago.

By the joys that cluster round,
By our vales with plenty crowned,
By our hill-tops, holy ground,
 Rescued from the foe,
Where of old the Indian strayed,
Where of old the Pilgrim prayed,
Where the patriot drew his blade,
 A hundred years ago.

Should again the war-trump peal,
There shall Indian firmness seal
Pilgrim faith and patriot zeal,
 Prompt to strike the blow ;
There shall valor's work be done ;
Like the sire shall be the son,
Where the fight was waged and won,
 A hundred years ago.

 11

A NIGHT OF TERROR.

PAUL LOUIS COURIER thus writes to a cousin, of a series of terrors experienced by him: —

"I was one day travelling in Calabria; a country of people who, I believe, have no great liking to anybody, and are particularly ill-disposed towards the French. To tell you why would be a long affair. It is enough that they hate us to death, and that the unhappy being who should chance to fall into their hands would not pass his time in the most agreeable manner. I had for my companion a worthy young fellow: I do not say this to interest you, but because it is the truth. In these mountains, the roads are precipices, and our horses advanced with the greatest difficulty. My comrade going first, a track, which appeared to him more practicable and shorter than the regular path, led us astray. It was my fault. Ought I to have trusted to a head of twenty years? We sought our way out of the wood while it was yet light; but the more we looked for the path, the farther we were off it.

"It was a very black night, when we came close upon a very black house. We went in, and not without suspicion. But what was to be done? There we found a whole family of charcoal-burners at table. At the first word, they invited us to join them. My young man did not stop for much ceremony. In a minute or two we were eating and drinking in right earnest — he at least; for my own part, I could not help glancing about at the place and the people. Our hosts, indeed, looked like charcoal-burners; but the house!

you would have taken it for an arsenal. There was
nothing to be seen but muskets, pistols, sabres, knives,
cutlasses. Everything displeased me, and I saw that
I was in no favor myself. My comrade, on the con-
trary, was soon one of the family. He laughed, he
chatted with them : and with an imprudence which I
ought to have prevented, he at once said where we
came from, where we were going, and that we were
Frenchmen. Think of our situation! Here we were
among our mortal enemies — alone, benighted, and
far from all human aid. That nothing might be
omitted that could tend to our destruction, he must,
forsooth, play the rich man, promising these folks to
pay them well for their hospitality : and then he must
prate about his portmanteau, earnestly beseeching
them to take care of it, and put it at the head of his
bed, for he wanted no other pillow. Ah, youth, youth!
how art thou to be pitied! Cousin, they might have
thought that we carried the diamonds of the crown :
and yet the treasure in his portmanteau, which gave
him so much anxiety, consisted only of some private
letters!

"Supper ended, they left us. Our hosts slept below ; we on the story where we had been eating. In
a sort of platform raised seven or eight feet, where we
were to mount by a ladder, was the bed that awaited
us — a nest into which we had to introduce ourselves
by jumping over barrels filled with provisions for all
the year. My comrade seized upon the bed above,
and was soon fast asleep, with his head upon the precious portmanteau. I was determined to keep awake,
so I made a good fire, and sat myself down. The
night was almost passed over tranquilly enough, and

I was beginning to be comfortable, when just at the time it appeared to me that day was about to break, I heard our host and his wife talking and disputing below me; and, putting my ear into the chimney, which communicated with the lower room, I perfectly distinguished these exact words of the husband : 'Well, well, let us see — *must we kill them both?*' To which the wife replied, 'Yes!' and I heard no more.

"How should I tell you the rest? I could scarcely breathe; my whole body was as cold as marble; had you seen me, you could not have told whether I was dead or alive. Even now, the thought of my condition is enough. We two were almost without arms; against us, were twelve or fifteen persons who had plenty of weapons. And then, my comrade was overwhelmed with sleep. To call him up, to make a noise, was more than I dared; to escape alone was an impossibility. The window was not very high; but under it were two great dogs, howling like wolves. Imagine, if you can, the distress I was in. At the end of a quarter of an hour, which seemed to be an age, I heard some one on the staircase, and, through the chink of the door, I saw the old man, with a lamp in one hand, and one of his great knives in the other.

"The crisis was now come. He mounted—his wife followed him, I was behind the door. He opened it; but before he entered, he put down the lamp, which his wife took up, and coming in, with his feet naked, she, being behind him, said, in a smothered voice, hiding the light partially with her fingers, 'Gently, go gently.' On reaching the ladder, he mounted, with his knife between his teeth, and going to the head of the bed where that poor young man lay, with his throat uncovered, with one hand he took the knife, and with the other — ah, my cousin ! — he SEIZED — a ham which hung from the roof, cut a slice, and retired as he had come in !

"When the day appeared, all the family, with a great noise, came to rouse us as we had desired. They brought us plenty to eat; they served us up, I assure you, a capital breakfast. Two chickens formed a part of it, the hostess saying, 'You must eat one, and carry away the other.' When I saw them, I at once comprehended the meaning of those terrible words, 'Must we kill them *both*?'"

THE UNFINISHED PRAYER.

"NOW I lay," repeat it, darling ;
   "Lay me," lisped the tiny lips
Of my daughter, kneeling, bending
   O'er her folded finger-tips.

"Down to sleep." "To sleep," she murmured,
   And the curly head dropped low ;
"I pray the Lord," I gently added,
   You can say it all, you know.

"Pray the Lord," the word came faintly,
   Fainter still, "My soul to keep ; "
Then the tired head fairly nodded,
   And the child fell fast asleep.

But the dewy eyes half opened
   When I clasped her to my breast,
And the dear voice softly whispered,
   "Mamma, God knows all the rest."

BLINDMAN'S BUFF.

THREE wags (whom some fastidious carpers
　　Might rather designate three sharpers)
Entered at York, the cat and fiddle ;
　　And finding that the host was out
On business for two hours or more,
While Sam, the rustic waiter, wore
　　The visage of a simple lout,
Whom they might safely try to diddle, —
They ordered dinner in a canter, —
　　Cold or hot. it mattered not,
Provided it was served *instanter*.

Sam soon produced a first-rate dinner,
On which an alderman might dine ;
Joints hot and cold, dessert and wine,
　　He spread before each hungry sinner.
With talking, laughing, eating, and quaffing,
　　The bottles stood no moment still.
They rallied Sam with joke and banter,
And, as they drained the last decanter,
　　Called for the bill.

'Twas brought, — when one of them, who eyed
And added up the items, cried,
　　" Extremely moderate, indeed !
I'll make a point to recommend
This inn to every travelling friend ;
　　And you, Sam, shall be doubly fee'd."
This said, a weighty purse he drew,
　　When his companion interposed.
" Nay, Harry, that will never do ;
　　Pray let your purse again be closed ;
You paid all charges yesterday ;
'Tis clearly now my turn to pay."
Harry, however, wouldn't listen
　　To any such insulting offer ;

His generous eyes appeared to glisten
 Indignant at the very proffer;
And though his friend talked loud, his clangor
Served but to aggravate Hal's anger.
" My worthy fellow," cried the third,
" Now, really, this is too absurd.
What! do you both forget
I haven't paid a farthing yet?
 Am I in every house to cram,
At your expense? 'Tis childish, quite.
I claim this payment as my right.
 Here, how much is the money, Sam?"

The others bawled out fierce negation,
And hot became the altercation;
Each in his purse his money rattling,
Insisting, arguing, and battling.
One of them cried, at last, " A truce!
Wrangling for trifles is no use.
 That we may settle what we three owe,
We'll blindfold Sam, and whichsoe'er
He catches of us first shall bear
 All the expenses of the trio,
With half a crown (if that's enough)
To Sam for playing blindman's buff."
Sam liked it hugely, — thought the ransom
For a good game of fun was handsome;
Gave his own handkerchief beside,
To have his eyes securely tied,
And soon began to grope and search;
 When the three knaves, I needn't say,
Adroitly left him in the lurch,
 Slipped down the stairs, and stole away.

Poor Sam continued hard at work.
 Now o'er a chair he gets a fall;
Now floundering forward with a jerk,
 He bobs his nose against the wall;

And now, encouraged by a subtle
　Fancy that they're near the door,
　He jumps behind it to explore,
And breaks his shins against the scuttle.
Just in the crisis of his doom,
The host, returning, sought the room ;
Sam pounced upon him like a bruin,
And almost shook him into ruin.
" Huzza ! I've caught you now ; so down
With cash for all, and my half crown !"
　Off went the bandage, and his eyes
Seemed to be goggling o'er his forehead,
While his mouth widened with a horrid
　Look of agonized surprise.
" You gudgeon!" roared his master; "gull! and dunce!
Fool, as you are, in that you're right for once ;
'Tis clear that I must pay the sum ;
　But this one thought my wrath assuages,
That every half-penny shall come,
　Dolt, from your wages !"
　　　　　　　　　　　　　　　　　HORACE SMITH.

──────◆◆◆──────

KEARNY AT SEVEN PINES.

SO that soldierly legend is still on its journey —
　That story of Kearny who knew not to yield !
'Twas the day when, with Jameson, fierce Berry and
　　　Birney,
　Against twenty thousand he rallied the field.
Where the red volleys poured, where the clamor rose
　　　highest,
　Where the dead lay in clumps through the dwarf-oak
　　　and pine ;
Where the aim from the thicket was surest and nighest,
　No charge like Phil Kearny's along the whole line.

When the battle went ill, and the bravest were solemn,
    Near the dark Seven Pines, where we still held our
        ground,
He rode down the length of the withering column,
    And his heart at our war-cry leaped up with a bound;
He snuffed, like his charger, the wind of the powder,
    His sword waved us on, and we answered the sign;
Loud our cheers as we rushed, but his laugh rang the
        louder, —
    " There's the devil's own fun, boys, along the whole
        line ! "

How he strode his brown steed ! How we saw his blade
    brighten
In the one hand still left — and the reins in his teeth !
He laughed like a boy when the holidays heighten,
    But a soldier's glance shot from his visor beneath.
Up came the reserves to the mellay infernal,
    Asking where to go in — through the clearing or pine ?
" O, anywhere ! Forward ! 'Tis all the same, colonel ;
    You'll find lovely fighting along the whole line ! "

O, evil the black shroud of night at Chantilly,
    That hid him from sight of his brave men and tried !
Foul, foul sped the bullet that clipped the white lily,
    The flower of our knighthood, the whole army's pride !
Yet we dream that he still, in that shadowy region,
    Where the dead form their ranks at the wan drummer's
        sign,
Rides on, as of old, down the length of his legion,
    And the word still is — Forward ! along the whole line.

EDMUND C. STEDMAN.

BABY FAITH.

O BEAUTIFUL faith of childhood!   How
   It beamed to-night on the upturned brow
Of my three-year Love, as she knelt to say
Her prayers, in her guileless, dreamy way.

"And wouldn't my darling like," I said,
As softly I stroked the bowing head,
"Like to be good, and by and by
Go to a home in the happy sky,
Away and away above yon star,
Where God and his holy angels are?"

She lifted her drowsy and dewy eyes,
And a shy, scared look of half surprise
Rippled and filmed their depth of blue,
And kept the gladness from breaking through;
"I think I would like to go," she said,
Yet doubtingly shook her golden head,
And clasped my hands in her fingers small,
"But then, *I'm afraid that I might fall
Out at the moon!*"

      Her baby eye
Saw only an opening in the sky —
A marvellous oriel, whence the light
Of heaven streamed out across the night —
Where the angels lean, as they come and go,
Agaze at our world so far below.

She mused a moment in tender thought,
Then suddenly every feature caught
A new, rare sparkle, and I could trace
The dawn of trust that flashed her face.
"But God is good.   He will understand
That Baby's afraid, and will take my hand
And lead me in at the shining door,
And then I shall be afraid no more."

Christian Observer.

BE PATIENT.

BE patient! O, be patient! Put your ear against the
earth ;
Listen there how noiselessly the germ o' the seed has
birth ;
How noiselessly and gently it upheaves its little way,
Till it parts the scarcely broken ground, and the blade
stands up in the day.

Be patient! O, be patient! The germs of mighty thought
Must have their silent undergrowth, must underground be
wrought ;
But as sure as there's a power that makes the grass appear,
Our land shall be green with liberty, the blade-time shall
be here.

Be patient! O, be patient! Go and watch the wheat
ears grow —
So imperceptibly that ye can mark nor change nor throe —
Day after day, day after day, till the ear is fully grown,
And then again, day after day, till the ripened field is
brown.

Be patient! O, be patient! though yet our hopes are
green,
The harvest fields of freedom shall be crowned with sunny
sheen.
Be ripening! be ripening! mature your silent way,
Till the whole broad land is tongued with fire or freedom's
harvest day.

FRENCH.

MY DOG "SPORT."

I HAVE always loved dogs, and dogs have always loved me. I cannot recall a time in my life when I was afraid of a dog, and I never knew a dog to be cross to me. We understand each other. Dogs, like people, soon find out who are their friends, and all the sympathy of their dog nature warms up to them. I endure cats. I fancy birds. I like horses. But I love dogs with a real human love. I have been the owner of a good many, and their memory is fragrant with me yet.

But the best and loveliest of them all was Sport. He was as handsome as a picture — of a rich brown color, with large, liquid eyes, full of inexpressible tenderness, long silken ears that reached nearly to the ground, a short pug nose, and square, intellectual head. He was a rare beauty. People would always stop and look round at him as he passed. Thieves tried to steal him; but he was too cunning for them.

He understood language, as far as his range of words went, as well as a man; yes, better than some men I know. He would watch my every motion, and at the slightest hint would be off like shot to do my bidding. If I told him to take a man's hat off in the street (which, I am sorry to say, I have done), he would give a spring to his shoulders, and bring me the hat before the man had time to get over his scare and look round. Sometimes, if I left home and had forgotten something, it would be enough to say, "Sport, 'handkerchief!' 'pocket-book!' 'gloves!'"

when away he would go, soon after returning with the article in his mouth.

I was once bathing in the Delaware. After I had dressed and gone a mile from the place, I found that I had left my necktie. I looked at Sport, pointed at my neck, and said, " Bring it." Before the words were fairly spoken he was off, and in a quarter of an hour returned with the tie in his mouth.

I used to play hide and seek with him. I would turn him out of the room, and then hide my handkerchief. He always beat me. I would put it under the carpet, inside the piano, stuff it down behind the sofa seat. But he always found it. Once I put it on top of the curtain cornice. He had a long hunt that time ; but at last he mounted on a chair, looked up, gave a long snuff, then wagged his tail and whined. He couldn't get it, but told me plainly enough where it was.

One Sunday night I came home from church very tired, and thought I would see if he could get my slippers. I took off my boots, and, pointing to my feet, said, " Sport, slippers ! " It was a new word to him. He looked at me sharply ; then at my feet ; then away he went to the bedroom and brought my nightgown. Seeing my boots off, and knowing that it was near bed-time, he thought that was what I wanted. I shook my head, " No, no ; " and again pointed to my feet. " Slippers, see ! " showing the uncovered foot. Away he went the second time, returning with the bootjack. I said, " No, no." He looked at me again inquiringly, turned his head on one side, then dashed off the third time with a sharp yelp. This time he got them ; and, O, how glad and proud he was when I patted him approvingly! He never made a mistake about slippers after that.

Of all dogs he was the most faithful. If I put anything in his charge, he would guard it for hours, and I believe he would have sacrificed his life rather than desert it. Put him beside a sleeping child, and say, "Watch!" and woe betide any one who should disturb that child!

Once I came to the city in a steamboat. I put my valise on the fore-deck, and told Sport to watch it. He lay down with his paw upon it, and his sharp eyes unclosed. When the boat reached the landing, a colored porter rushed up to me, crying out, "Baggage? baggage?" "Yes," I said; "take that valise." pointing to it. He sprang for it, but Sport made a snap at him that soon drove him back. He tried in vain to get possession of it by artifice. I stood by laughing.

The porter saw the joke, and went ashore to call a comrade. "Here, Pete," he said, "take that gen'l'-man's valise. I'm full!" Away the second fellow went for it; but Sport's teeth rattled more furiously than ever. I offered him double fare if he would get it; but it was of no use. Sport was too much for him; and even after I had called him off duty he eyed the man suspiciously, and never left him till the valise was safely home.

Once only was Sport disobedient. He was subjected to a temptation too great for even his great dog heart. We had sailed across and down the river in a large yacht; when anchoring, we took a small skiff to hunt in the reeds for ducks, bidding Sport remain on the yacht and keep watch. We were gone about an hour, had fired a few shots, then returned to the yacht. But Sport was not there. We called him, whistled for him, fired our guns, but in vain. We spent hours seeking for him among the reeds. Fruitless search! He was not there. We thought him lost to us forever, and with sad hearts at nightfall returned home. But Sport was ahead of us. He was lying on the grass at the landing, waiting; but too weary to rise even. He could only wag his tail, and that faintly.

We saw at once what the matter was. He had heard the shooting while on the yacht, and in a moment of excitement had forgotten the command to stay, and jumped into the water. Not being able to swim through the reeds to us, he returned to the yacht; but the sides were too high for him to climb up. After, probably, many fruitless efforts, he started for home on the side of the river—a long swim against the current; but he accomplished it. It cost him dearly, though. He grew quite deaf, and lost his ambition from that day.

Soon afterwards he was walking on the railroad, and, unable to hear an approaching train, he was run over and killed. How sad we were! I felt that I had lost a friend to whom I was all the world. I wonder sometimes if there is no after-life for one like him. The line between his instinct and a soul's intelligence was very faint. The depth of his affection was wonderful. Poor dear Sport! Would that my arms were around thy neck, and thy soft silken ears were resting on my cheek now! Thy place can never be filled. Rev. Thomas Street.

SCIPIO TO THE SENATE.

[Scipio the Great, when his brother was accused of peculation, with some suspicion of his own complicity, tore in pieces the accounts which he held in his hand, and flung them down before the senate, refusing to put his honor in question.]

QUESTIONED in trust and honor, I could speak,
   Nor aught that honor might disclose would spare ;
Questioned in doubt, excusing words were weak
   And coward breaths, to shame their kindred air.

Ye that can doubt me, pass in silence by ;
   Bury my name, nor greet me with a word !
My truth is deaf to challenge of a lie ;
   Not with *that* champion does it cross the sword.

Have I, then, lived among you all these years
   A dubious phantom, true or false unknown ?
And ye, forsooth ! would have to lay your fears
   My doubted faith by proof of parchment shown ?

Never from me !   I tear the proofs to shreds,
   And strew them here upon the senate floor ;
Ye that know not a man, *go* make your beds
   Upon your thorniest thoughts ; vex me no more

O, ye could trust me in your hour of need,
   When the grim foe was menacing your gates ;
But saved your rude suspicion for your meed,
   When I had made you master of your fates.

Asked ye for parchments when the power of Rome
   To foreign shores I led in stern array ?
Called ye for parchments when, returning home,
   I brought you victory, beauteous as the day ?

Your fate, as my sword's hilt, was in my hand ;
  I came a conqueror, but bent the knee,
By faith subdued, and lowly to my land
  Gave that in *power*, that came in want to me.

And now in power, behold, ye come to say,
  Hast thou not filched our coins? Speak, give us proof.
Nay, pawn your doubt to win another, play
  Your game of question : proud, I stand aloof.

There ! gather up these fragments, if ye will,
  And mouse among them, — *pore, compare*, and *scan*.
When of that labor ye have had your fill,
  Go, learn the art of arts — to know a man !

D. A. WASSON.

KING ROBERT OF SICILY.

ROBERT of Sicily, brother of Pope Urbane,
  And Valmond, emperor of Allemaine,
Apparelled in magnificent attire,
With retinue of many a knight and squire,
On St. John's eve, at vespers, proudly sat
And heard the priests chant the Magnificat.
And as he listened, o'er and o'er again
Repeated, like a burden or refrain,
He caught the words, " *Deposuit potentes
De sede, et exaltavit humiles* ; "
And slowly lifting up his kingly head,
He to a learnéd clerk beside him said,
" What mean these words? " The clerk made answer
    meet,
" He has put down the mighty from their seat,
And has exalted them of low degree."
Thereat King Robert muttered scornfully,
" 'Tis well that such seditious words are sung
Only by priests, and in the Latin tongue ;

12

For unto priests and people be it known,
There is no power can push me from my throne!"
And leaning back, he yawned and fell asleep,
Lulled by the chant monotonous and deep.

When he awoke, it was already night;
The church was empty, and there was no light,
Save where the lamps that glimmered, few and faint,
Lighted a little space before some saint.
He started from his seat and gazed around,
But saw no living thing, and heard no sound.
He groped towards the door, but it was locked;
He cried aloud, and listened, and then knocked,
And uttered awful threatenings, and complaints,
And imprecations upon men and saints.
The sounds re-echoed from the roof and walls,
As if dead priests were laughing in their stalls.

At length the sexton, hearing from without
The tumult of the knocking and the shout,
And thinking thieves were in the house of prayer,
Came with his lantern, asking, "Who is there?"
Half choked with rage, King Robert fiercely said,
"Open; 'tis I, the king! Art thou afraid?"
The frightened sexton, muttering with a curse,
"This is some drunken vagabond, or worse,"
Turned the great key, and flung the portal wide;
A man rushed by him at a single stride,
Haggard, half naked, without hat or cloak,
Who neither turned, nor looked at him, nor spoke,
But leaped into the blackness of the night,
And vanished like a spectre from his sight.

Robert of Sicily, brother of Pope Urbane,
And Valmond, emperor of Allemaine,
Despoiled of his magnificent attire,
Bare-headed, breathless, and besprent with mire,
With sense of wrong and outrage desperate,

Strode on and thundered at the palace gate;
Rushed through the court-yard, thrusting, in his rage,
To right and left each seneschal and page,
And hurried up the broad and sounding stair,
His white face ghastly in the torches' glare.
From hall to hall he passed with breathless speed;
Voices and cries he heard, but did not heed,
Until at last he reached the banquet-room,
Blazing with light, and breathing with perfume.

There on the dais sat another King,
Wearing his robes, his crown, his signet-ring,
King Robert's self in features, form, and height,
But all transfigured with angelic light!
It was an angel; and his presence there
With a divine effulgence filled the air,
An exaltation piercing the disguise,
Though none the hidden angel recognize.

A moment speechless, motionless, amazed,
The throneless monarch on the angel gazed,
Who met his looks of anger and surprise
With the divine compassion of his eyes;
Then said, "Who art thou? and why cam'st thou here?"
To which King Robert answered, with a sneer,
"I am the king, and come to claim my own
From an impostor, who usurps my throne!"
And suddenly, at these audacious words,
Up sprang the angry guests, and drew their swords;
The angel answered, with unruffled brow,
"Nay, not the king, but the king's jester; thou
Henceforth shalt wear the bells and scalloped cape,
And for thy counsellor shall lead an ape;
Thou shalt obey my servants when they call,
And wait upon my henchmen in the hall!"

Deaf to King Robert's threats, and cries, and prayers,
They thrust him from the hall, and down the stairs;

A group of tittering pages ran before,
And as they opened wide the folding-door,
His heart failed, for he heard, with strange alarms,
The boisterous laughter of the men-at-arms,
And all the vaulted chamber roar and ring
With the mock plaudits of " Long live the King ! "

Next morning, waking with the day's first beam,
He said within himself, " It was a dream ! "
But the straw rustled as he turned his head ;
There were the cap and bells beside his bed ;
Around him rose the bare, discolored walls ;
Close by, the steeds were champing in their stalls,
And in the corner, a revolting shape,
Shivering and chattering, sat the wretched ape.
It was no dream ; the world he loved so much
Had turned to dust and ashes at his touch !

Days came and went ; and now returned again
To Sicily the old Saturnian reign ;
Under the angel's governance benign
The happy island danced with corn and wine,
And deep within the mountain's burning breast
Enceladus, the giant, was at rest.
Meanwhile King Robert yielded to his fate,
Sullen, and silent, and disconsolate.
Dressed in the motley garb that jesters wear,
With looks bewildered and a vacant stare,
Close shaven above the ears, as monks are shorn,
By courtiers mocked, by pages laughed to scorn,
His only friend the ape, his only food
What others left, — he still was unsubdued.
And when the angel met him on his way,
And half in earnest, half in jest, would say,
Sternly, though tenderly, that he might feel
The velvet scabbard held a sword of steel,
" Art thou the king ? " the passion of his woe
Burst from him in resistless overflow,

And lifting high his forehead, he would fling
The haughty answer back, "I am, I am the king!"

Almost three years were ended, when there came
Ambassadors of great repute and name
From Valmond, emperor of Allemaine,
Unto King Robert, saying that Pope Urbane,
By letter summoned them forthwith to come
On Holy Thursday to his city of Rome.
The angel with great joy received his guests,
And gave them presents of embroidered vests,
And velvet mantles with rich ermine lined,
And rings and jewels of the rarest kind.
Then he departed with them o'er the sea,
Into the lovely land of Italy,
Whose loveliness was more resplendent made
By the mere passing of that cavalcade,
With plumes, and cloaks, and housings, and the stir
Of jewelled bridle and of golden spur.
And lo! among the menials, in mock state,
Upon a piebald steed, with shambling gait,
His cloak of fox-tails flapping in the wind,
The solemn ape demurely perched behind,
King Robert rode, making huge merriment
In all the country towns through which they went.

The pope received them with great pomp, and blare
Of bannered trumpets, on St. Peter's square,
Giving his benediction and embrace,
Fervent, and full of apostolic grace.
While with congratulations and with prayers,
He entertained the angel unawares,
Robert, the jester, bursting through the crowd,
Into their presence rushed, and cried aloud,
"I am the king! Look and behold in me
Robert, your brother, King of Sicily!
This man, who wears my semblance to your eyes,
Is an impostor in a king's disguise.

Do you not know me? does no voice within
Answer my cry, and say we are akin?"
The pope in silence, but with troubled mien,
Gazed at the angel's countenance serene;
The emperor, laughing, said, "It is strange sport
To keep a madman for thy fool at court!"
And the poor baffled jester in disgrace
Was hustled back among the populace.

In solemn state the holy week went by,
And Easter Sunday gleamed upon the sky;
The presence of an angel, with its light,
Before the sun rose, made the city bright,
And with new fervor filled the hearts of men,
Who felt that Christ indeed had risen again;
Even the jester, on his bed of straw,
With haggard eyes the unwonted splendor saw;
He felt within a power unfelt before,
And, kneeling humbly on his chamber floor,
He heard the rushing garments of the Lord
Sweep through the silent air, ascending heavenward.

And now the visit ending, and once more
Valmond returning to the Danube's shore,
Homeward the angel journeyed, and again
The land was made resplendent with his train,
Flashing along the towns of Italy
Unto Salerno, and from there by sea.
And when once more within Palermo's wall,
And seated on his throne in his great hall,
He heard the Angelus from convent towers,
As if the better world conversed with ours,
He beckoned to King Robert to draw nigher,
And with a gesture bade the rest retire;
And when they were alone, the angel said,
"Art thou the king?" Then bowing down his head,
King Robert crossed both hands upon his breast,
And meekly answered him, "Thou knowest best!

My sins as scarlet are ; let me go hence,
And in some cloister's school of penitence,
Across those stones that pave the way to heaven
Walk barefoot, till my guilty soul is shriven."
The angel smiled, and from his radiant face
A holy light illumined all the place,
And through the open window, loud and clear,
They heard the monks chant in the chapel near,
Above the stir and tumult of the street, —
" He has put down the mighty from their seat,
And has exalted them of low degree !"
And through the chant a second melody
Rose like the throbbing of a single string, —
" I am an angel, and thou art the king !"

King Robert, who was standing near the throne,
Lifted his eyes, and lo ! he was alone !
But all apparelled as in days of old,
With ermined mantle, and with cloth of gold ;
And when his courtiers came, they found him there
Kneeling upon the floor, absorbed in silent prayer.

OUR FATHERS.

O, MANY a time it hath been told,
   The story of those men of old.
For this fair Poetry hath wreathed
   Her sweetest, purest flower ;
For this proud Eloquence hath breathed
   His strain of loftiest power ;
Devotion, too, hath lingered round
Each spot of consecrated ground,
   And hill and valley blessed ;
There, where our banished fathers strayed,
There, where they loved, and wept, and prayed,
   There, where their ashes rest.

And never may they rest unsung,
While Liberty can find a tongue.
Twine, Gratitude, a wreath for them
More deathless than the diadem,
Who, to life's noblest end,   ·
    Gave up life's noblest powers,
And bade the legacy descend
    Down, down to us and ours.

By centuries now the glorious hour we mark,
When to these shores they steered their shattered bark;
And still, as other centuries melt away,
Shall other ages come to keep the day.
When we are dust, who gather round this spot,
Our joys, our griefs, our very names forgot,
Here shall the dwellers of the land be seen,
To keep the memory of the Pilgrims green.

Nor here alone their praises shall go round,
Nor here alone their virtues shall abound —
Broad as the empire of the free shall spread,
Far as the foot of man shall dare to tread,
Where oar hath never dipped, where human tongue
Hath never through the woods of ages rung,
There, where the eagle's scream and wild wolf's cry
Keep ceaseless day and night through earth and sky,
Even there, in after time, as toil and taste
Go forth in gladness to redeem the waste,
Even there shall rise, as grateful myriads throng,
Faith's holy prayer, and Freedom's joyful song;
There shall the flame that flashed from yonder Rock,
Light up the land, till Nature's final shock.

CHARLES SPRAGUE.

MOTIVES OF ACTION.

IT has been said by a noble lord, that I am running the race of popularity. If the noble lord means by popularity, that applause bestowed by after ages on good and virtuous actions, I have long been struggling in that race; to what purpose, all-trying Time can alone determine. But if the noble lord means that mushroom popularity that is raised without merit, and lost without crime, he is much mistaken in his opinion.

I defy the noble lord to point out a single instance in my life where the popularity of the times ever had the smallest influence on my determinations. I thank Heaven I have a more permanent and steady rule of conduct — the dictates of my own breast.

Those that have foregone that pleasing adviser, and given up their mind to be the slave of every popular impulse, I sincerely pity; I pity them still more, if their vanity leads them to mistake the shouts of a mob for the trumpet of fame. Experience might inform them that many who have been saluted with the huzzas of the crowd one day, have received their execrations the next; and many, who, by the popularity of their times, have been held up as spotless patriots, have, nevertheless, appeared upon the historian's page, when truth has triumphed over delusion, the assassins of liberty.

True liberty, in my opinion, can only exist when justice is equally administered to all — to the king and to the beggar. Where is the justice, then, or where is the law, that protects a member of Parlia-

ment, more than any other man, from the punishment
due to his crimes? The laws of this country allow
of no place, nor no employment, to be a sanctuary for
crimes; and where I have the honor to sit as judge,
neither royal favor nor popular applause shall ever
protect the guilty. LORD MANSFIELD.

IF I WERE A VOICE.

IF I were a Voice, — a persuasive Voice, —
That could travel the wide world through,
I would fly on the beams of the morning light,
And speak to men with a gentle might,
    And tell them to be true.
I'd fly, I'd fly o'er land and sea,
Wherever a human heart might be,
Telling a tale, or singing a song,
In praise of the Right—in blame of the Wrong.

If I were a Voice, — a consoling Voice, —
    I'd fly on the wings of air;
The homes of Sorrow and Guilt I'd seek,
And calm and truthful words I'd speak,
    To save them from Despair.
I'd fly, I'd fly o'er the crowded town,
And drop, like the happy sunlight, down
Into the hearts of suffering men,
And teach them to rejoice again.

If I were a Voice, — a convincing Voice, —
    I'd travel with the wind;
And whenever I saw the nations torn
By warfare, jealousy, or scorn,
    Or hatred of their kind,

I'd fly, I'd fly on the thunder-crash,
And into their blinded bosoms flash ;
And all their evil thoughts subdued,
I'd teach them Christian Brotherhood.

If I were a Voice, — a pervading Voice, —
  I'd seek the kings of earth ;
I'd find them alone on their beds at night,
And whisper words that should guide them right—
  Lessons of priceless worth.
I'd fly more swift than the swiftest bird,
And tell them things they never heard —
Truths which the ages for aye repeat,
Unknown to the statesmen at their feet.

If I were a Voice, — an immortal Voice, —
  I'd speak in the people's ear ;
And whenever they shouted " Liberty,"
Without deserving to be free,
  I'd make their error clear.
I'd fly, I'd fly on the wings of day,
Rebuking wrong on my world-wide way,
And making all the earth rejoice —
If I were a Voice — an immortal Voice.

CHARLES MACKAY.

THE SONG OF STEAM.

HARNESS me down with your iron bands ;
  Be sure of your curb and rein ;
For I scorn the power of your puny hands
  As the tempest scorns a chain.
How I laughed, as I lay concealed from sight
  For many a countless hour,
At the childish boast of human might,
  And the pride of human power !

Ha! ha! ha! They found me at last;
  They invited me forth at length,
And I rushed to my throne with thunder-blast,
  And laughed in my iron strength.
O! then ye saw a wondrous change
  On the earth and ocean wide,
Where now my fiery armies range,
  Nor wait for wind or tide.

Hurrah! hurrah! The waters o'er
  The mountains steep decline;
Time—space—have yielded to my power—
  The world! the world is mine!
The rivers the sun hath earliest blest,
  Or those where his beams decline,
The giant streams of the queenly West,
  Or the Orient floods divine.

I blow the bellows, I forge the steel,
  In all the shops of trade;
I hammer the ore, and turn the wheel,
  Where my arms of strength are made;
I manage the furnace, the mill, the mint;
  I carry, I spin, I weave;
And all my doings I put into print
  On every Saturday eve.

I've no muscle to weary, no breast to decay,
  No bones to be "laid on the shelf;"
And soon I intend you may "go and play,"
  While I manage the world by myself.
But harness me down with your iron bands;
  Be sure of your curb and rein;
For I scorn the strength of your puny hands,
  As the tempest scorns a chain.

THE WRECK OF THE HESPERUS.

IT was the schooner Hesperus,
    That sailed the wintry sea ;
And the skipper had taken his little daughter,
    To bear him company.

Blue were her eyes as the fairy flax,
    Her cheeks like the dawn of day,
And her bosom white as the hawthorn buds,
    That ope in the month of May.

Down came the storm, and smote amain
    The vessel in its strength —
She shuddered and paused, like a frighted steed,
    Then leaped her cable's length.

"Come hither! come hither! my little daughter,
    And do not tremble so,
For I can weather the roughest gale
    That ever wind did blow."

He wrapped her warm in his seaman's coat
    Against the stinging blast ;
He cut a rope from a broken spar,
    And bound her to the mast.

"O, father! I hear the church bells ring ;
    O, say, what may it be ?"
"'Tis a fog-bell on a rock-bound coast !" —
    And he steered for the open sea.

"O, father! I hear the sound of guns ;
    O, say, what may it be ?"
"Some ship in distress, that cannot live
    In such an angry sea !"

"O, father! I see a gleaming light ;
    O, say, what may it be ?"

But the father answered never a word, —
   A frozen corpse was he.

Then the maiden clasped her hands, and prayed
   That savéd she might be ;
And she thought of Christ, who stilled the wave
   On the lake of Galilee.

And fast through the midnight dark and drear,
   Through the whistling sleet and snow,
Like a sheeted ghost, the vessel swept
   Towards the reef of Norman's Woe.

To the rocks and breakers right ahead
   She drifted, a dreary wreck,
And a whooping billow swept the crew
   Like icicles from her deck.

She struck where the white and fleecy waves
   Looked soft as carded wool,
But the cruel rocks they gored her side
   Like the horns of an angry bull

At daybreak, on the bleak sea-beach,
   A fisherman stood aghast,
To see the form of a maiden fair,
   Lashed close to a drifting mast.

The salt sea was frozen on her breast,
   The salt tears in her eyes ;
And he saw her hair, like the brown sea-weed,
   On the billows fall and rise.

Such was the wreck of the Hesperus,
   In the midnight and the snow —
Christ save us from a death like this,
   On the reef of Norman's Woe !

                                   LONGFELLOW.

A GRECIAN FABLE.

ONCE on a time, a son and sire, we're told, —
The stripling tender and the father old, —
Purchased a donkey at a country fair,
To ease their limbs, and hawk about their ware ;
But as the sluggish animal was weak,
They feared, if both should mount, his back would break.
Up got the boy ; the father plods on foot,
And through the gazing crowd he leads the brute ;
Forth from the crowd the graybeards hobble out,
And hail the cavalcade with feeble shout :
"This the respect to feeble age you show ?
And this the duty you to parents owe ?
He beats the hoof, and you are set astride ;
Sirrah ! get down, and let your father ride !"

As Grecian lads were seldom void of grace,
The decent, duteous youth resigned his place.
Then a fresh murmur through the rabble ran ;
Boys, girls, wives, widows, all attack the man :
"Sure ne'er was brute so void of nature !
Have you no pity for the pretty creature ?
To your young child can you be so unkind ?
Here, Luke, Bill, Betty, put the child behind !"
Old Dapple next the clowns' compassion claimed :
"'Tis strange those boobies are not quite ashamed !
Two at a time upon a poor dumb beast !
They might as well have carried *him*, at least."
The pair, still pliant to the partial voice,
Dismount and bear the brute.   Then what a noise !
Huzzas, loud laughs, low gibe, and bitter joke,
From the yet silent sire these words provoke :
"Proceed, my boy, nor heed their further call ;
Vain his attempt who strives to please them all !"

THE COMING WOMAN.

A DIALOGUE FOR GIRLS.

First Voice.

NOBODY knows how I want to grow,
 How I count the days as they come and go,
Wishing and wishing that time had wings ;
For I've made up my mind to do great things
    When I'm a woman !
I won't be dull, and faded, and gray,
And drudge in the household from day to day,
    Like some of the women I know ;
But I mean to grow fresher every year,
And I'll be so smart that the people here
    Shall ask how I manage so.

Second Voice.

When *I*'m a woman I mean to show
What wonderful things a woman can know —
I'll know French and German to write and speak,
And I'll read all those funny old books in Greek,
    Besides what there are in Latin.
I'll learn all about what they call "High Art ;"
I'll have the Philosophy quite by heart,
    And Trigonometry, too.
I won't take a minute to work or play,
But I'll study by night, and I'll study by day,
    To show what a woman can do !

Third Voice.

A writer *I*'ll be, and I'll engage
To write not a single stupid page ;
But funny short stories for girls and boys,
And songs to be sung with a good deal of noise,
    And marvellous fairy tales.

I know all the children will buy my books,
And I'll write some, too, for the older folks,
   For the newspapers first, I guess ;
Letters, perhaps, from over the sea,
To tell the strange things that have happened to me,
   And how the queer people dress.

Fourth Voice.

Such a famous housekeeper *I* will be,
That all the ladies will call to see
How I ever make such *beautiful* bread !
For all my household shall be well fed
   When I'm a woman.
O, the sweetest jellies and cream I'll make,
And of daintiest puddings, and pies, and cake,
   I will always have great store ;
My kitchen-floor shall be snowy white,
And everything else shall be just right
   That you find inside my door.

Fifth Voice.

I'll be a lecturer, travelling about,
When it isn't too stormy for men to get out ;
I'll show them their sphere, and the women's, too,
And tell the young girls what they ought to do
   When *they* are women.
I'll let people see why the world goes wrong,
And make them all hope that it won't be long
   Till women can have their way.
Freedom to lecture, to vote, to preach,
To do everything now beyond our reach,
   We surely will have some day !

Sixth Voice.

I'll be a milliner, wrapped in a cloud
Of laces and ribbons, and sought by a crowd

13

Of beautiful ladies in velvet and pearls,
Who want exquisite hats for their dear little girls,
    In the style just fresh from Paris!
Such ravishing bonnets as I'll invent
Have never been seen on this continent!
    And, for customers to prepare them,
I'll have dozens of girls sewing night and day,
For fear the new fashion will grow *passé*
    Before folks get a chance to wear them.

Seventh Voice.

When *I*'m a woman, a teacher I'll be,
But I hope I shan't have much company;
O, if committees could only know
How glad we are when they rise to go!
    When I'm a woman
I expect that teachers will have great pay,
And they won't work more than three hours a day,
    And vacations will be so long!
And I'll caution my scholars to take great care
To study no more than their health will bear,
    For that would be very wrong.

All.

When *we* are women, you then will see
The *useful* things that women can be;
And though each of us in her own way tries,
We can all be happy, and good, and wise,
    When we are women.
But perhaps it is true that time has wings,
And, if we would do all these wonderful things,
    We must lose not a single day.
If our plans should go wrong, we'll have courage still,
For we think that somehow, where we've a will,
    We shall always find a way!

Christian Union.

THE AFFRAY IN KING STREET, BOSTON, 1770.

SOON after the French war, which closed in 1763, the king and Parliament of Great Britain began to treat the colonies very unjustly. The British government, being very much in debt, wanted to raise large sums of money, and so determined to get a part of it by taxing the Americans. Now, the latter maintained that England had no right to tax them.

The people of Boston were particularly excited; and fearing rebellion, General Gage, the British commander, assembled two regiments of soldiers to keep them in awe. In the spring of 1770, quarrels occurred almost every day between the soldiers and the populace.

A great tumult broke out, between seven and eight o'clock, on the evening of the 5th of March. The mob, armed with clubs, ran towards King Street, now State Street, crying, "Let us drive out these rascals! They have no business here! Drive them out! Drive out the rascals!"

About this time, some one cried out that the town had been set on fire. Then the bells rang, and the crowd became greater and more noisy. They rushed furiously to the custom-house, and, seeing an English soldier stationed there, shouted, "Kill him! kill him!" The people attacked him with snowballs, pieces of ice, and whatever they could find.

The sentinel called for the guard, and Captain Preston sent a corporal with a few soldiers to defend him. They marched with their guns loaded, and the captain

followed them.   They met a crowd of the people, led
on by a giant of a negro, named Attucks.   They
brandished their clubs, and pelted the soldiers with
snowballs, abused them with all manner of harsh
words, shouted in their faces, surrounded them, and
challenged them to fire.

They even rushed upon the points of the bayonets.
The soldiers stood like statues, the bells ringing, and
the mob pressing upon them.   At last, Attucks, with
twelve of his men, began to strike upon their muskets
with clubs, and cried out to the multitude, " Don't be
afraid !   They dare not fire — the miserable cowards !
Kill the rascals !   Crush them under foot ! "

Attucks lifted his arm against Captain Preston, and
seized upon a bayonet.   "They dare not fire !" shouted
the mob again.   At this instant the firing began.   The
negro dropped dead upon the ground.   The soldiers
fired twice more.   Three men were killed, and others
were wounded.   The mob dispersed, but soon returned
to carry off the bodies.

The whole town was now in an uproar.   Thousands
of men, women, and children rushed through the
streets.   The sound of drums, and cries of, " To arms !
to arms ! " were heard from all quarters.   The soldiers
who had fired on the people were arrested, and the
governor at last persuaded the multitude to go home
quietly.

TIT FOR TAT.

A MIGHTY elephant, that swelled the state
   Of Aurengzebe the Great,
One day was taken by his driver
To drink and cool him in the river ;
The driver on his neck was seated ;
   And, as he rode along,
   By some acquaintance in the throng,
With a ripe cocoa-nut was treated.

A cocoa-nut's a pretty fruit enough,
But guarded by a shell both hard and tough ;
The fellow tried, and tried, and tried,
   Working and sweating,
   Fuming and fretting,
To find out the inside,
And pick the kernel for his eating.

At length, quite out of patience grown,
" Who'll reach me up," he cries, " a stone,
   To break this tough old shell ?
But stay ; I've here a solid bone
   May do perhaps as well."
So, half in earnest, half in jest,
He banged it on the forehead of the beast.

An elephant, they say, has human feeling,
   And full as well as we he knows
   The difference between words and blows,
Between horse-play and civil dealing ;
Use him but well, he'll do his best
   To serve you faithfully and truly ;
But insults unprovoked he can't digest ,
   He studies o'er them, and repays them duly.

To make my head an anvil, thought the creature,
Was never, certainly, the will of Nature ;
So, master mine, you may repent ;
Then shaking his broad ears, away he went ;
The driver took him to the water,
And thought no more about the matter ;
The elephant within his memory hid it ;
He *felt* the wrong, the other only *did* it.

A week or two elapsed ; one market day,
Again the beast and driver took their way ;
Through rows of shops and booths they passed,
 With eatables and trinkets stored,
Till to a gardener's stall they came at last,
 Where cocoa-nuts lay piled upon the board.
" Ha ! " thought the elephant, " 'tis now my turn
 To show this method of nut breaking ;
My friend above will like to learn,
 Though at the cost of a head-aching."

Then in his curling trunk he took a heap,
And waved it o'er his neck with sudden sweep,
 And on the hapless driver's sconce
He laid a blow, so hard and full,
 He cracked the nuts at once,
But, at the same time, cracked the poor man's skull.

Young folks, whene'er you feel inclined .
 To rompish sports and freedom rough,
Bear tit for tat in mind ;
 Nor give an elephant a cuff,
To be repaid in kind.

TO WHOM SHALL WE GIVE THANKS?

A LITTLE boy had sought the pump
    From whence the sparkling water burst,
And drank with eager joy the draught
    That kindly quenched his raging thirst.
Then gracefully he touched his cap —
    "I thank you, Mr. Pump," he said,
"For this nice drink you've given me!"
    (This little boy had been well bred.)

Then said the Pump, "My little man,
    You're welcome to what I have done;
But I am not the one to thank —
    I only help the water run."
"O, then," the little fellow said
    (Polite he always meant to be),
"Cold Water, please accept my thanks;
    You have been very kind to me."

"Ah!" said Cold Water, "don't thank me;
    Far up the hill-side lives the Spring
That sends me forth with generous hand
    To gladden every living thing."
"I'll thank the Spring, then," said the boy,
    And gracefully he bowed his head.
"O, don't thank me, my little man,"
    The Spring with silvery accents said.

"O, don't thank me; for what am I
    Without the dew and summer rain?
Without their aid I ne'er could quench
    Your thirst, my little boy, again."
"O, well, then," said the little boy,
    "I'll gladly thank the Rain and Dew."
"Pray, don't thank us — without the sun
    We could not fill one cup for you."

" Then, Mr. Sun, ten thousand thanks
    For all that you have done for me."
" Stop !" said the Sun, with blushing face ;
    " My little fellow, don't thank me :
'Twas from the ocean's mighty stores
    I drew the draught I gave to thee."
" O, Ocean, thanks, then !" said the boy —
    It echoed back, " Not unto me.

" Not unto me ; but unto Him
    Who formed the depths in which I lie ;
Go, give thy thanks, my little boy,
    To Him who will thy wants supply."
The boy took off his cap, and said,
    In tones so gentle and subdued,
" O God, I thank Thee for this gift ;
    Thou art the Giver of all good."

THE DYNMOUTH FISHERMAN.

A TERRIFIC storm was raging on the wild coast
of North Devonshire, and the Dynmouth life-
boat was preparing to put out to a ship which, at
some distance from the land, was making signals of
distress.

"One more man is wanted — who will go?" was
shouted above the roar of the wind and waves.

"I will!" And a Dynmouth fisher-lad started forth
from a crowd of anxious spectators grouped upon the
beach.

The cry was taken up by the excited bystanders,
"Will Carew — he will go! He can pull an oar with
the best man in the boat!"

But just then a woman, pale as death, her black hair blown wildly back by the tempest, darted after him, and with a shriek caught the youth by the flap of his sailor's jacket.

"Mother! mother!" he said, "don't be foolish now! There's nobody else to go — don't you see?"

But the woman, having stopped him, flung herself on his neck.

"O, my Will! my poor fatherless boy! How can I let you go? You are all I have! The dreadful sea! Think of your father, and have pity on me!" And she sobbed and clung in an agony of distress.

Only a few months before, her husband, a brave and skillful fisherman, had gone out to pull his trawls, been overtaken by a violent storm, and never been heard from more. Only the broken pieces of his boat drifting upon the shore had brought her the dismal tidings of his fate. She had not yet recovered from the shock of that dreadful event; and now their boy — the brave Will, in whom all her affections, all her hopes, were centred — was going to risk his life upon the same treacherous, awful deep.

The spectators looked with compassionate respect upon her grief; and some one muttered, "The old wife is daft; and no wonder! Let somebody else go!"

But Will, who would not tear himself from her clinging arms by force, said kindly and earnestly, —

"The boat is waiting! O, mother, it is not the time for selfish sorrow. Think of the lives in that wrecked vessel! It may go to pieces at any moment, and we may be too late to save them."

"Can I let you? — can I? O, my brave boy, you are right, I know! There are men on board that ship as dear to their friends, perhaps, as your father was to us. And they *may* be saved — as he could not be! Go, go, my boy! and Heaven preserve you!"

Clasping her hands together as if to keep them from holding him back, she looked on in agony while he leaped aboard the boat, which was already pushing off, seized an oar, and pulled hastily away out into the darkness of the storm and the gathering night.

The widow watched the tossing boat disappear in the light of the beacon-fire, which shot its ruddy glare over the breakers; then suffered herself to be led away by kind neighbors to her desolate cottage, where she was left alone to struggle with her old sorrow and her new fear.

Some of those who remained on the shore to watch for the boat, — for it contained other lives as precious as Will's, — had promised to give her instant warning of its safe return; and suddenly in the dead of night came a loud knock on her door, and a shout, —

"They are coming back! the boat has lived through a terrible sea, and now if she pulls through the breakers again she is safe!"

The speaker disappeared in the storm; and the widow, who was at the door at the first sound of his voice, ran out after him, in the direction of the beacon-fire.

She was just in time to hear cries of welcome and triumph, and see the boat seized and dragged upon the shore, out of the jaws of the last foaming wave.

In a minute Will was half stifled in his mother's wild embrace.

"You are safe: thank God! thank God!" she sobbed.

"All safe, mother," Will replied. "And we have

brought off every one of the crew from the wreck —
we picked up the last man after he had been swept
off by a wave into the sea. They are lifting him from
the boat now; for he was exhausted and nearly
drowned. Shall he be taken to our house?"

"O, yes! and Heaven be praised that he—that you,
and all are saved! What do I hear — what do I hear,
Will?"

Will, standing in the light of the beacon-fire, watching anxiously his mother's face and the excited group
about the boat, replied, —

"There are some who know him; he was once a
Dynmouth fisherman. O, mother! mother! don't go
down there yet — wait till I tell you!"

Will was strangely agitated, as, keeping between his
mother and the group, he went on: —

"I saved him with my own hands -- caught him by
the hair as he was drifting by. It was after he had
revived a little that we found out who he was. He
went out from Dynmouth once in his fishing-boat —
was lost in a storm — picked up by a brig bound on a
foreign voyage — and now, on his way home, another
storm — O, mother! since *he* was saved, may not my
own father have been picked up, too. I sprang before
to tell you — "

Will tried to hold her back; but just then the red
light of the beacon fell upon the face of the rescued
man, as he staggered towards her, half supported by
two of his old neighbors.

"My husband!" And with a piercing scream of
joy she flew to receive in her arms the long-lost man,
who had that night been saved from a second peril of
death by the hands of his own son.

THREE LITTLE NEST-BIRDS.

WE meant to be very kind;
  But if ever we find
  Another soft, gray-green, feather-lined
  Nest in a hedge,
  We have taken a pledge, —
Susan, Jemmy, and I, — with remorseful tears at this
    very minute,
That if there are eggs or little birds in it, —
Robin or wren, thrush, chaffinch, or linnet, —
  We'll leave them there
  To their mother's care.

There were three of us, — Kate and Susan and Jem, —   .
  And three of them.
I don't know their names, for they couldn't speak,
Except with a little imperative squeak
    Exactly like Poll,
    Susan's squeaking doll;
But squeaking dolls will lie on the shelves
For years, and never squeak of themselves.
The reason we like little birds so much better than toys
Is because they are really alive, and know how to make
    a noise.

There were three of us, and three of them, —
Kate —that is, I— and Susan and Jem.
Our mother was busy making a pie;
And theirs we think was up in the sky.
But, for all Susan, Jemmy, or I can tell,
She may have been getting their dinner as well.
They were left to themselves (and so were we)
In a nest in the hedge by the willow-tree;
And when we caught sight of three red little fluff-tufted,
    hazel-eyed, open-mouthed, pink-throated heads,
    we all shouted for glee.

The way we really did wrong was this:
We took them for mother to kiss;
And she told us to put them back,
While out on the weeping-willow their mother was cry-
    'ing, " Alack ! "
        We really heard
Both what mother told us to do, and the voice of the
    mother-bird :
But we three — that is, Susan and I and Jem —
Thought we knew better than either of them ;
And in spite of our mother's command and the poor
    bird's cry,
We determined to bring up her three little nestlings our-
    selves on the sly.

        We each took one.
        It did seem such excellent fun !
Susan fed hers on milk and bread.
Jem got wriggling worms for his instead.
        I gave mine meat ;
For, you know, I thought, " Poor darling pet ! why
    shouldn't it have roast-beef to eat ? "
But, O dear ! O dear ! O dear ! how we cried,
When, in spite of milk and bread, and worms and roast-
    beef, the little birds died !

It's a terrible thing to have heart-ache !
I thought mine would break
As I heard the mother-bird's moan,
And looked at the gray-green, moss-coated, feather-lined
    nest she had taken such pains to make ;
And her three little children dead and cold as a stone !
Mother said, — and it's sadly true, —
" There are some wrong things one can never undo ; "
And nothing that we could do or say
Would bring back life to the birds that day.

The bitterest tears that we could weep
Wouldn't waken them out of their still, cold sleep :
     But then
We — Susan and Jem and I — mean never to be so self-
    ish and wilful and cruel again ;
And we three have buried that other three
In a soft, green, moss-covered, flower-lined grave at the
    foot of the willow-tree ;
And all the leaves which its branches shed
We think are tears because they are dead.

ANGER AND ENUMERATION.

A DANBURY man, named Reubens, recently saw
a statement, that counting one hundred when
tempted to speak an angry word would save a man
a great deal of trouble. This statement sounded a
little singular at first, but the more he read it over
the more favorably he became impressed with it, and
finally concluded to adopt it.

Next door to Reubens lives a man who has made
five distinct attempts in the past fortnight to secure
a dinner of green peas by the first of July, and every
time has been retarded by Reubens' hens. The next
morning after Reubens made his resolution, this man
found his fifth attempt to have miscarried. Then he
called on Reubens. He said, —

"What in thunder do you mean by letting your
hens tear up my garden?"

Reubens was prompted to call him a mud-snoot, —
a new name just coming into general use, — but he
remembered his resolution put down his rage, and
meekly observed, —

" One, two, three, four, five, six, seven, eight— "

Then the mad neighbor, who had been eying this answer with a great deal of suspicion, broke in again, —

" Why don't you answer my question, you rascal ? "

But still Reubens maintained his equanimity, and went on with the test.

" Nine, ten, eleven, twelve, thirteen, fourteen, fifteen, sixteen— "

The mad neighbor stared harder than ever.

" Seventeen, eighteen, nineteen, twenty, twenty-one — "

" You're a mean skunk ! " said the mad neighbor, backing towards the fence.

Reuben's face flushed at this charge, but he only said, —

" Twenty-two, twenty-three, twenty-four, twenty-five, twenty-six— "

At this figure the neighbor got up on the fence in some haste, but suddenly thinking of his peas, he opened his mouth, —

" You mean, low-lived rascal ! For two cents I could knock your cracked head over a barn, and I would— "

" Twenty-seven, twenty-eight," interrupted Reubens, " twenty-nine, thirty, thirty-one, thirty-two, thirty-three— "

Here the neighbor broke for the house, and entering it, violently slammed the door behind him : but Reubens did not dare let up on the enumeration, and so he stood out there alone in his own yard, and kept on counting, while his burning cheeks and flashing eyes eloquently affirmed his judgment. When he got up into the eighties, his wife came to the door in some alarm.

"Why, Reubens, man, what is the matter with you?" she said. "Do come into the house."

But he didn't let up. She came out to him, and clung tremblingly to him, but he only looked into her eyes, and said —

"Ninety-three, ninety-four, ninety-five, ninety-six, ninety-seven, ninety-eight, ninety-nine, one hundred — go into the house, old woman, or I'll bust ye!"

And she went.

JAMES M. BAILEY.

KING CHRISTIAN THE DANE.

HEARKEN while I sing
A song of a Danish King, —
 Christian the Fifth, and the best;
He wore, in shade and in sun,
The Cross of the Crucified One
 On his mailéd breast.

He was a sailor brave;
And he drove on the ocean wave
 Before the storms of the Lord, —
The crown of the land on his head,
On his breast the symbol of red,
 By his side the sword.

Wild blew the winter gale,
Rending at shroud and sail
 With a storm of snow and sleet;
And crouching like birds in fear
When the hawk of the hill swoops near,
 Lay the Danish fleet.

At anchor like birds they lay,
In a foul and open bay,
   Each with a folded wing ;
But out in the tempest's brawl,
In the noblest ship of all,
   Stood Christian the King.

Black came the winter night,
But the foam was driving white,
   And the breakers flashed ashore ;
And now and again o'erhead,
The electric forks ran red
   To the thunder's roar.

Down through the narrow sound
Flying, bound upon bound,
   Blown by the shrieking wind,
The ship fled, straining sore,
With the fatal rocks before
   And the storm behind.

Then into the open bay,
Where the ships at anchor lay
   She drove with tattered sail ;
Loudly the thunder rung —
The steersman shouted, and swung
   Her head to the gale.

Swift as thought, from her bow
They have hurled the anchor now,
   Huge and black and strong.
What's this ? The men turn pale —
Sideways before the gale
   She is driven along !

" Cast forth anchor ! " they cry, —
And the lightning from the sky
   Illumes them with its flash.

14

The great masts bend and groan —
The second anchor is thrown
   And sinks with a splash.

Leaning against the mast,
While the fluke is loosened and cast,
   The King stands still and pale.
Hark ! what is this they say ?
Still she is dragging away
   With the breath of the gale !

All that remaineth, all,
Is an anchor light and small,
   And a warp of hempen rope : —
" What booteth to cast it out ? "
The affrighted sailors shout,
   And abandon hope.

Then loud o'er the storm doth ring
The voice of Christian the King :
   " Nay — cast it overboard !
God made all things that be —
Yea, cast it into the sea,
   In the name of the Lord ! "

'Tis done !   All hold their breath —
For the foam-white eyes of death
   Flash to a sullen sound —
What's this ?   They raise their hands —
She swings to the gale, and stands,
   For it grips the ground !

A hundred yards from land
Behold the good ship stand,
   Held by that anchor small ! —
Ah, who shall answer " Nay,"
When He on the Throne says " Yea,"
   Being Lord of all ?

Honor to Christian the King!
Who knew that a little thing
    May serve when the mightiest fail.
Honor to Christian the Dane!
For he trusted the Lord of the main
    And the wind and the gale!

When thou despairest, sing
This song of a Christian King,
    And the Danish ship he trod.
Have great things failed thee so? —
Trust to the smallest, and throw
    —— In the name of God!

THE BRAHMIN AND THE TIGER.

A HINDOO STORY.

A TIGER, prowling in a forest, was attracted by a
bleating calf. It proved to be a bait, and the
tiger found himself trapped in a spring cage. There
he lay for two days, when a Brahmin happened to pass
that way.

"O, Brahmin!" piteously cried the beast, "have
mercy on me; let me out of this cage."

"Ah! but you will eat me."

"Eat you! Devour my benefactor? Never could
I be guilty of such a deed," responded the tiger.

The Brahmin, being benevolently inclined, was
moved by these entreaties and opened the door of the
cage. The tiger walked up to him, wagged his tail,
and said, —

"Brahmin, prepare to die; I shall now eat you."

"O how ungrateful! how wicked! Did I not save your life?" protested the trembling priest.

. "True," said the tiger, "very true; but it is the custom of my race to eat a man when we get a chance, and I cannot afford to let you go."

"Let us submit the case to an arbitrator," said the Brahmin. "Here comes the fox. The fox is wise; let us abide by his decision."

"Very well," replied the tiger.

The fox, assuming a judicial aspect, sat on his haunches with all the dignity he could muster, and, looking at the disputants, he said,—

"Good friends, I am somewhat confused at the different accounts which you give of this matter; my mind is not clear enough to render equitable judgment, but if you will be kind enough to act the whole transaction before my eyes, I shall attain unto a more definite conception of the case. Do you, Mr. Tiger, show me just how you approached and entered the cage, and then you, Mr. Brahmin, show me how you liberated him, and I shall be able to render a proper decision."

They assented, for the fox was solemn and oracular. The tiger walked into the cage, the spring door fell and shut him in. He was a prisoner. The judicial expression faded from the fox's countenance, and, turning to the Brahmin, he said,—

"I advise you to go home as fast as you can, and abstain, in future, from doing favors to rascally tigers. Good morning, Brahmin; good morning, tiger."

JINGLES.

WHO can tell what a baby thinks,
  When it wakes from its forty winks,
And rubs its face into numerous kinks,
And stares at the light that comes in at the chinks
Of its rockaby nest, and gapes and blinks, —
  Who can tell what a baby thinks?

Who has courage to venture a guess
As to what the baby may think of its dress,
Trimmed and ruffled to such excess?
Or what the baby may think of the mess
For headache, and toothache, and stomach distress,
  And for all its ailings, more or less?

What does it think when it wakes at night,
With all the pretty things out of sight,   .
With nobody stirring and " making a light"?
Does it think its condition is far from right,
And that big folks are not at all polite,
And treat their visitors far from right,
And that darkness is meant for a personal slight?
Is that the reason it takes delight
In screaming with all its personal might,
  And rousing the neighbors at dead of night?

And what do you think that the baby thinks?
Looking about like a mild-eyed lynx,
Watching the spoon that tinkles and clinks,
While papa is warming its catnip drinks
Over a candle that glimmers and blinks,
Humming and drumming out " Captain Jinks,"
That the children skate to now at the rinks, —
  What do you think that the baby thinks?

Did you say that babies are thinkless things,
With no other light than what instinct brings ;
With brains as downy as butterflies' wings,
And heads as empty as a bell that swings
Over and under, and rings, and sings
When muscular motion is moving the strings ?
Did you say that babies are thinkless things ?
Then when does the thing begin to grow ?
And when does the mind begin to show ?
And when does the baby begin to know
That this is true, or that is so ?
    Say, when you find out, please let me know.

Examiner and Chronicle.

———◆◇◆———

PRAYER AND POTATOES.

["If a brother or sister be naked, and destitute of daily food, and one of you say unto them, Depart in peace, be ye warmed and filled, notwithstanding ye give them not those things which are needful to the body, what doth it profit ? " — JAMES ii. 15, 18.]

AN old lady sat in her old arm-chair,
  With wrinkled visage and dishevelled hair,
    And hunger-worn features,
For days and for weeks her only fare,
As she sat in her old arm-chair,
    Had been potatoes.

But now they were gone : of bad or good
Not one was left for the old lady's food
    Of those potatoes.
And she sighed, and said, " What shall I do ?
Where shall I send, and to whom shall I go
    For more potatoes ? "

And she thought of the deacon over the way,
The deacon so ready to worship and pray,
    Whose cellar was full of potatoes.
She said, " I will send for the deacon to come ;
He'll not much mind to give me some
    Of such a store of potatoes."

And the deacon came over as fast as he could,
Thinking to do the old lady some good,
    But never for once of potatoes.
He asked her at once what was her chief want :
And she, simple soul, expecting a grant,
    Immediately answered, " Potatoes."

But the deacon's religion didn't lie that way ;
He was more accustomed to preach and to pray
    Than to give his hoarded potatoes.
So, not hearing, of course, what the old lady said,
He rose to pray, with uncovered head :
    But she only thought of potatoes.

He prayed for patience, goodness, and grace ;
But when he prayed, " Lord, give her peace,"
    She audibly sighed, " Give potatoes."
And at the end of each prayer which he said,
He heard, or thought he heard, in its stead,
    That same request for potatoes.

The deacon was troubled, knew not what to do ;
'Twas very embarrassing to have her act so,
    And about those carnal potatoes.
So, ending his prayers, he started for home ;
The door closed behind ; he heard a deep groan :
    " O, give to the hungry potatoes ! "

And the groan followed him all the way home ;
In the midst of the night it haunted his room :
.   " O, give to the hungry potatoes ! "

He could bear it no longer ; arose and dressed,
From his well-filled cellar taking in haste
    A bag of his best potatoes.

Again he went to the widow's lone hut ;
Her sleepless eyes she had not yet shut ;
But there she sat in the old arm-chair,
With the same wan features, same wan air.
And entering in, he poured on the floor
A bushel or more from his goodly store
    Of choicest potatoes.

The widow's heart leaped up for joy ;
Her face was pale and haggard no more.
" Now," said the deacon, " shall we pray ? "
" Yes," said the widow, " now you may."
And he knelt him down on the sanded floor,
Where he had poured out his goodly store,
And such a prayer the deacon prayed
As never before his lips essayed.
No longer embarrassed, but free and full,
He poured out the voice of a liberal soul ;
And the widow responded a loud " Amen ! "
    But said no more of potatoes.

And would you who hear this simple tale,
Pray for the poor, and praying, prevail ?
Then preface your prayer with alms and good deeds ;
Search out the poor, their wants and needs ;
Pray for their peace and grace, spiritual food,
For wisdom and guidance — all these are good ;
    But don't forget the potatoes !

MICE AT PLAY.

FOUR children sat around a wood-fire, in an old-fashioned country house. The red embers blazed up merrily, and showed four flushed little faces, four very tangled heads of hair, eight bright, merry eyes, and — I regret extremely to add — eight very dirty little hands, belonging, respectively, to Bess, Bob, Archie, and Tom. Mamma was away, you may be sure. If she were at home, the children would have made a very different appearance. O yes, indeed, quite and entirely different.

The round table was wheeled in front of the fire, and the student lamp in the centre shed its light on Tom's letter, which he was writing to his mother.

Archie was leaning back in the large chair; his arm, which he had broken in riding the trick mule of the circus the day before, was in a splint; but, judging from the rapid disappearance of the gingerbread on the plate near him, it is to be doubted if new cider, trick mules, or broken arms seriously impair the appetite.

"Bess, stop jogging the table! How on earth can a fellow write with you around?"

"Read what you've written," said Bess.

"Yes, do," chimed in Archie. They were both anxious to know what account their mother would receive of their performance.

"Wait till it's done," answered Tom. Writing a letter was no joke for Thomas Bradley, junior.

"How on earth do you spell *circus?*" he asked.

"S-u-r-k-e-ss," answered Bess, promptly.

"No you don't," cried Tom. "I know better."

"If you know so much, why do you ask?" retorted Bess.

"O, come, Bess! do think, can't you?"

"There is a c in it," put in Archie; "for I saw the big red-and-blue posters in the village, and I know there was a c in circus."

"Then it's c-i-r-k-i-s," said Bess.

"Yes; I guess that's right," said Tom, thoughtfully, writing the word, and then holding his head back from the paper, first on one side and then on the other, to see if it looked natural.

"I'm not exactly sure," he said, at last. "It looks kinder queer. And mamma does make such a row if I don't spell right! What's the use in spelling, any way? If the folks know what you mean, that's enough — one way is as good as another. Pshaw!" he continued, "I don't believe it is right. See here, Bob! you're a first-rate little boy — a real, regular first-rate good boy, you are."

"If it's up-stairs, I won't," declared Bob, who knew that flattery always preceded errands. Bob was one of the kind who learned by experience.

"O, yes, Bobby! That's a lovely harness you've made for pussy. I couldn't have done better myself. You know where my dictionary is, up in my room, on the table. Run along and get it, — that's a good boy."

Bob kept on with his work.

"Come, Bobby," said Tom, encouragingly.

"Go yourself," was Bob's polite suggestion.

"O, I'm so tired. I've done nothing but run for doctors all day long. Come, Bob, I'll tell mamma what a good boy you are if you will."

" Won't you tell her I dropped the teapot down the well?" asked Bob.

" O, did you?" cried Tom, Bess, and Archie, all in a breath.

Bob nodded his head, and looked at them all with a calm stare.

" Which one?" asked the three children, anxiously.

" The big silver one," said Bob.

" How? Why? What were you doing with it?"

" The gardener wouldn't lend me the watering-pot, and I wanted to water my garden, so I just thought that would do instead; and I went to fill it at the well, and the bucket hit it right over into the well. It was the bucket's fault. I ain't to blame."

" Whe-e-ew!" at last whistled Tom.

" If you won't tell mamma, I'll go for your book," said Bob.

" Well, I won't tell her in this letter, any way."

" Don't tell her at all," insisted Bob.

" If you don't go right off and get it, I'll write it this moment."

" I'll go, I'll go!" cried Bob.

" That's the worst scrape yet," said Bess. " For if I did get lost, I was found again; and if I did tear my clothes, they are all mended now; and if Archie did break his arm, he's got it mended now, too; but the teapot! That's dropped down the well, and there it is."

Bessie's argument was convincing. There was no more to be said.

After a while, Tom's letter was finished, and ran as follows: —

"DEAR MAMMA: I wish you was home. We have dun a good menny bad things. Bess got lost in the woods, and most drowned in Rainy Pond. I shot Kate thru the head with a squirt of water, and most killed her. Archie broke his arm trying to wride the trik mule at the curkis. Bob has dun worst of all; but I sed I woodn't tel that. Bob has dun a dredful thing; but I sed I woodn't tel, so I won't. It's orful. Papa is very good to us, and don't make us wash too much. The bred is orful; Maggy is cross. But we're all wel, except Archy's arm, and Dr. Jarvis says if he don't get fever he wil get wel.

"Your loveing son,   TOM.

"P. S. You wil feel orful bad about what Bob's dun."

The next morning all four children were gathered around the well, at the bottom of which lay the silver teapot.

"I see it, I see it!" cried Tom, eagerly. "It's down at the bottom."

"Did you suppose it would float?" asked Bess.

"Let me see," cried Bob.

"You clear out," said Archie; "you've made all this mischief. You'd better go before you tumble in yourself, you little goose. I can't go after it, with my broken arm."

"Now, I suppose we will hear of nothing but your broken arm for a month, and you'll shirk everything for it. 'I can't study 'cause my arm's broken; I can't go errands 'cause my arm's broken; I can't go to church 'cause my arm's broken;' that will be your whim, Archie; but don't try your dodges on me, for I

won't stand it. If it really hurts you, I'm sorry, and
I'll lick any fellow that touches you till you get well
again; but none of your humbug. Of course you can't
go down the well, you couldn't if your arm wasn't
broken."

Meanwhile Bess had gone to the house for a long
fishing-pole, and soon returned carrying it.

" We'll fasten a hook to the end of it, and fish the
teapot up," said she.

" Ho, ho! Do you suppose it will bite like a fish?"
laughed Tom.

" No, I do not, Tom Bradley. But I suppose if I
tie a string to the pole, and fasten an iron hook to one
end, that I can wiggle it round in the water till the
hook catches in the handle, and then we can draw it
up. That's what I suppose."

" There's something in that, Bess. Let me try."

" No; go and get one for yourself."

" But where can I find one?"

" In the smoke-house, where I got mine."

" O, get me one, too," cried Bob.

" And me one, too," cried Archie.

Before half an hour had passed, the four children,
all armed with fishing-poles, were intently wiggling
in the water, catching their hooks in the stones by the
side of the well, entangling their lines, digging their
elbows into each other's sides, in their frantic attempts
to pull their hooks loose, scolding, pushing, and getting generally excited.

Every few minutes Tom would pull Bess back by
her sun-bonnet, and save her from tumbling over in
her eagerness; but so far from being grateful to her
deliverer, Bess resented the treatment indignantly.

"Stop jerking my head so!" she cried.

"You'll be in, in a minute; you'd have been in then, if I hadn't jerked you," answered Tom.

"Well, what if I had? Let me alone. If I go in, that's my own lookout."

"Your own look in, you mean. My gracious! wouldn't you astonish the toads down there! But you'd get your face clean."

"Now, Tom, you let me be. I 'most had it that time."

"So you've said forty times. This is all humbug. I'm going down on the rope for it."

"O, no, Tom, please don't. Indeed you'll be drowned; the rope will break; you'll kill yourself; you'll catch cold," cried Bess, in alarm.

"Pooh! girl! coward!" retorted thankless Tom. "Who's afraid of what? Stand back, small boys, I'm going in."

"You'll poison the water," suggested Archie.

"It will be so cold," moaned Bob.

"I'll scream for a hundred years without stopping, Tom," cried Bess, wildly. "You shan't go down — you shan't; I'll call some one. Murray! Peter! Maggie! c-o-o-o-o-o-o-me! O-o-o-o-h, c-o-o-o-o-o-me!"

"Stop screaming, and help. Now, do you three hold on tight to this bucket; don't let go for a moment; pull away as hard as you can when I tell you to. Now for it."

And, without more ado, Tom clung to the other rope with his hands, and twisted his feet around the bucket-handle.

"Hold on tight, and let me down easy," said Tom, and the three children lowered him little by little.

A sudden splash and shiver told them he had reached water, and a shout of triumph declared that the teapot was rescued.

As Tom shouted, all the children let go the rope, and rushed to the side of the well to look at the victorious hero.

It was a most fortunate circumstance that the water in the well was low. As it was, he stood in the cold water up to his shoulders.

"What made you let go?" roared Tom.

"O, Tom, have you got it? Have you really? Ain't it cold? Are you hurt? Were you scared? Is the teapot broken?"

"Draw me up! You silly children! You goose of a Bess! Why don't you draw me up?"

"I will, Tom; I'm going to," answered Bess.

But all the united efforts could not raise Tom.

"I'll run next door and call Mr. Wilson," said Bess, hopefully, and started.

As Bess ran, she was suddenly stopped at the gate by the sight of a carriage which had just driven up, and out of which now stepped Aunt Maria and Aunt Maria's husband, Uncle Daniel. These were the very grimmest and grandest of all the relations.

For one awful moment Bess stood stunned. Then her anxiety for Tom overcame every other consideration, and before Aunt Maria could say, "How do you do, Elizabeth?" she had caught her uncle by his august coat-tail, and, in a piteous voice, besought him to come and pull on the rope.

"Pull on a rope, Elizabeth!" said Uncle Daniel, who was a very slow man; "why should I pull on a rope, my dear?"

" O, come quick ! hurry faster ! Tom's down in the well!" cried Bess.

" Tom down a well ! How did he get there ? "

" He went down for the teapot," sobbed Bess ; " the silver teapot, and we can't pull him up again ; and he's cramped with cold. O, do hurry ! "

Uncle Daniel leisurely looked down at Tom. Then he slowly took off his coat, and as slowly carried it into the house, stopped to give an order to his coach-man, came with measured pace to the three frightened children : then took hold of the rope, gave a long, strong, calm pull, and in an instant, Tom, " dripping with coolness, arose from the well."

THE PETRIFIED FERN.

IN a valley, centuries ago,
    Grew a little fern leaf, green and slender,
    Veining delicate, and fibres tender,
Waving when the wind crept down so low :
    Rushes tall, and moss and grass grew round it,
    Playful sunbeams darted in and found it,
    Drops of dew stole in by night and crowned it,
    But no foot of man e'er trod that way ;
    Earth was young, and keeping holiday.

Monster fishes swam the silent main,
    Stately forests waved their giant branches,
    Mountains hurled their snowy avalanches,
Mammoth creatures stalked across the plain ;
    Nature revelled in grand mysteries ;
    But the little fern was not one of these,
    Did not number with the hills and trees ;
    Only grew and waved its sweet, wild way ;
    No one came to note it day by day.

Earth one time put on frolic mood,
   Heaved the rocks, and changed the mighty motion
   Of the deep, strong currents of the ocean ;
Moved the plain, shook the haughty wood,
   Crushed the little fern in soft, moist clay ;
   Covered it, and hid it safe away.
   O, the long, long centuries since that day !
   O, the agony ! O, life's bitter cost,
   Since that useless little fern was lost !

Useless ? Lost ? There came a thoughtful man,
   Searching out Nature's secrets far and deep.
   From a fissure in a rocky steep
He withdrew a stone, o'er which there ran
   Fairy pencillings, a quaint design,
   Veining and leafage, fibres clear and fine,
   And the fern's life lay traced in every line !
   Just so, I think, God hides some souls away,
   Sweetly to surprise us at the last day.

THE BLACKSMITH'S STORY.

WELL, no ! My wife ain't dead, sir ; but I've lost her
   all the same ;
She left me voluntarily, and neither was to blame.
It's rather a queer story, and I think you will agree —
When you hear the circumstances — 'twas rather rough
   on me.

She was a soldier's widow. He was killed at Malvern
   Hill ;
And when I married her she seemed to sorrow for him
   still.
But I brought her here to Kansas, and I never want to
   see
A better wife than Mary was, for five bright years, to me !

15

The change of scene brought cheerfulness, and soon a
　　rosy glow
Of happiness warmed Mary's cheeks, and melted all their
　　snow.
I think she loved me some, — I'm bound to think that of
　　her, sir, —
And as for me, — I can't begin to tell how I loved her !

Three years ago the baby came, our humble home to
　　bless ;
And then I reckon I was nigh to perfect happiness.
'Twas hers — 'twas mine — but I've no language to
　　explain to you
How that little girl's weak fingers. our hearts together
　　drew !

Once we watched it through a fever, and, with each gasp-
　　ing breath,
Dumb with an awful, wordless woe, we waited for its
　　death ;
And though I'm not a pious man, our souls together
　　there,
For Heaven to spare our darling, went up in voiceless
　　prayer.

And when the doctor said 'twould live, our joy what
　　words could tell !
Clasped in each other's arms our grateful tears together
　　fell.
Sometimes, you see, the shadow fell across our little nest,
But it only made the sunshine seem a doubly welcome
　　guest.

Work came to me a plenty, and I kept the anvil ringing.
Early and late you'd find me there, a-hammering and
　　singing.
Love nerved my arm to labor, and moved my tongue to
　　song ;
And though my singing wasn't sweet, it was almighty
　　strong.

One day a one-armed stranger stopped to have me nail a
    shoe;
And while I was at work, we passed a compliment or
    two.
I asked him how he lost his arm. He said 'twas shot
    away
At Malvern Hill. "At Malvern Hill! Did you know
    Robert May?"

"That's me!" said he. "You! you!" I gasped, chok-
    ing with horrid doubt;
"If you're a man, just follow me; we'll try this mystery
    out."
With dizzy steps I led him to Mary. God! 'Twas true!
Then the bitterest pangs of misery unspeakable I knew.

Frozen with deadly horror, she stared with eyes of stone,
And from her quivering lips there broke one wild, despair-
    ing moan.
'Twas he! the husband of her youth, new risen from the
    dead;
But all too late! And with that bitter cry her senses
    fled.

What could be done? He was reported dead. On his
    return
He strove in vain some tidings of his absent wife to
    learn.
'Twas well that he was innocent, else *I'd* have killed
    him too,
So dead he never would have rose till Gabriel's trumpet
    blew!

It was agreed that Mary between us should decide,
And each by her decision would sacredly abide.
No sinner at the Judgment-Seat, waiting eternal doom,
Could suffer what I did while waiting sentence in that
    room.

Rigid and breathless there we stood, with nerves as tense
    as steel,
While Mary's eyes sought each white face in piteous
    appeal.
God! Could not woman's duty be less hardly reconciled
Between her lawful husband and the father of her child?

Ah, how my heart was chilled to ice when she knelt
    down and said,
"Forgive me, John! He is my husband! Here! Alive!
    not dead!"
I raised her tenderly, and tried to tell her she was right;
But somehow in my aching breast the prisoned words
    stuck tight!

"But, John, I can't leave baby —" "What! Wife and
    child!" cried I;
"Must I yield all? Ah, cruel! Better that I should
    die!
Think of the long, sad, lonely hours waiting in gloom
    for me —
No wife to cheer me with her love — no babe to climb
    my knee!

"And yet — 'you are her mother; and the sacred mother-
    love
Is still the purest, tenderest tie that Heaven ever wove.
Take her; but promise, Mary, — for that will be no
    shame, —
My little girl shall bear, and learn to lisp, her father's
    name."

It may be in the life to come I'll meet my child and wife;
But yonder, by my cottage gate, we parted for this life.
One long hand-clasp from Mary, and my dream of love
    was done!
One long embrace from baby, and my happiness was
    gone!

FRANK CLIVE.

NAMING THE CHICKENS.

THERE were two little chickens hatched out by one hen,
    And the owner of both was our little boy Ben;
So he set him to work, as soon as they came,
To make them a house and find them a name.

As for building a house, Benny knew very well
That he couldn't do that; but his big brother Phil
Must be handy at tools, for he'd been to college,
Where boys are supposed to learn all sorts of knowledge.

Phil was very good-natured, and soon his small brother
Had a nice cosy home for his chicks and their mother;
And a happier boy in the country just then
Could not have been found than our dear little Ben.

But a *name* for his pets it was harder to find,
At least such as suited exactly his mind;
No mother of twins was ever more haunted
With trouble to find just the ones that she wanted.

There were plenty of names, no doubt about that,
But a name that would do for a dog or a cat
Would not answer for chickens so pretty as these;
Or else our dear boy was not easy to please.

These two tiny chickens looked just like each other:
To name them so young would be only a bother.
But with one in each hand, said queer little Ben,
" I want *this* one a *rooster* and *that* one a *hen*."

Benny knew them apart by a little brown spot
On the head of the one that the other had not;
They grew up like magic, each fat feathered chick:
One at length was named Peggy, and the other named
    Dick.

Benny watched them so closely, not a feather could grow
In the dress of those chickens that he did not know ;
And he taught them so well, they would march at com-
    mand,
Fly up on his shoulder, or eat from his hand.

But a funny thing happened concerning their names.
Rushing into the house one day, Benny exclaims,
" O mother! O Phil! such a blunder there's been,
For *Peggy's* the *rooster*, and *Dick* is the *hen!*"

MRS. L. B. BACON.

THE ADVERTISEMENT ANSWERED.

GOOD mornin' til yez, yer honor! And are yez the
    gintlemon
    As advertised, in the paper, fur an active, intilligint
        b'y ?
Y' are ?   Thin I've brought him along wid me, — a raal,
    fine sprig iv a wan : —
    As likely a b'y iv his age, sur, as iver ye'd wish ti em-
        pl'y.

That's him.   Av coorse I'm his mother!   Yez can see
    his resimblance til me,
    Fur ivery wan iv his faytures, and mine, are alike as
        two paze, —
Barrin' wan iv his hivenly eyes, which he lost in a bit iv
    a spree
    Wid Hooligan's b'y, which intinded to larrup me
        Teddy with aize ;

And his taythe, which hung out on his lip, like a pair iv
    big, shinin', twin pearls,
    Till wan iv thim taythe was removed by the fut iv a
        cow he was tazin' ;

And his hair, that we niver cu'd comb, along iv bewil-
dcrin' curls,
So we kape it cropped short to save combin', and that
makes our intercoorse plazin'.

And is it rid-headed ye call him? Belike he *is* foxy,
is Ted,
And goold-colored hair is becomin' til thim that's com-
plicted wid blonde!
But who cares fur color? Sure contints out-vally the
rest iv the head!
And Ted has a head full iv contints, as lively as t'hrout
in a pond!

Good-timpered? Sure niver a bett'her.—The peace-
ablest, quietest lamb
As lives the whole lin'th iv our st'hrate, where the b'ys
is that kane fur a row
That Ted has to fight iv'ry day, though he'd quarrel no
more than a clam —
Faith, thim b'ys 'ud provoke the swate angels in hiven
to fight onyhow!

Thim Hooligan b'ys is that d'hirty, they have to be
washed wanst a wake : —
Faith, Hooligan finds it convanient to live down fer-
ninst the canall
Where the wat'her fur scrubbin' the mud off his chil-
d'hers is not far til sake, —
But Teddy is always that nate that he niver nades
washin' at all!

Can he rade? Sure, me Ted has the makin' iv a beautiful
rader, indade,
And lairn't all the lett'hers, but twinty, in three
months' attindance at school :

But the mast'her got mad at me Teddy, becase iv a joke
    that was played
  Wid a pin, that persuaded the mast'her quite suddint
    to rise from his stool.

Teddy niver cu'd plaze that schoolmast'her wid ony iv
    thim playful t'hricks ;
  So, wid his edication unfinished, Ted found it convan-
    ient to lave.
But, barrin' the larnin', I'll match him, fur kaneness,
    ferninst ony six,
  In butt'herin' paple wid blarney, and playin' nate
    t'hricks to desave.

Thim Hooligan b'ys is all raders, but Teddy jist skins 'em
    alive :
  Wid their marbles, and paynuts, and pennies, iv'ry
    wan iv his pockets he'll fill
By the turn iv his wrist, ur such tactics as Teddy knows
    how til contrive : —
  They'd gladly t'hrade off their book-laruin' for Ted-
    dy's suparior skill !

Politeness comes aisy til Ted, fur he's had me to tache
    him the t'hrick
  Iv bowin' and spakin' and scrapin' to show paple
    proper respict.
Spake up til the gintlemon, Teddy! Whist! Aff wid
    your cap first, ye stick!
  He's shapish a t'hrifle, yer honor; he's allus been
    brought up that strict.

Come! Spake up and show yer foine bradin'! Och!
    Hear that! " How are yez, Owld Moke? "
  Arrah, millia murther! Did ever yez hear jist the
    aqual iv that?

"How are yez, Owld Moke?" says he.   Ha! ha!
    Sure, yer honor, he manes it in joke!
He's the playfullest b'y!   Faith it's laughin' at Teddy
    that makes me so fat.

Honest?   Troth, he is that!   He's that honest, he was
    niver tuk by the perlace,
    Barrin' wanst that Owld Hooligan swore that Teddy
        had stole his b'y's knife
Wid divil a blade.   And the jidge he remarked wid
    contimpt, 'twas the t'hriflinest case
    To bod'her a dignified Coort wid, he iver had known
        in his life!

Yez can t'hrust him wid onything.   Honest!   Does he
    luk like a b'y that 'ud stale?
    Jist luk in the swate, open face iv him, barrin' the eye
        wid the wink : —
Och!   Teddy!!   Phat ugly black st'hrame is it runnin'
    down there by yer hale! . . .
    Murtheration!   Yer honor, me Teddy has spilt yer
        fine bottle iv ink!!

Phat?   How. kem the ink in his pocket?   I'm thinkin'
    he borry'd it, sur : —
    And yez saw him pick up yer pen-howlder and stick
        it inside iv his slave!
And yez think that Teddy mint til purline 'em!!   Ah!
    wirra! the likes iv that slur
    Will d'hrive me — poor, tinder, lone widdy — wid
        sorrow down until me grave!

Bad 'cess til yez, Teddy, ye spalpeen!   Why c'udn't yez
    howld on, the day —
    Ye thafe iv the world! — widout breakin' the heart iv
        me?   No.   Yez *must* stale!

I'll tache ye a t'hrick, ye rid-headed, pilferin', gimlet-
eyed flay! —
Ye freckle-faced, impident bla'guard! — Och! whin
we get home, yez'll squale!

FRANK M. THORN, in *Scribner's Magazine.*

LOVE IN A BALLOON.

SOME time ago I was staying with Sir George
Flasher, with a great number of people there —
all kinds of amusements going on. Driving, riding,
fishing, shooting, everything, in fact. Sir George's
daughter, Fanny, was often my companion in these
expeditions, and I was considerably struck with her,
for she was a girl to whom the epithet "stunning"
applies better than any other that I am acquainted
with. She could ride like Nimrod, she could drive
like Jehu, she could row like Charon, she could dance
like Terpsichore, she could row like Diana, she walked
like Juno, and she looked like Venus. I've even
seen her smoke.

O, she was a stunner! You should have heard that
girl whistle, and laugh — you should have heard her
laugh. She was truly a delightful companion. We
rode together, drove together, fished together, walked
together, danced together, sang together; I called her
Fanny, and she called me Tom. All this could have
but one termination, you know. I fell in love with
her, and determined to take the first opportunity of
proposing. So, one day, when we were out together,
fishing on the lake, I went down on my knees amongst

the gudgeons, seized her hand, pressed it to my waistcoat, and in burning accents entreated her to become
my wife.

"Don't be a fool," she said. "Now drop it, do, and
put me a fresh worm on."

"O, Fanny!" I exclaimed; "don't talk about worms
when marriage is in question. Only say — "

"I tell you what it is, now," she replied, angrily:
"if you don't drop it, I'll pitch you out of the boat."

Gentlemen, I did not drop it, and I give you my
word of honor, with a sudden shove she sent me flying into the water; then, seizing the sculls, with a
stroke or two she put several yards between us, and
burst into a fit of laughter that fortunately prevented
her from going further. I swam up, and climbed into
the boat. "Jenkins," said I to myself, "revenge!
revenge!" I disguised my feelings. I laughed —
hideous mockery of mirth — I laughed, pulled to the
bank, went to the house, and changed my clothes.
When I appeared at the dinner-table, I perceived that
every one had been informed of my ducking. Universal laughter greeted me. During dinner, Fanny
repeatedly whispered to her neighbor, and glanced
at me. Smothered laughter invariably followed.
"Jenkins," said I, "revenge!" The opportunity
soon offered. There was to be a balloon ascent from
the lawn, and Fanny had tormented her father into
letting her ascend with the aeronaut. I instantly took
my plans; bribed the aeronaut to plead illness at the
moment when the machine should have risen; learned
from him the management of the balloon, though I
understood that pretty well before, and calmly awaited
the result. The day came. The weather was fine.

The balloon was inflated. Fanny was in the car. Everything was ready, when the aeronaut suddenly fainted. He was carried into the house, and Sir George accompanied me. Fanny was in despair.

"Am I to lose my air expedition?" she exclaimed, looking over the side of the car; "some one understands the management of this thing, surely? Nobody! Tom!" she called out to me, "you understand it — don't you?"

"Perfectly," I answered.

"Come along, then," she cried; "be quick, before papa comes back."

The company in general endeavored to dissuade her from her project, but of course in vain. After a decent show of hesitation, I climbed into the car. The balloon was cast off, and rapidly sailed heavenward. There was scarcely a breath of wind, and we rose almost straight up. We rose above the house, and she laughed and said, "How jolly!"

We were higher than the highest trees, and she smiled, and said it was very kind of me to come with her. We were so high that the people below looked mere specks, and she hoped that I thoroughly understood the management of the balloon. Now was my time.

"I understand the going up part," I answered; "to come down is not so easy;" and I whistled.

"What do you mean?" she cried.

"Why, when you want to go up faster, you throw some sand overboard," I replied, suiting the action to the word.

"Don't be foolish, Tom," she said, trying to appear quite calm and indifferent, but trembling uncommonly.

"Foolish!" I said. "O dear, no; but whether I go along the ground or up in the air, I like to go the pace, and so do you, Fanny, I know. Go it, you cripples!" and over went another sand-bag.

"Why, you're mad, surely," she whispered, in utter terror, and tried to reach the bags, but I kept her back.

"Only with love, my dear," I answered, smiling pleasantly; "only with love for you. O, Fanny, I adore you! Say you will be my wife."

"I gave you an answer the other day," she replied; "one which I should have thought you would have remembered," she added, laughing a little, notwithstanding her terror.

"I remember it perfectly," I answered; "but I intend to have a different reply from that. You see those five sand-bags. I shall ask you five times to become my wife. Every time you refuse I shall throw over a sand-bag; so, lady fair, as the cabmen would say, reconsider your decision, and consent to become Mrs. Jenkins."

"I won't," she said; "I never will; and let me tell you that you are acting in a very ungentlemanly way to press me thus."

"You acted in a very ladylike way the other day, did you not," I rejoined, "when you knocked me out of the boat?" She laughed again, for she was a plucky girl, and no mistake — a very plucky girl. "However," I went on, "it's no good arguing about it: will you promise to give me your hand?"

"Never!" she answered; "I'll go to Ursa Major first, though I've got a big enough bear here, in all conscience. Stay! you'd prefer Aquarius, wouldn't you?"

She looked so pretty that I was almost inclined to let her off. (I was only trying to frighten her, of course: I knew how high we could go safely, well enough, and how valuable the life of Jenkins was to his country); but resolution is one of the strong points of my character, and when I've begun a thing, I like to carry it through; so I threw over another sand-bag, and whistled the Dead March in Saul.

"Come, Mr. Jenkins," she said, suddenly, — "come, Tom, let us descend now, and I'll promise to say nothing whatever about all this."

I continued the execution of the Dead March.

"But if you do not begin the descent at once, I'll tell papa the moment I set foot on the ground."

I laughed, seized another bag, and, looking steadily at her, said, "Will you promise to give me your hand?"

"I've answered you already," was the reply.

Over went the sand, and the solemn notes of the Dead March resounded through the car.

"I thought you were a gentleman," said Fanny, rising up in a terrible rage from the bottom of the car, where she had been sitting, and looking perfectly beautiful in her wrath. "I thought you were a gentleman, but I find I was mistaken. Why, a chimney-sweeper would not treat a lady in such a way. Do you know that you are risking your own life as well as mine by your madness?"

I explained that I adored her so much that to die in her company would be perfect bliss, so that I begged she would not consider my feelings at all. She dashed her beautiful hair from her face, and standing perfectly erect, looking like the Goddess of Anger or

Boadicea, — if you can imagine that personage in a balloon, — she said, "I command you to begin the descent this instant!"

The Dead March, whistled in a manner essentially gay and lively, was the only response. After a few minutes' silence I took up another bag, and said, —

"We are getting rather high. If you do not decide soon, we shall have Mercury coming to tell us that we are trespassing. Will you promise me your hand?"

She sat in sulky silence in the bottom of the car. I threw over the sand. Then she tried another plan. Throwing herself upon her knees, and bursting into tears, she said, —

"O, forgive me for what I did the other day. It was very wrong, and I am very sorry. Take me home, and I will be a sister to you."

"Not a wife?" said I.

"I can't! I can't!" she answered.

Over went the fourth bag, and I began to think she would beat me after all, for I did not like the idea of going much higher. I would not give in just yet, however. I whistled for a few moments, to give her time for reflection, and then said, "Fanny, they say that marriages are made in heaven: if you do not take care, ours will be solemnized there."

I took up the fifth bag. "Come," I said, "my wife in life, or my companion in death. Which is it to be?" and I petted the sand-bag in a cheerful manner. She held her face in her hands, but did not answer. I nursed the bag in my arms as if it had been a baby.

"Come, Fanny, give me your promise." I could hear her sobs. I'm the softest-hearted creature breathing, and would not pain any living thing, and

I confess she had beaten me. I forgave her the ducking; I forgave her for rejecting me. I was on the
point of flinging the .bag back into the car, and saying, "Dearest Fanny, forgive me for frightening you.
Marry whomsoever you wish. Give your lovely hand
to the lowest groom in your stables; endow with
your priceless beauty the chief of the Panki-wanki
Indians. Whatever happens, Jenkins is your slave —
·your dog — your footstool. His duty, henceforth, is
to go whithersoever you shall order, to do whatever
you shall command." I was just on the point of saying this, I repeat, when Fanny suddenly looked up, and
said, with a queerish expression upon her face, —

"You need not throw that last bag over. I promise
to give you my hand."

"With all your heart?" I asked, quickly.

"With all my heart," she answered, with the same
strange look.

I tossed the bag into the bottom of the car, and
opened the valve. The balloon descended. Gentlemen, will you believe it? — when we had reached the
ground, and the balloon had been given over to its recovered master — when I had helped Fanny tenderly
to the earth, and turned towards her to receive anew
the promise of her affection and her hand, — will you
believe it? — she gave me a box on the ear that upset
me against the car, and, running to her father, who
at that moment came up, she related to him and the
assembled company what she called my disgraceful
conduct in the balloon, and ended by informing me
that all of her hand that I was likely to get had been
already bestowed upon my ear, which she assured me
had been given with all her heart.

"You villain!" said Sir George, advancing towards
me with a horsewhip in his hand. "You villain!
I've a good mind to break this over your back."

"Sir George," said I, "villain and Jenkins must
never be coupled in the same sentence; and as for the
breaking of this whip, I'll relieve you of the trouble;"
and snatching it from his hand, I broke it in two, and
threw the pieces on the ground. "And now I shall
have the honor of wishing you a good morning. Miss
Flasher, I forgive you;" and I retired. Now, I ask
you whether any specimen of female treachery equal
to that has ever come within your experience, and
whether any excuse can be made for such conduct?

LITCHFIELD MOSELEY.

TOM'S COME HOME.

WITH its heavily rocking and swinging load,
The stage-coach rolls up the mountain road.
The mowers lean on their scythes and say,
"Hallo! what brings Big George this way?"
The children climb the slats, and wait
To see him drive past the door-yard gate;
When, four in hand, sedate and grand,
He brings the old craft like a ship to land.
At the window, mild grandmotherly eyes
Beam from their glasses with quaint surprise,
Grow wide with wonder, and guess, and doubt;
Then a quick, half-stifled voice shrieks out,
  "Tom! Tom's come home!"

The face at the casement disappears,
To shine at the door, all joy and tears,
As a traveller, dusty and bearded and brown,
Over the wheel steps lightly down.

16

"Well, mother!" "My son!" And to his breast
A forward-tottering form is pressed.
She lies there, and cries there; now at arm's-length
Admires his manly size and strength
(While he winks hard one misty eye);
Then calls to the youngsters staring nigh —
"Quick! go for your gran'ther! run, boys, run!
Tell him your uncle — tell him his son —
        Our Tom's come home!"

The stage-coach waits; but little cares she
What faces pleasantly smile to see
Her jostled glasses and tumbled cap.
Big George's hands the trunk unstrap
And bear it in; while two light-heeled
Young Mercuries fly to the mowing field,
And shriek and beckon, and meet half-way
The old gran'ther, lame and gaunt and gray,
Coat on arm, half in alarm,
Striding over the stony farm.
The good news clears his cloudy face,
And he cries, as he quickens his anxious pace,
        "Tom? Tom come home?"

With twitching cheek and quivering lid
(A soft heart under the hard lines hid),
And "Tom, how d'e do?" in a husky voice,
He grasps with rough, strong hand the boy's —
A boy's no more. "I shouldn't have known
That beard." While Tom's fine barytone
Rolls out from his deep chest cheerily,
"You're hale as ever, I'm glad to see."
In the low back porch the mother stands,
And rubs her glasses with trembling hands,
And, smiling with eyes that blear and blink,
Chimes in, "I never!" and "Only think!
        Our Tom's come home!"

With question and joke and anecdote,
He brushes his hat, they dust his coat,
While all the household gathers near :
Tanned urchins eager to see and hear,
And large-eyed, dark-eyed, shy young mother,
Widow of Tom's unlucky brother,
Who turned out ill, and was drowned at the mill :
The stricken old people mourn him still,
And the hope of their lives in him undone ;
But grief for the dissolute ruined son —
Their best-beloved and oldest boy —
Is all forgotten, or turned to joy,
  Now Tom's come home.

Yet Tom was never the favored child,
Though Tom was steady, and Will was wild ;
But often his own and his brother's share
Of blows and blame he was forced to bear ;
Till at last he said, " Here is no room
For both — I go !" Now he to whom
Scant grace was shown has proved the one
Large-hearted, upright, trusty son ;
And well may the old folks joy to find
His brow so frank and his eye so kind,
No shadow of all the past allowed
To trouble the present hour, or cloud
  His welcome home.

His trunk unlocked, the lid he lifts,
And lays out curious, costly gifts ;
For Tom has prospered since he went
Into his long self-banishment.
Each youngster's glee, as he hugs his share,
The widow's surprise, and the old folks' air
Of affectionate pride in a son so good,
Thrill him with generous gratitude.
And he thinks, " Am I that lonely lad
Who went off friendless, poor, and sad,

That dismal day, from my father's door ? "
And can it be true he is here once more
   In his childhood's home ?

'Tis hard to think of his brother dead,
And a widow and orphans here in his stead —
So little seems changed since they were young!
The row of pegs where the hats were hung ;
The checkered chimney and hearth of bricks ;
The sober old clock with its lonesome ticks,
And shrill, loud chime for the flying time ;
The stairs the bare feet used to climb,
Tom chasing his wild bedfellow Will ;
And there is the small low bedroom still,
And the table he had when a little lad :
Ah, Tom, does it make you sad or glad,
     This coming home ?

Tom's heart is moved. " Now don't mind me !
I am no stranger guest," cries he.
" And, father, I say ! " — with the old-time laugh —
" Don't kill for me any fatted calf !
But go now and show me the sheep and swine,
And the cattle — where is that colt of mine ? —
And the farm and crops — is harvest over ?
I'd like a chance at the oats and clover !
I can mow, you'll find, and cradle and bind,
Load hay, stow away, pitch, rake behind ;
For I know a scythe from a well-sweep yet.
In an hour I'll make you quite forget
     That I've been from home."

He plucks from its peg an old farm hat,
And with cordial chat upon this and that,
Tom walks with his father about the place.
There's a pensive grace in his fine young face
As they loiter under the orchard trees,
As he breathes once more the mountain breeze,

And looks from the hill-side far away,
Over pasture and fallow, and field of hay,
To the hazy peaks of the azure range,
Which change forever, yet never change;
The wild sweet winds his welcome blow:
Even old Monadnock seems to know
    That Tom 's come home.

The old man stammers and speaks at last:
" You notice your mother is failing fast,
Though she can't see it.   Poor Will's disgrace
And debts, and the mortgage on the place;
His sudden death — 'Twas a dreadful blow;
She couldn't bear up like a man, you know.
She's talked of you since the trouble came:
Some things in the past she seems to blame
Herself for; what, it is hard to tell.
I marvel how she keeps round so well,
For often all night she lies awake.
I'm thankful, if only for her sake,
    That you've come home."

They visit the field : Tom mows with the men;
And now they come round to the porch again.
The mother draws Tom aside; lets sink
Her voice to a whisper, and — " What do you think?
You see," she says, " he is broken quite.
Sometimes he tosses and groans all night,
And — Tom, it is hard, it is hard indeed!
The mortgage, and so many mouths to feed!
But tell him he must not worry so,
And work so hard, for he don't know
That he hasn't the strength of a younger man.
Counsel him, comfort him, all you can,
    While you're at home."

Tom's heart is full; he moves away,
And ponders what he will do or say.

And now at evening all are met,
The tea is drawn, the table set;
But when the old man with bended head,
In reverent, fervent tones has said
The opening phrase of his simple grace,
He falters, the tears course down his face;
For the words seem cold, and the sense of the old
Set form is too weak his joy to hold;
And broken accents best express
The upheaved heart's deep thankfulness,
    Now Tom's come home.

The supper done, Tom has his say:
"I heard of some matters first to-day;
And I call it a shame — you're both to blame —
That a son, who has only to sign his name,
To lift the mortgage and clear the score,
Should never have had that chance before.
From this time forth you are free from care;
Your troubles I share; your burdens I bear.
So promise to quit hard work, and say
That you'll give yourselves a holiday.
Now, father! now, mother! you can't refuse;
For what's a son for, and what's the use
    Of his coming home?"

And so there is cheer in the house to-night.
It hardly can hold so much delight.
Tom wanders forth across the lot,
And, under the stars — though Tom is not
So pious as some boys have been —
Thanks Heaven, that turned his thoughts from sin,
And blessed him, and brought him home once more.
And now he knocks at a cottage-door,
For one who has waited many a year
In hope that thrilling sound to hear;
Who, happy as other hearts may be,
Knows well there is none so glad as she
    That Tom's come home.

J. T. TROWBRIDGE.

WYATT'S HARANGUE TO THE LONDON CROWD.

MEN of Kent; England of England; you that have kept your old customs upright, while all the rest of England bowed theirs to the Norman: the cause that hath brought us together is not the cause of a county or a shire, but of this England, in whose crown our Kent is the fairest jewel. Philip shall not wed Mary; and ye have called me to be your leader. I know Spain. I have been there with my father; I have seen them in their own land; have marked the haughtiness of their nobles, the cruelty of their priests. If this man marry our Queen, however the Council and the Commons may fence round his power with restriction, he will be King, King of England, my masters; and the Queen, and the laws, and the people, his slaves. What? shall we have Spain on the throne and in the parliament; Spain in the pulpit and on the law-bench; Spain in all the great offices of state; Spain in our ships, in our forts, in our houses, in our beds?

But, say you, must we levy war against the Queen's Grace?

No, my friends; war *for* the Queen's Grace — to save her from herself and Philip — war against Spain. And think not we shall be alone — thousands will flock to us. The Council, the Court itself, is on our side. The Lord Chancellor himself is on our side. The King of France is with us; the King of Denmark is with us; the world is with us — war against Spain! And if we move not now, yet it will be known that we

have moved; and if Philip come to be King, O, my
God! the rope, the rack, the thumb-screw, the stake,
the fire. If we move not now, Spain moves, bribes
our nobles with her gold, and creeps, creeps, snake-
like, about our legs till we cannot move at all; and ye
know, my masters, that wherever Spain hath ruled she
hath withered all beneath her.   Look at the New
World — a paradise made hell; the red man, that good
helpless creature, starved, maimed, flogged, flayed,
burned, boiled, buried alive, worried by dogs; and
here, nearer home, the Netherlands, Sicily, Naples,
Lombardy.   I say no more — only this, their lot is
yours.   Forward to London with me! forward to London! If ye love your liberties or your skins, forward
to London!

TENNYSON.

WAKING.

I HAVE done at length with dreaming;
   Henceforth, O thou soul of mine,
Thou must take up sword and gauntlet,
   Waging warfare most divine!
Life is struggle, combat, victory;
   Wherefore have I slumbered on,
With my forces all unmarshalled,
   With my weapons all undrawn!
O how many a glorious record
   Had the angels of me kept,
Had I done instead of doubted,
   Had I warred instead of wept!
But begone regret bewailing;
   Ye but weaken at the best;
I have tried the trusty weapons
   Rusting erst within my breast;

I have wakened to my duty,
  To a knowledge, strong and deep,
That I dreamed not of aforetime,
  In my long, inglorious sleep;
For to live is something awful,
  And I knew it not before;
And I dreamed not how stupendous
  Was the secret that I bore, —
The great, deep, mysterious secret
  Of a life to be wrought out
Into warm, heroic action,
  Weakened not by fear or doubt.
In this subtle sense of being,
  Newly-stirred within my vein,
I can feel a throb electric,
  Pleasure half allied to pain.
'Tis so great, and yet so awful,
  So bewildering, yet brave,
To be king in every conflict
  When before I crouched a slave.
'Tis so glorious to be conscious
  Of a glowing power within
Stronger than the rallying forces
  Of a charged and marshalled sin.
O those olden days of dalliance,
  When I wantoned with my fate,
When I trifled with a knowledge
  That had well-nigh come too late!
But, my soul, look not behind thee,
  Thou hast work to do at last;
Let the brave toil of the Present
  Overarch the crumbled Past.
Build thy great acts high and higher,
  Build them on the conquered soil
Where thy weakness first fell, bleeding,
  And thy prayers arose to God.

MRS. CAROLINE MASON.

THE ANGEL'S STORY.

THROUGH the blue and frosty heavens
　　Christmas stars were shining bright;
Glistening lamps through the great city
　　Almost matched their gleaming light;
While the winter snow was lying,
And the winter winds were sighing,
　　Long ago one Christmas night.

While from every tower and steeple
　　Pealing bells were sounding clear,
Never with such tones of gladness,
Save when Christmas time draws near.
Many a one that night was merry,
　　Who had toiled through all the year.

　　.　　.　　.　　.　　.　　.

Yet one house was dim and darkened;
　　Gloom, and sickness, and despair
Were dwelling in the gilded chamber,
　　Creeping up the marble stair,
Stilling even the voice of mourning:
　　For a child lay dying there!

Silken curtains fell around him,
　　Velvet carpets hushed the tread;
Many costly toys were lying
　　All unheeded by his bed;
And his tangled golden ringlets
　　Were on downy pillows spread.

All the skill of the great city
　　To save that little life was vain;
That little thread from being broken,
That fatal word from being spoken;

Nay, his very mother's pain,
And the mighty love within her,
　Could not give him health again.

* * * * * *

Suddenly an unseen Presence
　Checked those constant moaning cries,
Stilled the little heart's quick fluttering,
　Raised those blue and wandering eyes,
Fixed on some mysterious vision,
　With a startled, sweet surprise.

For a radiant angel hovered
　Smiling o'er the little bed ;
White his raiment, from his shoulders
　Snowy, dove-like pinions spread,
And a star-like light was shining
　In a Glory round his head.

While with tender love the angel,
　Leaning o'er the little nest,
In his arms the sick child folding,
　Laid him gently on his breast,
Sobs and wailings told the mother
　That her darling was at rest.

So the angel, slowly rising,
　Spread his wings, and through the air
Bore the smiling child, and held him
　On his heart with loving care ;
A red branch of blooming roses
　Placing softly by him there.

While the child, thus clinging, floated
　Towards the mansions of the Blest,
Gazing from his shining guardian
　To the flowers upon his breast,
Thus the angel spake, still smiling
　On the little heavenly guest :

* * * * * *

"Once in that great town below us,
  In a poor and narrow street,
Dwelt a little sickly orphan;
  Gentle aid, or pity sweet,
Never in life's rugged pathway
  Guided his poor tottering feet.

.   .   .   .   .   .

"All too weak for childish pastimes,
  Drearily the hours sped;
On his hands, so small and trembling,
  Leaning his poor aching head,
Or, through dark and painful hours,
  Lying sleepless on his bed.

.   .   .   .   .   .

"One bright day, with feeble footsteps,
  Slowly forth he dared to crawl,
Through the crowded city's pathways,
  Till he reached a garden wall,
Where, 'mid princely halls and mansions,
  Stood the lordliest of all.

.   .   .   .   .

"He against the gate of iron
  Pressed his wan and wistful face,
Gazing with an awe-struck pleasure
  At the glories of the place;
Never had his brightest day-dream
  Shone with half such wondrous grace.

"You were playing in that garden,
  Throwing blossoms in the air,
And laughing when the petals floated
  Downwards on your golden hair;
And the fond eyes watching o'er you,
And the splendor spread before you,
  Told a House's Hope was there.

" When your servants, tired of seeing
    His pale face of want and woe,
Turning to the ragged Orphan,
    Gave him coin, and bade him go,
Down his cheek, so thin and wasted,
    Bitter tears began to flow.

" But that look of childish sorrow
    On your tender child-heart fell,
And you plucked the reddest roses
    From the tree you loved so well ;
Passing them through the stern grating,
    With the gentle word, ' Farewell ! '

" Dazzled by the fragrant treasure,
    And the gentle voice he heard,
In the poor, forlorn boy's spirit,
    Joy, the sleeping Seraph, stirred ;
In his hand he took the flowers,
    In his heart the loving word.

" So he crept to his poor garret,
    Poor no more, but rich and bright ;
For the holy dreams of childhood —
    Love, and Rest, and Hope, and Light —
Floated round the Orphan's pillow
    Through the starry summer night.

" Day dawned, yet the visions lasted ;
    All too weak to rise he lay ;
Did he dream that none spake harshly —
    All were strangely kind that day ?
And he thought his treasured roses
    Must have charmed all ills away.

"And he smiled, though they were fading?
  One by one their leaves were shed ;
'Such bright things could never perish ;
  They would bloom again,' he said.
When the next day's sun had risen,
  Child and flowers both were dead !

"Know, dear little one, our Father
  Does no little deed disdain ;
And in hearts that beat in heaven,
  Still all tender thoughts remain.
Love on the cold earth beginning,
  Lives divine and pure again !"

Thus the angel ceased, and gently
  O'er his little burden leant ;
While the child gazed from the shining,
  Loving eyes that o'er him bent,
To the blooming roses by him,
  Wondering what that mystery meant.

Then the radiant angel answered,
  And with tender meaning smiled,
"Ere your child-like, loving spirit,
  Sin and the hard world defiled,
God has given me leave to seek you : —
  I was once that little child !"

    .   . .   .   .   .

ADELAIDE PROCTER.

HOW TOM SAWYER GOT HIS FENCE WHITEWASHED.

TOM SAWYER, having offended his sole guardian, Aunt Polly, is by that sternly affectionate dame punished by being set to whitewash the fence in front of the garden. The world seemed a hollow mockery to Tom, who had planned fun for that day, and he knew that he would be the laughing-stock of all the boys as they came past and saw him set to work like a "nigger." But a great inspiration burst upon him, and he went tranquilly to work. What that inspiration was will appear from what follows.

One of the boys, Ben Rogers, comes by and pauses, eating a particularly fine apple. Tom does not see him. Ben stared a moment, and then said, —

"Hi-yi! you're a stump, ain't you?"

No answer. Tom surveyed his last touch with the eye of an artist, then he gave another gentle sweep, and surveyed the result as before. Ben ranged up alongside of him. Tom's mouth watered for the apple, but he stuck to his work. Ben said, —

"Hello, old chap: you got to work, hey!"

"Why, it's you, Ben: I wasn't noticing."

"Say, I'm going in a-swimming, I am. Don't you wish you could? But, of course, you'd ruther work, wouldn't you? Course you would!"

Tom contemplated the boy a bit, and said, —

"What do you call work?"

"Why, ain't that work?"

Tom resumed his whitewashing, and answered carelessly, —

"Well, maybe it is, and maybe it ain't. All I know is, it suits Tom Sawyer."

"O, come now, you don't mean to let on that you like it?"

The brush continued to move.

"Like it? Well, I don't see why I oughtn't to like it. Does a boy get a chance to whitewash a fence every day?"

That put the thing in a new light. Ben stopped nibbling his apple. Tom swept his brush daintily back and forth — stepped back to note the effect — added a touch here and there — criticised the effect again. Ben watching every move, and getting more and more interested, more and more absorbed. Presently he said, —

"Say, Tom, let me whitewash a little."

Tom considered; was about to consent, but he altered his mind. "No, no; I reckon it wouldn't hardly do, Ben. You see, Aunt Polly's awful particular about this fence — right here on the street, you know — but if it was the back fence I wouldn't mind, and she wouldn't. Yes, she's awful particular about this fence; it's got to be done very careful; I reckon there ain't one boy in a thousand, maybe two thousand, that can do it in the way it's got to be done."

"No — is that so? O, come now; lemme just try, only just a little. I'd let you, if you was me, Tom."

"Ben, I'd like to; honest Injun; but Aunt Polly — well, Jim wanted to do it, but she wouldn't let him. Sid wanted to do it, but she wouldn't let Sid. Now, don't you see how I am fixed? If you was to tackle this fence, and anything was to happen to it — "

"O, shucks! I'll be just as careful. Now lemme try. Say — I'll give you the core of my apple."

" Well, here.   No, Ben ; now don't; I'm afeard —"
" I'll give you all of it !"

Tom gave up the brush with reluctance in his face,
but alacrity in his heart.   And while Ben worked and
sweated in the sun, the retired artist sat on a barrel
in the shade close by, dangling his legs, munched his
apple, and planned the slaughter of more innocents.
There was no lack of material; boys happened along
every little while ; they came to jeer, but remained to
whitewash.   By the time Ben was fagged out, Tom
had traded the next chance to Billy Fisher for a kite
in good repair ; and when he played out, Johnny Miller
bought it for a dead rat and a string to swing it with ;
and so on, and so on, hour after hour.   And when the
middle of the afternoon came, from being a poor pov-
erty-stricken boy in the morning, Tom was literally
rolling in wealth.   He had, besides the things I have
mentioned, twelve marbles, part of a jews-harp, a piece
of blue bottle-glass to look through, a spool cannon, a
key that wouldn't unlock anything, a fragment of
chalk, a glass stopper of a decanter, a tin soldier, a
couple of tadpoles, six fire-crackers, a kitten with only
one eye, a brass door-knob, a dog collar — but no dog
— the handle of a knife, four pieces of orange peel,
and a dilapidated old window sash.   He had had a
nice, good, idle time all the while — plenty of company
— and the fence had three coats of whitewash on it !
If he hadn't run out of whitewash, he would have
bankrupted every boy in the village.

Tom said to himself that it was not such a hollow
world after all.   He had discovered a great law of
human action without knowing it, namely, that in
order to make a man or a boy covet a thing, it is only
necessary to make it difficult to attain.   MARK TWAIN.

17

OUR ORIOLE NEIGHBORS.

THERE'S an oriole's nest in the elm-tree boughs ;
    And the flurry and flutter are such that it seems
As if the young husband were telling his spouse,
In an air-castle way, of his householding schemes.
Don't he talk like a tipsy one telling his dreams ?
    But what does he care for the lore of the schools
While his thoughts are busy with family cares ?
    So, disregarding grammatical rules,
      (No Lord of the Birch has our hero to fear,)
He winds up his story of household affairs
      With, " Here I be, here I be, — right up here ! "

Do matters go smoothly ?   Well, once in a while
Our neighbor is down with a touch of the blues ;
    Then he talks to himself in a very queer style,
But is dumb when his lady solicits the news.
He mopes, and he sulks, and he stares at his shoes,
    And he vows that this world is a very dull place.
But 'tis easier by far for our friend to rejoice ;
    So, just as his goodwife, with sorrowful face,
      Is wondering whether her partner is near,
He shouts from his perch, at the top of his voice,
      " Why, here I be, here I be, — right up here ! "

" But never," he says, " in my love-making days,
When I was a youngster, and Mrs. was Miss,
    And the bright world abounded in all its glad ways,
With song and with sunshine, with beauty and bliss, —
Never once did I think that it *could* come to this !
    'Tis a serious question, this matter of bread ;
And soon the demand will be, — ' rations for five ! '
    Shall I give up the fight, and go down with the dead,
      And leave you a widow ?   Say, Tooty, my dear !
No ; I am determined to strive and to thrive ;
      So, here I be, here I be, — right up here ! "

O, the wind blows east, and the wind blows west,
And the days and the weeks and the months go by ;
   In the yellowing elm there's a desolate nest,
For its builders have flown to a pleasanter sky ;
And I hardly know whether to smile or to sigh
   At the thought that when I shall have left this abode,
And passed, like the birds, from the Old to the New,
   Some friend, losing sight of my face on the road,
   May puzzle his brain to determine my sphere,
And get for all answer, (I hope 'twill be true !)
   " Why, here I be, here I be, — right up here ! "

BEVERLY MOORE.

DEFENCE OF HOFER, THE TYROLESE PATRIOT.

YOU ask what I have to say in my defence — *you* who glory in the name of France, who wander through the world to enrich and exalt the land of your birth, — *you* demand how I could dare to arm myself against the invaders of my native rocks? Do you confine the love of home to yourselves? Do you punish in others the actions which you dignify and reward among yourselves? Those stars which glitter on your breasts, do they hang there as a recompense for patient servitude?

I see the smile of contempt which curls your lips. You say, " This brute, — he is a ruffian, a beggar ! That patched jacket, that ragged cap, that rusty belt: — shall barbarians such as *he* close the pass against *us*, shower rocks on our heads, and single out our leaders with unfailing aim, — these grovelling mountaineers, who know not the joys and brilliance of life, creeping

amid eternal snows, and snatching with greedy hand
their stinted ear of corn?"

Yet, poor as we are, we never envied our neighbors
their smiling sun, their gilded palaces; *we* never
strayed from our peaceful huts to blast the happiness
of those who had not injured us. The traveller who
visited our valleys, met every hand outstretched to
welcome him; for him every hearth blazed with delight as we listened to his tale of distant lands. Too
happy for ambition, we were not jealous of wealth; we
have even refused to partake of it.

Frenchmen! you have wives and children. When
you return to your beautiful cities, amid the roar of
trumpets, the smiles of the lovely, and the multitudes
shouting their triumph, *they* will ask, "Where have
you roamed? What have you achieved? What have
you brought back to us?" Those laughing babes
who climb upon your knees, will you have the heart
to tell them, "We have pierced the barren crags; we
have entered the naked cottage to level it to the
ground; we found no treasures but honest hearts, and
those we have broken because they throbbed with
love for the wilderness around them? Clasp this old
firelock in your little hands, it was snatched from a
peasant of Tyrol, who died in the vain effort to stem
the torrent!" Seated by your fireside, will you boast
to your generous and blooming wives, that you have
extinguished the last ember which enlightened our
gloom?

Happy scenes! I shall never see you more! In
those cold and stern eyes I read my fate. Think not
that your sentence can be terrible to *me!* But I have
sons, daughters, and a wife who has shared all my

labors; she has shared, too, my little pleasures, — such pleasures as that humble roof can yield, — pleasures that *you* cannot understand.

My little ones! should you live to bask in the sunshine of manhood (you are sporting by the brook that washes our door), dream not of your father's doom! Should you live to know it, know, too, that the man who has served his God and country with all his heart, can smile at the musket levelled to pierce it. What is death to ME? I have not revelled in pleasures wrung from innocence or want; rough and discolored as are these hands, they are pure. My death is nothing. O that my country could live! O that ten thousand such deaths could make her immortal!

Do I despair, then? No; we have rushed to the sacrifice, and the offering has been vain for *us;* but our children shall burst these fetters; the blood of virtue was never shed in vain. Freedom can never die! I have heard that *you* killed your king once, because he enslaved you; yet now, again, you crouch before a single man who bids you trample on all who abjure his yoke, and shoots you if you have courage to disobey. Do you think that, when I am buried, there shall breathe no *other* Hofers? Dream you that, if *to-day* you prostrate Hofer in the dust, *to-morrow* Hofer is no more?

In the distance I see the liberty which I shall not taste; behind, I look on my slaughtered countrymen, on my orphans, on my desolate fields; but a star rises before my aching sight, which points to justice, and it shall come. Before the sun has sunk below yon mountains, I shall awake in a paradise which *you*, perhaps, may never reach.

THE LITTLE HERO.

A TALE OF THE ATLANTIC, AS TOLD BY OLD BEN.

NOW, lads, a short yarn I'll just spin you,
   As happened on our very last run,
'Bout a boy as a man's soul had in him,
   Or else I'm a son of a gun !

From Liverpool port out three days, lads,
   The good ship floating over the deep,
The skies bright with sunshine above us,
   The waters beneath us asleep ;

Not a bad-tempered lubber among us,
   A jollier crew never sailed ;
'Cept the first mate, a bit of a savage,
   But good seaman as ever was hailed.

Regulation, good order, his motto,
   Strong as iron, and steady as quick,
With a couple of bushy black eyebrows,
   And eyes fierce as those of Old Nick !

One day he comes up from below deck,
   A-graspin' a lad by the arm,
A poor little ragged young urchin,
   As ought to be home with his marm !

An' the mate asks the boy pretty roughly,
   " How he dared for to be stowed away ?
A-cheating the owners and captain,
   Sailin', eatin', and all without pay !"

The lad had a face bright and sunny,
　An' a pair o' blue eyes like a girl's,
An' looks up at the scowling first mate, boys,
　An' shakes back his long shining curls.

An' says he, in a voice clear and pretty,
　"My stepfather brought me aboard,
And hid me away down the stairs there,
　For to keep me he couldn't afford.

"And he told me the big ship would take me
　To Halifax town, O, so far!
And he said, ' Now the Lord is your Father,
　Who lives where the good angels are!'"

"It's a lie!" says the mate, — "not your father,
　But some o' the big skulkers here ;
Some milk-hearted, soft-headed sailor!
　Speak up! tell the truth! d'ye hear!"

" 'Twarn't us," growled the tars as stood round
　　'em.
　"What's your age?" says one son of the brine.
" And your name?" says another old saltfish.
　Says the small chap, "I'm Frank — just turned
　　nine!"

" O, my eyes!" says another bronzed seaman
　To the mate, who seemed staggered hisself,
" Let him go free to old Novy Scoshy,
　An' I'll work out his passage myself!"

" Belay!" says the mate ; " shut your mouth, man ;
　I'll sail this here craft, bet your life!
An' I'll fit the lie on to ye somehow,
　As square as a fork fits a knife!"

Then a-knitting his black brows with anger,
  He tumbles the poor slip below,
An' says he, " P'raps to-morrow 'll change you;
  If it don't, back to England you go ! "

I took him some dinner, be sure, mates;
  Just think — only nine years of age !
An' next day, just as soon as six bells tolled,
  The mate brings him out of his cage.

An' he plants him afore us amidships,
  His eyes like two coals all alight,
An' he says, through his teeth — mad with passion,
  An' his hand lifted ready to smite :

" Tell the truth, lad, and then I'll forgive you ;
  But the truth I *will* have — speak it out ;
It wasn't your father as brought you,
  But some of these men here about ? "

Then that pair o' blue eyes bright and winning,
  Clear and shady with innocent youth,
Looks up at the mate's bushy eyebrows,
  An' says he, " Sir, I've told you the truth ! "

'Twarn't no use — the mate didn't believe him,
  Though every man else did aboard ;
With rough hand by the collar he seized him,
  And cried, " You shall hang, by the Lord ! "

An' he snatched his watch out of his pocket,
  Just as if he'd bin drawin' a knife ;
" If in ten minutes more you don't speak, lad,
  There's the rope ! and good-by to dear life ! "

There ! — you never see such a sight, mates,
  As that boy with his pale, pretty face :
Proud, though, and steady with courage,
  Never thinking of asking for grace !

Eight minutes went by, all in silence.
  Says the mate, then, "Speak, lad : say your say!"
His eyes slowly filling with tear-drops,
  He, faltering, says, " May I pray ? "

I'm a rough and a hard old tarpaulin
  As any blue-jacket afloat,
But the salt water springs to my eyes, lads,
  And I felt my heart rise in my throat!

The mate kind o' trembled and shivered,
  And nodded his head in reply,
And his cheek went all white of a sudden,
  And the hot light was quenched in his eye.

An' he stood like a figure of marble,
  With his watch tightly grasped in his hand,
An' the passengers all still around him —
  Ne'er the like was on sea or on land !

An' the little chap kneels on the deck there,
  An' his hands he clasps over his breast,
As he must ha' done often at home, lads,
  At night-time, when goin' to rest.

And soft comes the first words, " Our Father,"
  Low and soft from that dear baby-lip,
But low as they was, heard like trumpet
  By each true man aboard o' that ship.

Ev'ry bit o' that prayer, mates, he goes through,
  To " Forever and ever.   Amen ! "
And for all the bright gold of the Indies
  I wouldn't ha' heard him agen !

An' says he, when he'd finished, uprising,
  An' lifting his blue eyes above,
" Dear Lord Jesus, O, take me to heaven,
  Back again to my own mother's love ! "

For a minute or two, like to magic,
  We stood every man like the dead,
Then back to the mate's face comes running
  The life-blood again, warm and red.

Off his feet was that lad sudden lifted,
  An' clasped to the mate's rugged breast,
And his husky voice muttered, " God bless you ! "
  As his lips to his forehead he-pressed.

If the ship hadn't been a good sailor,
  An' gone by herself right along,
All had gone to old Davy, for all, lads,
  Was gathered around in that throng.

Like a man, says the mate, " God forgive me,
  That ever I used you so hard ;
It's myself as had ought to be strung up
  Taut and sure to that ugly old yard ! "

" You believe me now ? " then said the youngster.
  " Believe you ! " — he kissed him once more ;
" You'd have laid down your life for the truth, lad.
  Believe you ! From now evermore ! "

An' p'raps, mates, he wasn't thought much on
  All that day, and the rest of the trip ;
P'raps he paid, after all, for his passage !
  P'raps he wasn't the pet of the ship !

And if that little chap ain't a model
  For all, young or old, short or tall,
And if that ain't the stuff to make men of,
  Old Ben he knows naught after all !

THE HISTORICAL BUTCHER.

WHAT d'ye buy, what d'ye buy — well, how are
you? How do you do? I wery glad to see
you; how are all the family? This is wery kind to
call in this here way. I've been reading as usual all
this here blessed morning, that favorite book of mine,
Hume's History in England; what a book that 'ere
is! How hinstructive and hentertaining Hume's History in England is — ten pence a pound, ma'am. I've
been reading the fourth wolum; it's a wery thick
un, wery thick indeed — make nice soup, ma'am.
Queen Mary — make nice Scotch collops, ma'am. Sir
Isaac Newton was a great man; he knew all about
the pole-axe of the fixed stars, and how long it would
take a man to go in a taxed cart to the moon. Queen
Elizabeth went to St. Paul's on a pillion — that saddle
of mutton's just your weight, ma'am. I've been reading, dear me, — I've been reading King Charles;
you've heard of him, han't you? Hid himself in St.
James's Park ever since; no, it warn't St. James's
Park, war it? However, I know it was in some park;
but the wicked rascals caught him and cut off his head
— make a capital hash, with parsley garnish, ma'am.
Cardinal Wolsey's father was a butcher; so am I.
There's a curious coincidence, an't it? And Henry
the Eighth married Queen Elizabeth; no, he didn't
though, for she war his mother; no, that couldn't be
— she warn't his mother — but she war some relation.
King Henry the Eighth — that's a nice fat bit, ma'am;
take it wi' you.

BABIE BELL.

HAVE you not heard the poets tell
    How came the dainty Babie Bell
  Into this world of ours?
The gates of heaven were left ajar:
    With folded hands and dreamy eyes,
    Wandering out of Paradise,
She saw this planet, like a star,
    Hung in the glittering depths of even,
Its bridges, running to and fro,
O'er which the white-winged angels go,
    Bearing the holy dead to heaven!
She touched a bridge of flowers, those feet,
    So light they did not bend the bells
    Of the celestial asphodels!
They fell like dew upon the flowers,
    Then all the air grew strangely sweet;
And thus came dainty Babie Bell
  Into this world of ours.

She came and brought delicious May,
    The swallows built beneath the eaves;
    Like sunlight in and out the leaves,
The robins went, the livelong day;
The lily swung its noiseless bell,
    And o'er the porch the trembling vine
    Seemed bursting with its veins of wine;
How sweetly, softly, twilight fell!
O, earth was full of singing birds,
    And opening spring-tide flowers,
When the dainty Babie Bell
  Came to this world of ours!

O Babie, dainty Babie Bell,
How fair she grew from day to day !
    What woman-nature filled her eyes,
What poetry within them lay !
Those deep and tender twilight eyes,
    So full of meaning, pure and bright,
    As if she yet stood in the light
Of those ope'd gates of Paradise !
And so we loved her more and more ;
Ah, never in our hearts before
    Was love so lovely born ;
We felt we had a link between
This real world and that unseen,
    The land beyond the morn.

    .   .   .   .

And now the orchards, which were white
    And red with blossoms when she came,
Were rich in autumn's mellow prime,
    The clustered apples burnt like flame,
The soft-cheeked peaches blushed and fell,
The ivory chestnut burst its shell,
The grape hung purpling in the grange,
And time wrought just as rich a change
    In little Babie Bell.
Her lissome form more perfect grew,
    And in her features we could trace,
    In softened curves, her mother's face.
Her angel-nature ripened too,
We thought her lovely when she came,
    But she was holy, saintly now,
    Around her pale angelic brow
We saw a slender ring of flame !

God's hand had taken away the seal
    That held the portals of her speech ;
And oft she said a few strange words,
    Whose meaning lay beyond our reach.

She never was a child to us,
 We never held her being's key ;
We could not teach her holy things,
 She was Christ's self in purity.

It came upon us by degrees,
 We saw its shadow ere it fell,
The knowledge that our God had sent
 His messenger for Babie Bell.
 We shuddered with unlanguaged pain,
And all our thoughts ran into tears,
 Like sunshine into rain.
 We cried aloud in our belief,
" O, smite us gently, gently, God !
Teach us to bend and kiss the rod,
 And perfect grow through grief."
Ah, how we loved her, God can tell ;
Her heart was folded deep in ours ;
 Our hearts are broken, Babie Bell.

At last he came, the messenger,
 The messenger from unseen lands ;
And what did dainty Babie Bell ?
 She only crossed her hands,
She only looked more meek and fair !
We parted back her silken hair ;
We wove the roses round her brow,
White buds, the summer's drifted snow,
 Wrapped her from head to foot in flowers,
And thus went dainty Babie Bell
 Out of this world of ours !

THOMAS BAILEY ALDRICH.

JIMMY BUTLER AND THE OWL.

'TWAS in the summer of '46 that I landed at
Hamilton, fresh as a new pratie just dug from
the " ould sod," and wid a light heart and a heavy
bundle I sot off for the township of Buford, tiding a
taste of a song, as merry a young fellow as iver took
the road. Well, I trudged on and on, past many a
plisint place, pleasin' meself wid the thought that
some day I might have a place of me own, wid a
world of chickens and ducks and pigs and childer
about the door ; and along in the afternoon of the
sicond day I got to Buford village. A cousin of me
mother's, one Dennis O'Dowd, lived about sivin miles
from there, and I wanted to make his place that night,
so I inquired the way at the tavern, and was lucky to
find a man who was goin' part of the way, an' would
show me the way to find Dennis. Sure he was very
kind indade, an' when I got out of his wagon he
pointed me through the wood, and tould me to go
straight south a mile and a half, and the first house
would be Dennis's.

"An' you've no time to lose now," said he, " for the
sun is low, and mind you don't get lost in the woods."

" Is it lost now," said I, " that I'd be gittin', an' me
uncle as great a navigator as iver steered a ship across
the thrackless say ! Not a bit of it, though I'm
obleeged to ye for your kind advice, and thank yiz
for the ride."

An' wid that he drove off an' left me alone. I shouldered me bundle bravely, an' whistlin' a bit of time for

company like, I pushed into the bush. Well, I went a
long way over bogs, an' turnin' among the bush an'
trees, till I began to think I must be well-nigh to Dennis's. But, bad 'cess to it! all of a sudden I came out
of the woods at the very identical spot where I started
in, which I knew by an ould crotched tree that seemed
to be standin' on its head an' kickin' up its heels to
make divarsion of me. By this time it was growin'
dark, and as there was no time to lose, I started in a
second time, detarmined to keep straight south this
time, an' no mistake. I got on bravely for a while,
but och hone! och hone! it got so dark I couldn't see
the trees, an' I bumped me nose an' barked me shins,
while the miskaties bit me hands and face to a blister;
an' afther tumblin' an' stumblin' around till I was fairly
bamfoozled, I sat down on a log, all of a trimble, to
think that I was lost intirely, an' that maybe a lion or
some other wild craythur would devour me before
mornin'.

Just then I heard somebody a long way off say,
"Whip poor Will!" "Bedad," sez I, "I'm glad it
isn't Jamie that's got to take it, though it seems it's
more in sorrow than in anger they are doin' it, or why
should they say 'poor Will'? An' sure they can't be
Injin, haythin, or naygur, for it's plain English they're
afther spakin'. Maybe they might help me out o'
this;" so I shouted at the top o' my voice, "A lost
man!" Thin I listened. Prisently an answer came.

"Who? Who-o? Who-o-o?"

"Jamie Butler, the waiver," sez I, as loud as I could
roar, an' snatchin' up me bundle an' stick, I started in
the direction of the voice. Whin I thought I had got
near the place, I stopped and shouted again, "A lost
man!"

"Who! Who-o! Who-o-o!" said a voice right over me head.

"Sure," thinks I, "it's a mighty quare place for a man to be at this time of night; maybe it's some settler scrapin' sugar off a sugar-bush for the children's breakfast in the mornin'. But where's Will and the rest of 'em?" All this wint through me head like a flash, an' thin I answered his inquiry.

"Jamie Butler, the waiver," sez I; "an' if it wouldn't inconvanience yer honor, would yez be kind enough to stop down and show me the way to the house of Dennis O'Dowd?"

"Who! Who-o! Who-o-o!" sez he.

"Dennis O'Dowd," sez I, civil enough; "an' a dacint man he is, an' first cousin to me own mother."

"Who! Who-o! Who-o-o!" sez he again.

"Me mother." sez I; "an' as fine a woman as iver peeled a biled pratie wid her thumb-nail; an' her maiden name was Molly McFiggin."

"Who! Who-o! Who-o-o!"

"Paddy McFiggin! bad luck to yer deaf ould head. Paddy McFiggin, I say: do ye hear that? An' he was the tallest man in all the county Tipperary, excipt Jim Doyle, the blacksmith."

"Who! Who-o! Who-o-o!"

"Jim Doyle, the blacksmith," sez I, "ye good-for-nothin' blaggurd naygur; an' if yiz don't come down and show me the way this min't, I'll climb up there an' break every bone in yer skin, ye spalpeen, so sure as me name is Jamie Butler!"

"Who! Who-o! Who-o-o!" sez he, as impident as iver.

I said niver a word, but layin' down me bundle, an'

18

takin' me stick in me teeth, I began to climb the tree.
Whin I got among the branches I looked quietly
around till I saw a pair of big eyes just forninst me.

"Whist," sez I, "an' I'll let him have a taste of an
Irish stick;" an' wid that I let dhrive, and lost me balance, an' came tumblin' to the ground, nearly breakin'
me neck wid the fall. Whin I came to me sinsis I had
a very sore head, wid a lump on it like a goose-egg,
and half of me Sunday coat-tail torn off intirely. I
spoke to the chap in the tree, but could git niver an
answer at all at all.

"Sure," thinks I, "he must have gone home to rowl
up his head, for by the powers I didn't throw me stick
for nothin'."

Well, by this time the moon was up, and I could see
a little, and I determined to make one more effort to
reach Dennis's.

I wint on cautiously for a while, an' thin I heard a
bell. "Sure," sez I, "I'm comin' to a settlement now,
for I hear the church-bell." I kept on toward the
sound till I came to an ould cow wid a bell on. She
started to run, but I was too quick for her, and got
her by the tail and hung on, thinkin' that maybe she
would take me out of the woods. On we wint, like an
ould country steeple-chase, till, sure enough, we came
out to a clearin', an' a house in sight wid a light in it.
So, leavin' the ould cow puffin' and blowin' in a shed,
I wint to the house, and, as luck would have it, whose
should it be but Dennis's.

He gave me a rael Irish welcome, and introduced
me to his two daughters, as purty a pair of girls as
iver ye clapped an eye on. But whin I tould him me
adventure in the woods, and about the fellow who

made fun of me, they all laughed and roared, and Dennis said it was an owl.

"An ould what?" sez I.

"Why, an owl — a bird," sez he.

"Do ye tell me now?" sez I. "Sure it's a quare country and a quare bird."

An' thin they all laughed again, till at last I laughed myself, that hearty like, and dropped right into a chair between the two purty girls, and the ould chap winked at me and roared again.

Dennis is me father-in-law now, and he often yet delights to tell our children about their daddy's adventure wid the owl.

BACHELOR'S HALL.

BACHELOR'S hall! What a quare-lookin' place it is!
   Save me from sich all the days o' my life!
Sure, but I think what a burnin' disgrace it is
   Niver at all to be gettin' a wife!

Pots, dishes, an' pans, an' sich grasy commodities,
   Ashes and pratie-skins, kiver the floor;
The cupboard's a storehouse of comical oddities,
   Things that had niver been neighbors before.

Say the ould bachelor, gloomy an' sad enough,
   Placin' his tay-kettle over the fire;
Soon it tips over — Saint Patrick! he's mad enough,
   If he were prisent, to fight with the squire!

He looks for the platter — Grimalkin is scourin' it;
   Sure, at a baste like that, swearin 's no sin!
His dish-cloth is missing. — the pigs are devourin' it.
   Thunder and turf! what a pickle he's in!

Late in the aiv'nin' he goes to bed shiverin';
Niver a bit is the bed made at all;
He crapes like a terrapin under the kiverin';
Bad luck to the picture of bachelor's hall!

SHELLING PEAS.

NO, Tom, you may banter as much as you please;
But it's all the result of the shellin' them peas.
Why, I hadn't the slightest idea, do you know,
That so serious a matter would out of it grow.
I tell you what, Tom, I do feel kind o' scared.
I dreamed it, I hoped it, but never once dared
To breathe it to her.   And, besides, I must say
I always half fancied *she* fancied Jim Wray.
So I felt kind o' stuffy and proud, and took care
To be out of the way when that feller was there
A-danglin' around; for thinks I, if it's him,
That Katy likes best, what's the use lookin grim
At Katy or Jim, for it's all up with me;
And I'd better jest let 'em alone, do you see?
But you wouldn't have thought it; that girl never
        keered
The snap of a pea-pod for Jim's bushy beard.
Well, here's how it was.   I was takin' some berries
Across near her garden to leave at Aunt Mary's,
When, jest as I come to the old ellum-tree,
All alone in the shade that June mornin' was she,
Shellin' peas — setting there on a garden settee.
I swan, she was handsomer 'n ever I seen,
Like a rose all alone in a moss-work of green.
Well, there wasn't no use; so says I, " I'll jest linger
And gaze at her here, behind a syringa."
But she heard me a-movin', and looked a bit frightened,
So I come and stood near her.   I fancied she brightened,

And seemed sort o' pleased. So I hoped she was well,
And — would she allow me to help her to shell ?
For she sat with a monstrous big dish full of peas,
Jest fresh from the vines, which she held on her knees.
" May I help you, Miss Katy ?" says I. "As you please,
Mr. Baxter," says she.   " But you're busy, I guess," —
Glancin' down at my berries, and then at her dress.
" Not the least. There's no hurry. It ain't very late ;
And I'd rather be here ; and Aunt Mary can wait."
So I sot down beside her ; an' as nobody seen us,
I jest took the dish and I held it between us.
And I thought to myself, " I must make an endeavor
To know which she likes, Jim or me, now or never."
But I couldn't say nothin'. We sot there and held
That green pile between us. She shelled and I shelled ;
And *pop* went the pods ; and I couldn't help thinkin'
Of popping the question. A kind of a sinkin'
Come over my spirits, till at last I got out
" Mister Wray 's an admirer of yours, I've no doubt :
You see him quite often.". " Well, sometimes. But why ?
And what if I did ? " " O, well, nothin'," says I.
" Some folks says you're goin' to marry him, though."
" Who says so ? " says she ; and she flared up like tow
When you throw in a match. " Well, some folks that I
            know."
" 'Tain't true, sir," says she. And she snapped a big
            pod,
Till the peas, right and left, flew all over the sod.
Then I looked in her eyes ; but she only looked down,
With a blush that she tried to chase off with a frown.
" Then it's somebody else you like better," says I.
" No, it ain't, though," says she ; and I thought she
            would cry.
Then I tried to say somethin' ; it stuck in my throat,
And all my ideas were upset and afloat.
But I said I knew somebody 'd loved her so long —
Though he never had told her — with feelin's so strong,
He was ready to die at her feet, if she chosed,
If she only could love him ! — I hardly supposed

That she cared for him much, though.   And so, Tom, —
 '   and so, —
For I thought that I saw how the matter would go, —
With my heart all a-jumpin' with rapture, I found
I had taken her hand, and my arm was around
Her waist ere I knew it ; and she with her head
On my shoulder, — but no, I won't tell what she said.
The birds sang above us ; our secret was theirs ;
The leaves whispered soft in the wandering airs.
I tell you the world was a new world to me.
I can talk of these things like a book now, you see.
But the peas ?   Ah, the peas *in* the pods were a mess
Rather bigger than those that we shelled, you may guess.
It's risky to set with a girl shellin' peas.
You may tease me now, Tom, just as much as you please.

C. P. CRANCH.

THE TWO WEAVERS.

AS at their work two weavers sat,
  Beguiling time with friendly chat,
They touched upon the price of meat,
So high a weaver scarce could eat.

" What with my babes and sickly wife,"
Quoth Dick, " I'm almost tired of life ;
So hard we work, so poor we fare,
'Tis more than mortal man can bear.

" How glorious is the rich man's state !
His house so fine, his wealth so great !
Heaven is unjust, you must agree :
Why all to him, and none to me ?

" In spite of what the Scripture teaches,
In spite of all the pulpit preaches,
This world — indeed, I've thought so long —
Is ruled, methinks, extremely wrong.

" Where'er I look, howe'er I range,
'Tis all confused, and hard, and strange ;
The good are troubled and opprest,
And all the wicked are the blest."

Quoth John, " Our ignorance is the cause
Why thus we blame our Maker's laws ;
Parts of his ways alone we know.
'Tis all that man can see below.

" Seest thou that carpet, not half done,
Which thou, dear Dick, hast well begun ?
Behold the wild confusion there !
So rude the mass, it makes one stare !

"A stranger, ignorant of the trade,
Would say, no meaning 's there conveyed ;
For where's the middle, where's the border ?
Thy carpet is now all disorder."

Quoth Dick, " My work is yet in bits,
But still in every part it fits ;
Besides, you reason like a lout ;
Why, man, that carpet 's inside out."

Says John, " Thou sayst the thing I mean ;
And now I hope to cure thy spleen :
This world, which clouds thy soul with doubt,
Is but a carpet inside out.

"As when we view the shreds and ends,
We know not what the whole intends ;
So, when on earth things look but odd,
They're working still some scheme of God.

" No plan, no pattern can we trace ;
All wants proportion, truth, and grace.
The motley mixture we deride,
Nor see the beauteous upper side.

" But when we reach the world of light,
And view these works of God aright,
Then shall we see the whole design,
And own the Workman is divine.

" What now seem random strokes, will there
All order and design appear ;
Then shall we praise what here we spurned,
For then the carpet will be turned."

" Thou'rt right," quoth Dick ; " no more I'll
          grumble
That this world is so strange a jumble.
My impious doubts are put to flight,
For my own carpet sets me right."

HANNAH MORE.

THE ART OF CONVERSATION.

FIRST party (opening conversation): " 'Ave you 'eard
as Jim Bates's father says he'll give 'im the sack ?"
Second ditto (after pause) : " Whose father ?"—First
ditto : "Why, Jim Bates's !" — Second ditto (after
pause) : " Jim Bates's who ? " — First ditto : " Why,
Jim Bates's father !" — Second ditto (after pause) :
" Jim Bates's father ! Well, what does he say ? " —
First ditto : " Says he'll give 'im the sack !"—Second
ditto (after pause) : " Give 'im the what ? " — First
ditto : " Give 'im the sack !" — Second ditto (after
pause) : " Give who the sack ? " — First ditto : " Why,
Jim Bates !" — Second ditto (after long pause) : " Ah,
I 'eard that the day before yesterday !"

Punch.

BOBBY.

A HIGHLAND family of some dignity, but not
much means, was to receive a visit from some
English relations for the first time. Great was the
anxiety and great the efforts to make things wear a
respectable appearance before these assumedly fastidious strangers. The lady had contrived to get up a
pretty good dinner ; but, either from an indulgent dis-
position, or from some defect in her set of servants,
she allowed her son Bobby, a little boy, to be present,
instead of remanding him to the nursery. But little
was she aware of Bobby's power of torture.

Bobby, who was dressed in a new jacket and a pair
of buff-colored trousers, had previously received strict
injunctions to sit at a side table quietly, and on no
account to join in conversation. For a little while he
carried out these instructions by sitting perfectly
quiet till the last guest had been helped to soup,
whereupon, during a slight lull in the general conversation, Bobby quietly said, —

" I want some soup, mamma."

" You can't be allowed to have any soup, Bobby.
You must not always be asking for things."

" If you don't give me some soup immediately, I'll
tell *yon !*"

The lady seemed a little troubled, and instead of
sending Bobby out of the room, quietly yielded to his
demand. Soup being removed, and fish introduced,
there was a fresh demand.

" Mamma, I want some sea-fish " (a rarity in the
Highlands).

"Bobby," said the mother, "you are very forward.
You can't get any fish. You must sit quietly, and not
trouble us so much."

"Well, mamma, if I don't get some fish, mind I'll tell
you!"

"O Bobby, you're a plague!" and then she gave
him the fish.

A little further on in the dinner, Bobby, observing
his papa and the guests taking wine, was pleased to
break in once more.

"Papa, I would like a glass of wine!"

By this time, as might well be supposed, the attention of the company had been pretty fully drawn to
Bobby, about whom, in all probability, there prevailed
but one opinion. The father was irritated at the
incident.

"Bobby, you must be quiet; you can have no
wine."

"Well, papa, if I don't get some wine, mind — I'll
tell *you.*"

"You rascal, you shall have no wine."

"You had better do it," answered Bobby, firmly.
"Once, twice — will you give me the wine? Come
now, mind I'll tell *you.* Once, twice — "

The father looked canes and lashes at his progeny.
Bobby, however, was not to be daunted.

"Here goes now! Once — twice — will you do it?
Once — twice — thrice! My trousers were made
out of mother's old window curtains!"

Stiff English party dissolves in unconstrainable
merriment.

DR. ROBERT CHAMBERS.

THE LEGEND OF THE ORGAN-BUILDER.

DAY by day the Organ-Builder in his lonely chamber
wrought;
Day by day the soft air trembled to the music of his
thought;

Till at last the work was ended; and no organ voice so
grand
Ever yet had soared responsive to the master's magic hand.

Ay, so rarely was it builded that whenever groom and
bride,
Who in God's sight were well-pleasing, in the church stood
side by side,

Without touch or breath the organ of itself began to play,
And the very airs of heaven through the soft gloom
seemed to stray.

He was young, the Organ-Builder, and o'er all the land
his fame
Ran with fleet and eager footsteps, like a swiftly rushing
flame.

All the maidens heard the story; all the maidens blushed
and smiled,
By his youth and wondrous beauty and his great renown
beguiled.

So he sought and won the fairest, and the wedding-day
was set:
Happy day — the brightest jewel in the glad year's coronet!

But when they the portal entered, he forgot his lovely
bride —
Forgot his love, forgot his God, and his heart swelled
high with pride.

"Ah!" thought he, "how great a master am I! When
    the organ plays,
How the vast cathedral-arches will re-echo with my praise!"

Up the aisle the gay procession moved. The altar shone
    afar,
With its every candle gleaming through soft shadows
    like a star.

But he listened, listened, listened, with no thought of
    love or prayer,
For the swelling notes of triumph from his organ stand-
    ing there.

All was silent. Nothing heard he save the priest's low
    monotone,
And the bride's robe trailing softly o'er the floor of
    fretted stone.

Then his lips grew white with anger. Surely God was
    pleased with him
Who had built the wondrous organ for his temple vast
    and dim!

Whose the fault, then? Hers — the maiden standing
    meekly at his side!
Flamed his jealous rage, maintaining she was false to
    him — his bride.

Vain were all her protestations, vain her innocence and
    truth;
On that very night he left her to her anguish and her ruth,

   .   .   .   .

Far he wandered to a country wherein no man knew his
    name:
For ten weary years he dwelt there, nursing still his
    wrath and shame.

Then his haughty heart grew softer, and he thought by
    night and day
Of the bride he had deserted, till he hardly dared to pray;

Thought of her, a spotless maiden, fair and beautiful and
    good ;
Thought of his relentless anger, that had cursed her
    womanhood ;

Till his yearning grief and penitence at last were all
    complete,
And he longed, with bitter longing, just to fall down at
    her feet.

. . . .

Ah ! how throbbed his heart when, after many a weary
    day and night,
Rose his native towers before him, with the sunset glow
    alight !

Through the gates into the city on he pressed with eager
    tread ;
There he met a long procession — mourners following
    the dead.

"Now why weep ye so, good people ? and whom bury
    ye to-day ?
Why do yonder sorrowing maidens scatter flowers along
    the way ?

"Has some saint gone up to heaven ? " "Yes," they
    answered, weeping sore ;
"For the Organ-Builder's saintly wife our eyes shall see
    no more ;

"And because her days were given to the service of
    God's poor,
From His church we mean to bury her. See ! yonder is
    the door."

No one knew him ; no one wondered when he cried out,
    white with pain ;
No one questioned when, with pallid lips, he poured his
    tears like rain.

"'Tis some one whom she has comforted who mourns
    with us," they said,
As he made his way unchallenged, and bore the coffin's
    head ;

Bore it through the open portal, bore it up the echoing
    aisle,
Let it down before the altar, where the lights burned
    clear the while :

When, O, hark ! the wondrous organ of itself began to
    play
Strains of rare, unearthly sweetness never heard until
    that day !

All the vaulted arches rang with the music sweet and
    clear ;
All the air was filled with glory, as of angels hovering
    near ;

And ere yet the strain was ended, he who bore the
    coffin's head,
With the smile of one forgiven, gently sank beside it—
    dead.

They who raised the body knew him, and they laid him
    by his bride ;
Down the aisle and o'er the threshold they were carried,
    side by side ;

While the organ played a dirge that no man ever heard
    before,
And then softly sank to silence — silence kept for ever-
    more.

Harper's Magazine.

UNDER THE WAGON.

"COME, wife," says good old Farmer-Gray,
 " Put on your things ; 'tis market-day ;
Let's be off to the nearest town —
There and back ere the sun goes down.
Spot! No, we'll leave old Spot behind."
But Spot he barked, and Spot he whined,
And soon made up his doggish mind
 To steal away under the wagon.

Away they went at a good round pace,
And joy came into the farmer's face.
" Poor Spot," said he, " did want to come,
But I'm very glad he's left at home.
He'll guard the barn and guard the cot,
And keep the cattle out of the lot."
" I'm not so sure of that," growled Spot,
 The little dog under the wagon.

The farmer all his produce sold,
And got his pay in yellow gold,
Then started home, just after dark —
Home through the lonely forest. Hark !
A robber springs from behind a tree :
" Your money or else your life !" said he.
The moon was out, yet he didn't see
 The little dog under the wagon.

Old Spot he barked, old Spot he whined,
And Spot he grabbed the thief behind
And dragged him down in mud and dirt.
He tore his coat and tore his shirt ;
He held him with a whisk and bound,
And he couldn't rise from the miry ground ;
While his legs and arms the farmer bound,
 And tumbled him into the wagon.

Old Spot he saved the farmer's life,
The farmer's money, the farmer's wife ;

And now a hero, grand and gay,
A silver collar he wears to-day ;
And everywhere his master goes,
Among his friends, among his foes,
He follows upon his horny toes,
    The little dog under the wagon !

A BOY'S JOURNAL.

THERE is much to be said in favor of keeping a regular account of our doings from day to day. The following is an American boy's attempt in this line : —

March 12. Have resolved to keep a journal.

March 13. Had rost befe for diner, and cabages, and potato, and appel sawse, and rice puding. I do not like rice puding when it is like ours. Charley Slack's kind is rele good. Mush and sirup for tea.

March 19. Forgit what did. John and me saved our pie to take to schule.

March 21. Forgit what did. Gridel cakes for breakfast. Debby didn't fry enuff.

March 24. This is Sunday. Corn befe for diner. Studdied 'my Bible lesson. Aunt Issy said I was gredy. Have resollved not to think so much about things to ete. Wish I was a better boy. Nothing pertikeler for tea.

March 25. Forgit what did.

March 27. Forgit what did.

March 29. Played.

March 31. Forgit what did.

April 1. Have dissided not to keep a journal no more.

THE LAST SERPENT.

AN IRISH LEGEND.

EVERYBODY has heard of St. Patrick, and how he bothered the vermin of Ireland, and drove all manner of venomous things out of the land into the sea.

But there was one old serpent too cunning to be talked out of the country, and to drown himself. The Saint did not know well how to manage this fellow; but at last he bethought him of getting a strong iron chest, with nine bolts to it. So one fine morning the Saint takes a walk to where the serpent used to sleep. Not liking his reverence in the least, the brute began to hiss and show his teeth.

"O," says St. Patrick, "what is the use of making so much ado about a gentleman like myself coming to see you? Here is a nice house that I have got for you to winter in; for I am to civilize the whole country, man and beast."

Hearing such smooth words, the serpent thought no harm meant to himself; so, fair and easy, he comes up to see the saint and his house. But the sight of the nine bolts made him think of making off with himself.

" 'Tis a warm house, you see," says St. Patrick, "and a good friend I am to you."

"I thank you kindly for your civility," says the serpent, turning away, "but it is too small for me."

"Too small!" cried the saint; "you are out there,

19

my boy, anyhow. I stake a gallon of porter that if you only try to get in you will find in it plenty of room."

The serpent was thirsty, and with great joy he set himself to do St. Patrick out of the gallon of porter; so, swelling himself up as big as he could, he got into the chest all but a little bit of his tail.

"There, now," cried he, "I have won the gallon, for I cannot get in my tail."

What does St. Patrick do? Coming behind the great heavy lid, and putting his two hands to it, he slaps it down with a bang like thunder. The rogue of a serpent, when the lid was coming down, whipped in his tail, for fear it might be whipped off; and the Saint at once began to bolt the nine bolts.

"O, murder! let me out! let me out! St. Patrick," cried the serpent; "I have lost the gallon, and I will pay for it like a man."

"Let you out, my darling!" cried the Saint; "to be sure I will, by all manner of means; but I have no time now, so you must wait till to-morrow." Then he pitched the chest into the lake, where it is to this hour; and it is the serpent struggling at the bottom that makes the waves upon it.

Many a living man has heard the serpent crying from under the water, "Is it to-morrow yet? Is it to-morrow yet?" which, to be sure, it never can be; and this is the way that St. Patrick settled the last of the serpents.

T. CROFTON CROKER.

A DOMESTIC SCENE.

CHILD. — Mother, I want a piece of cake.

MOTHER. — I haven't got any; it's all gone.

CHILD. — I know there's some in the cupboard; I saw it when you opened the door.

MOTHER. — Well, you don't need any more. Cake hurts children.

CHILD. — No it don't (*whining*). I do want a piece. Mother, mayn't I have a piece?

MOTHER. — Be still; I can't get up now. I'm busy.

CHILD (*crying aloud*). — I want a piece of cake! I want a piece of cake!

MOTHER. — Be still, I say. I shan't give you a bit if you don't leave off crying.

CHILD (*still crying*). — I want a piece of cake! I want a piece of cake!

MOTHER (*rising hastily, and reaching a piece*).— There, take that; and hold your tongue. Eat it up quick. There's Ben coming. Don't tell him you have had some cake, now.

(BEN *enters.*)

CHILD. — I've had a piece of cake, Ben; you can't have any.

BEN. — Yes, I will. Mother, give me a piece.

MOTHER (*very cross*). — There, take that! It seems as if I never could keep a bit of anything in the house. You'll see, sir, if I give you any another time.

(*Another room.*)

CHILD. — I've had a piece of cake.

YOUNGER SISTER. — O, I want some, too.

CHILD. — Well, you *bawl*, and mother'll give you a bit. I did.

THE SWEETS OF LIBERTY.

A GENEROUS tar, who long had been
   In foreign prison pent,
Released at length, returned again
   Brimful of merriment. .

A man who had some birds to sell
   Was just then passing by ;
Jack glanced at the poor fluttering things
   With sorrowing, pitying eye.

He paused amid the gaping throng,
   Before the seller's stall :
" Now hark ye, friend, just name your price
   For birds and cage and all."

The price was named, the sum was paid,
   The sailor seized the prize ;
And quickly from the opened door
   A young canary flies.

" Stop ! " cried the bird-seller, amazed,
   " They're all escaping fast."
" That's right," said Jack, and held the door
   Till all were gone at last.

" Had you," said Jack, " been doomed, like me,
   In prison long to lie,
You'd better understand, my friend,
   The sweets of liberty."

A LETTER OF BLUNDERS.

PERHAPS the best collection of blunders, such as occur in all nations, but which, of course, are fathered upon Paddy wholesale, as if by common consent, is the following: —

Copy of a Letter written during the Rebellion by an Irish Member of Parliament, to his friend in London.

My dear Sir: Having now a little peace and quietness, I sit down to inform you of the dreadful bustle and confusion we are in from these bloodthirsty rebels, most of whom are, I am glad to say, killed and dispersed. We are in a pretty mess, can get nothing to eat, nor wine to drink, except whiskey, and when we sit down to dinner we are obliged to keep both hands armed. Whilst I write this, I hold a sword in each hand and a pistol in the other. I concluded from the beginning that this would be the end of it, and I see I was right, for it is not half over yet. At present there are such goings on that everything is at a standstill.

I should have answered your letter a fortnight ago, but I did not receive it till this morning. Indeed, scarcely a mail arrives safe without being robbed. No longer ago than yesterday the coach with the mails from Dublin was robbed near this town; the bags had been judiciously left behind for fear of accident, and by good luck there was nobody in it but two outside passengers, who had nothing for the thieves to take.

Last Thursday notice was given that a gang of rebels was advancing here under the French standard, but they had no colors , nor any drums except bagpipes. Immediately every man in the place, including women and children, ran out to meet them. We soon found our force much too little ; we were far too near to think of retreating. Death was in every face, but to it we went, and by the time half our little party were killed, we began to be all alive again. Fortunately the rebels had no guns, except pistols, cutlasses, and pikes, and as we had plenty of muskets and ammunition, we put them all to the sword. Not a soul of them escaped, except some that were drowned in an adjacent bog, and, in a very short time, nothing was to be heard but silence. Their uniforms were all different colors, but mostly green. After the action we went to rummage a sort of camp, which they had left behind them. All we found was a few pikes without heads, a parcel of empty bottles full of water, and a bundle of French commissions filled up with Irish names. Troops are now stationed all round the country, which exactly squares with my ideas.

I have only time to add that I am in great haste.

Yours truly,

————

P. S. If you do not receive this, of course it must have miscarried, therefore I beg you will write to let me know.

"ON THE RAMPARTS BARE, STOOD THE LADY FAIR."

ON the ramparts bare, stood the lady fair,
  And the cold winds around her blew.
She called to the warder to take good care,
  And the warder was bold and true.

"O warder! guard the watch-lights well —
  Not a star 's to be seen to-night,
But the breezes swell, and the signals tell
  That the fleet of my lord is in sight."

"O lady dear! The fire burns clear,
  And the drawbridge is ready to fall,
And the yeomen stand by the road on the sand
  To guard thy lord to his hall."

"Methinks I hear the battle rage
  And the fugitives fly o'er the strand."
"'Tis only a page who brings this gage
  That the fleet of thy lord is at hand."

"And dost thou tell that my lord is well?
  Doth conquest crown his toil?"
"On victory's wings he met the sea-kings,
  And fought with the lord of the Isle."

"Let the castle-gate be opened straight,
  And the blazing torches light;
And haste, Montjoie, and wake my boy! —
  He shall see his dear father to-night.

"And dost thou weep, when awaked from sleep,
  On the night of such festal glee;
Thou didst oft inquire if thou hadst a sire,
  And a noble sire thou shalt see.

" So straight and so tall he stands in the hall,
    The chief of a thousand for grace,
Though the deeds he hath done and the battles he
            hath won
    Have marred and scarred his face.

" Betray no fear when the trumpets cheer,
    For a soldier's boy thou art ;
Thy blood must not quail at the cold iron mail
    When pressed to a hero's heart.

" Thou wast but a babe when he went to fight ;
    Thou art now a sprightly boy ;
Thy father will clasp thee with fond delight,
    And thy mother will weep for joy.

" When weak and pale with many an ail
    I held thee in my arms ;
While others slept I prayed and wept,
    And gazed on thy faded charms.

" ' Sir Arthur's race will be lost,' I said,
    ' His honors a stranger shall seize ;
The father will die in victory's bed,
    And the boy will die of disease.'

" But rosy and sleek is thy youthful cheek,
    And thy sire is crowned with success ;
And unborn swains who till these plains
    The line of Sir Arthur shall bless.

" Through the dubious gloom I see his plume,
    And his well-known voice I hear ; —
From the battle's strife to thy son and wife,
    Now welcome my lord most dear."

COUNT CANDESPINA'S STANDARD.

"The King of Aragon now entered Castile, by way of Soria and Osma, with a powerful army; and, having been met by the queen's forces, both parties encamped near Sepulveda, and prepared to give battle.

"This engagement, called, from the field where it took place, (de la Espina,) is one of the most famous of that age. The dastardly Count of Lara fled at the first shock, and joined the queen at Burgos, where she was anxiously awaiting the issue; but the brave Count of Candespina (Gomez Gonzalez) stood his ground to the last, and died on the field of battle. His standard-bearer, a gentleman of the house of Olea, after having his horse killed under him, and both hands cut off by sabre-strokes, fell beside his master, still clasping the standard in his arms, and repeating his war-cry of 'Olea!'"—ANNALS OF THE QUEENS OF SPAIN.

SCARCE were the splintered lances dropped,
    Scarce were the swords drawn out,
Ere recreant Lara, sick with fear,
    Had wheeled his steed about:

His courser reared, and plunged, and neighed,
    Loathing the fight to yield;
But the coward spurred him to the bone,
    And drove him from the field.

Gonzalez in his stirrups rose:
    "Turn, turn, thou traitor knight!
Thou bold tongue in a lady's bower,
    Thou dastard in a fight!"

But vainly valiant Gomez cried
    Across the waning fray:
Pale Lara and his craven band
    To Burgos scoured away.

"Now, by the God above me, sirs,
    Better we all were dead,
Than a single knight among ye all
    Should ride where Lara led!

"Yet ye who fear to follow me,
   As yon traitor turn and fly;
For I lead ye not to win a field:
   I lead ye forth to die.   .

"Olea, plant my standard here—
   Here on this little mound;
Here raise the war-cry of thy house,
   Make this our rallying ground.

"Forget not, as thou hop'st for grace,
   The last care I shall have
Will be to hear thy battle-cry,
   And see that standard wave."

Down on the ranks of Aragon
   The bold Gonzalez drove,
And Olea raised his battle-cry,
   And waved the flag above.

Slowly Gonzalez' little band
   Gave ground before the foe;
But not an inch of the field was won
   Without a deadly blow;

And not an inch of the field was won
   That did not draw a tear
From the widowed wives of Aragon,
   That fatal news to hear.

Backward and backward Gomez fought,
   And high o'er the clashing steel,
Plainer and plainer rose the cry,
   "Olea for Castile!"

Backward fought Gomez, step by step,
   Till the cry was close at hand,
Till his dauntless standard shadowed him;
   And there he made his stand.

Mace, sword, and axe rang on his mail,
    Yet he moved not where he stood,   -
Though each gaping joint of armor ran
    A stream of purple blood.

As, pierced with countless wounds, he fell,
    The standard caught his eye,
And he smiled, like an infant hushed asleep,
    To hear the battle-cry.

Now one by one the wearied knights
    Have fallen, or basely flown ;
And on the mound where his post was fixed
    Olea stood alone.

" Yield up thy banner, gallant knight !
    Thy lord lies on the plain ;
Thy duty has been nobly done,
    I would not see thee slain."

"Spare pity, King of Aragon !
    I would not hear thee lie :
My lord is looking down from heaven
    To see his standard fly."

" Yield, madman, yield ! thy horse is down,
    Thou hast nor lance nor shield ;
Fly ! I will grant thee time."   " This flag
    Can neither fly nor yield ! "

They girt the standard round about,
    A wall of flashing steel ;
But still they heard the battle-cry,
    " Olea for Castile ! "

And there, against all Aragon,
    Full-armed with lance and brand,
Olea fought until the sword
    Snapped in his sturdy hand.

Among the foe, with that high scorn
　　Which laughs at earthly fears,
He hurled the broken hilt, and drew
　　His dagger on the spears.

They hewed the hauberk from his breast,
　　The helmet from his head;
They hewed the hands from off his limbs;
　　From every vein he bled.

Clasping the standard to his heart,
　　He raised one dying peal,
That rang as if a trumpet blew, —
　　" Olea for Castile ! "

GEO. H. BOKER.

A CLEVER TRICK.

A YOUNG man, of eighteen or twenty, a student in
the university, took a walk one day with a professor, who was commonly called the student's friend,
such was his kindness to the young men whom it was
his office to instruct.

While they were walking together, and the professor was seeking to lead the conversation to grave
subjects, they saw a pair of old shoes lying in the
path, which they supposed belonged to a poor man
who was at work in the field close by, and who had
nearly finished his day's work.

The young student turned to the professor, saying,
" Let us play the man a trick. We will hide his shoes,
and conceal ourselves behind those bushes, and watch
to see his perplexity when he cannot find them."

"My dear friend," answered the professor, "we must never amuse ourselves at the expense of the poor. But you are rich, and you may give yourself a much greater pleasure by means of this poor man. Put a dollar in each shoe, and then we will hide ourselves."

The student did so, and then placed himself with the professor, behind the bushes hard by, through which they could easily watch the laborer, and see whatever wonder or joy he might express.

The poor man soon finished his work, and came across the field to the path, where he had left his coat and shoes. While he put on the coat, he slipped one foot into one of his shoes; but feeling something hard, he stooped down, and found the dollar. Astonishment and wonder were seen upon his countenance; he gazed upon the dollar, turned it round, and looked again and again; then he looked around on all sides but could see no one. Now he put the money into his pocket, and proceeded to put on the other shoe; but how great was his astonishment when he found the other dollar! His feelings overcame him: he fell upon his knees, looked up to heaven, and uttered aloud a fervent thanksgiving, in which he spoke of his wife, sick and helpless, and his children without bread, whom this timely bounty from some unknown hand would save from perishing.

The young man stood there deeply affected, and tears filled his eyes.

KATIE LEE AND WILLIE GRAY.

TWO brown heads with tossing curls,
　Red lips shutting over pearls,
Bare feet, white, and wet with dew,
Two eyes black, and two eyes blue —
Little boy and girl are they,
Katie Lee and Willie Gray.

They were standing where a brook,
Bending like a shepherd's crook,
Flashed its silver, and thick ranks
Of willow fringed its banks,
Half in thought and half in play,
Katie Lee and Willie Gray.

They had cheeks like cherries red ;
He was taller 'most a head ;
She, with arms like wreaths of snow,
Swung a basket to and fro
(As they loitered, half in play),
Chattering to Willie Gray.

" Pretty Katie," Willie said, —
And there came a dash of red
Through the brownness of the cheek, —
" Boys are strong, and girls are weak,
And I'll carry, so I will,
Katie's basket up the hill."

Katie answered, with a laugh, —
" You shall only carry half ; "
Then said, tossing back her curls,
" Boys are weak as well as girls."
Do you think that Katie guessed
Half the wisdom she expressed ?

Men are only boys grown tall ;
Hearts don't change much, after all ;
And when, long years from that day,
Katie Lee and Willie Gray
Stood again beside the brook
Bending like a shepherd's crook, —

Is it strange that Willie said,
While again a dash of red
Crowned the brownness of his cheek,
" I am strong and you are weak ;
Life is but a slippery steep,
Hung with shadows cold and deep.

" Will you trust me, Katie dear —
Walk beside me without fear ?
May I carry, if I will,
All your burdens up the hill ? "
And she answered, with a laugh,
" No, but you may carry half."

Close beside the little brook,
Bending like a shepherd's crook,
Working with its silver hands
Late and early at the sands,
Stands a cottage, where to-day
Katie lives with Willie Gray.

In the porch she sits, and, lo !
Swings a basket to and fro,
Vastly different from the one
That she swung in years agone :
This is long, and deep, and wide,
And has — rockers at the side.

THE SAILOR'S CONSOLATION.

ONE night came on a hurricane,
  The sea was mountains rolling,
When Barney Buntline slued his quid,
  And said to Billy Bowline,
" A strong nor'-wester 's blowing, Bill ;
  Hark ! don't ye hear it roar now ?
Lord help 'em, how I pities them
  Unhappy folks on shore now !

" Foolhardy chaps as live in towns,
  What danger they are all in,
And now lie quaking in their beds
  For fear the roof should fall in ;
Poor creaturs ! how they envies us,
  And wishes — I've a notion —
For our good luck in such a storm,
  To be upon the ocean !

" And as for them that's out all day
  On business from their houses,
And late at night returning home,
  To cheer their babes and spouses ;
While you and I, Bill, on the deck
  Are comfortably lying,
My eyes ! what tiles and chimney-pots
  About their heads are flying !

" Both you and I have ofttimes heard
  How men are killed and undone,
By overturns from carriages,
  By thieves, and fires in London.
We know what risks these landsmen run,
  From noblemen to tailors :
Then, Bill, let us thank Providence
  That you and I are sailors."

                                    WILLIAM PITT.

THE LANGUAGE OF SIGNS, OR TWO SIDES TO A STORY.

KING James the Sixth, on removing to London, was waited upon by the Spanish ambassador, a man of learning, but who had an odd notion in his head that every country should have a professor of signs, to enable men of all languages to communicate with each other without the aid of speech.

One day he lamented before the king that such people were not to be met with in all Europe. King James t en said, " Why, I have a professor of signs in the most remote college in my dominions; it is at Aberdeen, a great way off — perhaps six hundred miles from here."

" Were it ten thousand leagues off, I shall see him," said the ambassador, and expressed his determination to set out instanter, in order to have an interview with the Scottish professor of signs.

The king, perceiving he had committed himself, caused an intimation to be written to the University of Aberdeen, stating the case, and desiring the professors to put him off, or make the best of him they could.

The ambassador arrived, and was received with great solemnity. He immediately inquired which of them had the honor to be " Professor of Signs ; " but was told that the professor was absent in the Highlands, and would return nobody could say when.

" I will," said he, " wait his return, though it were not for twelve months."

20

The professors, seeing this would not do, contrived the following stratagem. There was one Geordie, a butcher, blind of an eye, a droll fellow, with much wit and roguery about him. The butcher was told the story, and instructed how to comport himself in his new situation of "Professor of Signs." And he was enjoined on no account to utter a syllable. Geordie willingly undertook the office for a small bribe. The ambassador was then told to his infinite delight that the professor of signs was expected to arrive the next day.

The next day came. Geordie, gowned and wigged, was placed in state in a room of the college. The Spaniard was then shown in, and left to converse with him as best he could, all of the professors waiting the issue with considerable anxiety.

An amusing scene commenced. The ambassador held up one of his fingers to Geordie; Geordie answered by holding up two of his. The ambassador held up three; Geordie clinched his fist and looked stern. The ambassador then took an orange from his pocket, and showed it to Geordie, who, in return, pulled out a piece of barley-bread from his pocket, and exhibited it in a similar manner. The ambassador then bowed to him and retired.

When the ambassador entered the room in which the professors were, they gathered about him and inquired his opinion of their learned brother.

"He is a perfect miracle!" said the ambassador. "I would not give him for the wealth of the Indies."

"Well!" exclaimed one of the professors, "how has he edified you?"

"Why," said the ambassador, "I first held up

one finger, denoting that there is one God; he
held up two, signifying that there are Father and
Son; I held up three, meaning the Father, Son, and
Holy Ghost; he clinched his hand to say that these
three are one. I then took out an orange, signifying
the goodness of God, who gives his creatures not only
the necessaries, but the luxuries of life, upon which
the wonderful man presented a piece of bread, showing that it was the staff of life, and preferable to every
luxury."

The professors were glad that matters had turned
out so well; and having got quit of the ambassador,
who set out again for London that night, they called
in Geordie to hear his version.

"Well, Geordie, how have you come on, and what
do you think of the man?"

"The scoundrel!" exclaimed the butcher, "what
did he do first, think ye? He held up one finger, as
much as to say you have only one eye! Then I held
up two, meaning that my one was as good as his two.
Then the fellow held up three of his fingers, to say
there were but three eyes between us: and then I
was so mad at him that I shut my fist and was going
to strike him, and would have done it too, but for your
sakes. He didn't stop there, but, forsooth, he took out
an orange, as much as to say, your poor beggarly country can't grow that! I showed him a piece of a barley
bannock, meaning that I didn't care a farthing for him
or his trash either, so long as I had that. But by all
that's good," continued Geordie, "I'm angry yet that
I didn't break every bone in his body."

Could two sides of a story be more opposed to one
another?

THE RAVEN.

ONCE upon a midnight dreary, while I pondered, weak
    and weary,
Over many a quaint and curious volume of forgotten lore ;
While I nodded, nearly napping, suddenly there came a
    tapping,
As of some one gently rapping, rapping at my chamber
    door.
" 'Tis some visitor," I muttered, " tapping at my cham-
    ber door —
        Only this, and nothing more."

Ah, distinctly I remember, it was in the bleak December,
And each separate dying ember wrought its ghost upon
    the floor.
Eagerly I wished the morrow : vainly I had sought to
    borrow
From my books surcease of sorrow — sorrow for the lost
    Lenore —
For the rare and radiant maiden whom the angels name
    Lenore —
        Nameless here for evermore.

And the silken, sad, uncertain rustling of each purple
    curtain,
Thrilled me — filled me with fantastic terrors never felt
    before ;
So that now, to still the beating of my heart, I stood re-
    peating,
" 'Tis some visitor entreating entrance at my chamber
    door —
Some late visitor entreating entrance at my chamber
    door ;
        This it is, and nothing more."

Presently my soul grew stronger : hesitating then no
    longer,
" Sir," said I, " or Madam, truly your forgiveness I im-
    plore ;
But the fact is, I was napping, and so gently you came
    rapping,
And so faintly you came tapping, tapping at my chamber
    door,
That I scarce was sure I heard you " — Here I opened
    wide the door :
        Darkness there, and nothing more.

Deep into that darkness peering, long I stood there, won-
    dering, fearing,
Doubting, dreaming dreams no mortal ever dared to dream
    before ;
But the silence was unbroken, and the darkness gave no
    token,
And the only word there spoken was the whispered word
    " Lenore ! "
This *I* whispered, and an echo murmured back the word
    " LENORE ! "
        Merely this, and nothing more.

Back into the chamber turning, all my soul within me
    burning,
Soon again I heard a tapping, something louder than
    before.
" Surely," said I, " surely that is something at my win-
    dow-lattice ;
Let me see then what thereat is, and this mystery ex-
    plore —
Let my heart be still a moment, and this mystery ex-
    plore ; —
        'Tis the wind, and nothing more."

Open then I flung the shutter, when, with many a flirt and
    flutter,
In there stepped a stately raven of the saintly days of
    yore.

Not the least obeisance made he ; not an instant stopped
    or stayed he ;
But, with mien of lord or lady, perched above my cham-
    ber door —
Perched upon a bust of Pallas, just above my chamber
    door —
        Perched, and sat, and nothing more.

Then this ebony bird beguiling my sad fancy into smiling,
By the grave and stern decorum of the countenance it
    wore, —
" Though thy crest be shorn and shaven, thou," I said,
    " art sure no craven ;
Ghastly, grim, and ancient raven, wandering from the
    nightly shore,
Tell me what thy lordly name is on the Night's Plutonian
    shore ? "
        Quoth the raven, " Nevermore ! "

Much I marvelled this ungainly fowl to hear discourse so
    plainly,
Though its answer, little meaning — little relevancy bore ;
For we cannot help agreeing that no living human being
Ever yet was blessed with seeing bird above his chamber
    door —
Bird or beast upon the sculptured bust above his chamber
    door —
        With such name as " Nevermore."

But the raven sitting lonely on the placid bust, spoke only
That one word, as if his soul in that one word he did
    outpour.
Nothing further then he uttered — not a feather then he
    fluttered —
Till I scarcely more than muttered, " Other friends have
    flown before —
On the morrow *he* will leave me, as my hopes have flown
    before."
        Then the bird said, " Nevermore ! "

Startled at the stillness, broken by reply so aptly spoken,
"Doubtless," said I, "what it utters is its only stock
    and store,
Caught from some unhappy master, whom unmerciful
    disaster
Followed fast and followed faster, till his song one burden
    bore —
Till the dirges of his hope that melancholy burden bore,
        Of ' Never — nevermore ! ' "

But the raven still beguiling all my sad soul into smiling,
Straight I wheeled a cushioned seat in front of bird, and
    bust, and door,
Then, upon the velvet sinking, I betook myself to linking
Fancy unto fancy, thinking what this ominous bird of
    yore —
What this grim, ungainly, ghastly, gaunt, and ominous
    bird of yore
        Meant in croaking " Nevermore ! "

Thus I sat engaged in guessing, but no syllable expressing
To the fowl, whose fiery eyes now burned into my
    bosom's core ;
This and more I sat divining, with my head at ease re-
    clining
On the cushion's velvet lining that the lamp-light gloated
    o'er,
But whose velvet violet lining, with the lamp-light gloat-
    ing o'er,
        She shall press — ah ! nevermore !

Then methought the air grew denser, perfumed from an
    unseen censer
Swung by seraphim, whose foot-falls tinkled on the tufted
    floor.
" Wretch ! " I cried, " thy God hath lent thee — by these
    angels he hath sent thee
Respite — respite and nepenthe from thy memories of
    Lenore !

Quaff, O quaff this kind nepenthe, and forget this lost
    Lenore !"
        Quoth the raven, " Nevermore ! "

" Prophet ! " said I, " thing of evil ! — prophet still, if
    bird or devil !
Whether tempter sent, or whether tempest tossed thee
    here ashore,
Desolate, yet all undaunted, on this desert land enchant-
    ed —
On this home by Horror haunted — tell me truly, I im-
    plore —
Is there — is there balm in Gilead ? — tell me — tell me,
    I implore ! "
        Quoth the raven, " Nevermore ! "

" Prophet ! " said I, " thing of evil ! — prophet still, if
    bird or devil !
By that heaven that bends above us — by that God we
    both adore,
Tell this soul with sorrow laden, if, within the distant
    Aidenn,
It shall clasp a sainted maiden, whom the angels name
    Lenore ;
Clasp a fair and radiant maiden, whom the angels name
    Lenore ! "
        Quoth the raven, " Nevermore ! "

" Be that word our sign of parting, bird or fiend ! " I
    shrieked, upstarting —
" Get thee back into the tempest and the Night's Plu-
    tonian shore !
Leave no black plume as a token of that lie thy soul hath
    spoken !
Leave my loneliness unbroken ! — quit the bust above my
    door !
Take thy beak from out my heart, and take thy form from
    off my door ! "
        Quoth the raven, " Nevermore ! "

And the raven, never flitting, still is sitting, still is sitting
On the pallid bust of Pallas, just above my chamber door;
And his eyes have all the seeming of a demon that is
    dreaming,
And the lamp-light o'er him streaming throws his shadow
    on the floor;
And my soul from out that shadow that lies floating on
    the floor
        Shall be lifted — NEVERMORE !
                        EDGAR A. POE.

AN EVENING WITH HELEN'S BABIES.

WITH a head full of pleasing fancies, I went down
to supper. My new friends, Helen's babies, were
unusually good. There were two of them. Budge,
the elder, was five years of age, and Toddie had seen
but three summers. Their ride seemed to have toned
down their boisterousness and elevated their little
souls; their appetites exhibited no diminution of force;
but they talked but little, and all that they said was
smart, funny, or startling — so much so that when,
after supper, they invited me to put them to bed, I
gladly accepted the invitation. Toddie disappeared
somewhere, and came back very disconsolate.

"Can't find my dolly's k'adle," he whined.

"Never mind, old pet," said I, soothingly. "Uncle
will ride you on his foot."

"But I *want* my dolly's k'adle," said he, piteously
rolling out his lower lip.

I remembered my experience when Toddie wanted
to "shee wheels go wound," and I trembled.

"Toddie," said I, in a tone so persuasive that it
would be worth thousands a year to me, as a salesman, if I could only command it at will: "Toddie,
don't you want to ride on uncle's back?"

"No; want my dolly's k'adle."

"Don't you want me to tell you a story?"

For a moment Toddie's face indicated a terrible internal conflict between old Adam and mother Eve, but curiosity finally overpowered natural depravity, and Toddie murmured, —

"Yesh."

"What shall I tell you about?"

"'Bout Nawndeark."

"About *what?*"

"He means Noah an' the ark," exclaimed Budge.

"Datsh what *I* shay — Nawndeark," declared Toddie.

"Well," said I, hastily refreshing my memory by picking up the Bible, — for Helen, like most people, is pretty sure to forget to pack her Bible when she runs away from home for a few days, — "well, once it rained forty days and nights, and everybody was drowned from the face of the earth excepting Noah, a righteous man, who was saved with all his family, in an ark which the Lord commanded him to build."

"Uncle Harry," said Budge, after contemplating me with open eyes and mouth for at least two minutes after I had finished, "do you think that's Noah?"

"Certainly, Budge; here's the whole story in the Bible."

"Well, *I* don't think it's Noah one single bit," said he, with increasing emphasis.

"I'm beginning to think we read different Bibles, Budge; but let's hear *your* version."

"Huh?"

"Tell *me* about Noah, if you know so much about him."

"I will, if you want me to. Once the Lord felt so

uncomfortable cos folks was bad that he was sorry he
ever made anybody, or any world, or anything. But
Noah wasn't bad ; the Lord liked him first-rate ; so he
told Noah to build a big ark, and then the Lord would
make it rain so everybody should be drownded but
Noah an' his little boys an' girls, an' doggies an' pus-
sies, an' mamma-cows, an' little-boy-cows an' little-girl-
cows, an' hosses, an' everything; they'd go in the
ark, an' wouldn't get wetted a bit when it rained.
An' Noah took lots of things to eat in the ark ; cook-
ies, an' milk, an' oatmeal, an' strawberries, an' porgies,
an' — O, yes — an' plum-puddins, an' pumpkin-pies.
But Noah didn't want everybody to get drownded, so
he talked to folks, an' said, 'It's goin' to rain *awful*
pretty soon; you'd better be good, an' then the Lord'll
let you come into my ark.' An' they jus' said, ' O, if
it rains we'll go in the house till it stops ;' an' other
folks said, ' *We* ain't afraid of rain ; we've got an um-
brella.' An' some more said, they wasn't goin' to be
afraid of just a rain. But it *did* rain though, an' folks
went in their houses, an' the water came in, an' they
went upstairs, an' the water came up there, an' they
got on the tops of the houses, an' up in big trees, an'
up in mountains, an' the water went after 'em everywhere an' drownded everybody, only just except
Noah and the people in the ark. An' it rained forty
days an' nights, an' then it stopped ; an' Noah got out
of the ark, an' he and his little boys an' girls went
wherever they wanted to, and everything in the
world was all theirs ; there wasn't anybody to tell 'em
to go home, nor no Kindergarten schools to go to,
nor no bad boys to fight 'em, nor nothin'. Now tell
us 'nother story."

                                              J. HABBERTON.

"HAS NOT SINCE BEEN HEARD OF."

BLOW, blustering wind ! thy loud alarms,
    They have no terrors for me ;
Thy gales will waft to my longing arms
    My darling over the sea.
Bluster thy might, thou lusty wight,
    I've never a thought for thee !

When first we parted, my darling and I,
    The gentlest breeze I cursed,
And gazed in fear on a stormy sky
    As I witnessed the tempest burst,
And the breakers roar on the dread lee shore,
    Of a bark by the billows tossed.

But now I welcome the wind that brings
    My love ever nearer home ;
Though sea-birds strive, with quivering wings,
    To battle the rising foam.
But blow, O gale ! and fill the sail ;
    No more shall my darling roam !

The sea is speaking ! The distant main
    Is scanned by an anxious crowd ;
And with a terrible shuddering pain
    Many a head is bowed !
But what care I — my darling nigh —
    For fisher-folks' weary load ?

The sea is silent ! A strange, sad tale
    Is writ on the pebbly strand !
Why do the storm-worn faces pale,
    While some of the fisher band
In sympathy point silently —
    There's drift on the " Shivering Sand!"

Speak out, man, speak ! what dost thou say,
  " Gone down ! — all hands ! " — all gone ?
Not one permitted to see the day,
  Never a glimpse of the sun !
The ship ! — her name ? No, not the same,
  It *cannot* have been that one !

O sea ! what terrible deed is thine !
  My love hast thou cast away ?
Lies he deep in yon treacherous brine,
  A toy for thy monstrous play ?
No tidings yet ? From rise till set,
  Wearily drags the day !

THE DISCONTENTED BUTTERCUP.

DOWN in a field, one day in June,
  The flowers all bloomed together,
Save one, who tried to hide herself,
  And drooped, that pleasant weather.

A robin who had soared too high,
  And felt a little lazy,
Was resting near a buttercup
  Who wished she were a daisy.

For daisies grow so trig and tall ;
  She always had a passion
For wearing frills about her neck
  In just the daisies' fashion.

And buttercups must always be
  The same old tiresome color,
While daisies dress in gold and white,
  Although their gold is duller.

" Dear robin," said this sad young flower,
  " Perhaps you'd not mind trying
To find a nice white frill for me,
  Some day, when you are flying ? "

"You silly thing!" the robin said;
  "I think you must be crazy!
I'd rather be my honest self
  Than any made-up daisy.

"You're nicer in your own bright gown;
  The little children love you;
Be the best buttercup you can,
  And think no flower above you.

"Though swallows leave me out of sight,
  We'd better keep our places;
Perhaps the world would all go wrong
  With one too many daisies.

"Look bravely up into the sky,
  And be content with knowing
That God wished for a buttercup,
  Just here where you are growing."

SARAH O. JEWETT.

A WEDDING-MARCH ON TRIAL.

DAY with dewy eve was blending,
  Clouds lay piled in radiant state,
When a fine young German farmer
  Rode up to the parson's gate.

Clinging to him on a pillion
  Was a maiden fair and tall,
Blushing, trembling, palpitating,
  Smiling brightly through it all.

Said the farmer, "Goot Herr Pastor,
  Marguerite and I vas coome
Diesen evening to be married,
  Dhen mit her I make mine home."

Soon the nuptial tie was fastened,
  Soon the kiss received and given.

In that moment earth had vanished ;
  They had caught a glimpse of heaven.

But the prudent German farmer
  First recalled his tranced wits —
Said, "Herr Pastor, here's von shilling,
  Choost at present ve vas quits.

"But dake notice, if I finds her
  Marguerite, mine fraw, mine queen,
Ven der year vas gone, is petter
  As goot, vy dhen I coomes again."

Twelve months sped with wildering fleetness
  Down Time's pathway past recall,
Then there came a barrel rolling
  Thundering through the parson's hall ;

With this note : "I send, Herr Pastor,
  Mit ein parrel of pesten flour
Dhem five dollars; for mine Marguerite
  More petter as goot is every hour.

"Dot schmall leetle paby is ein darling ;
  If dhey shtay so goot, vy dhen,
Vhen dot year vas gone, Herr Pastor,
  Quick, booty soon, you hear again."

On the wedding-march went singing
  Sweeter, tenderer than before ;
At the year's end it came drumming
  Gayly at the parson's door ;

With this note : "Here is five dollars
  Und ein parrel of pesten flour ;
Marguerite und dot dear paby
  More petter as goot is — more and more

"Now dot funny leetle paby
  Sucks de ink vots in mine pen,
Makes me laugh — I dink, Herr Pastor,
  Next year I vill come again."

Down the years the pair went marching
  Hand in hand from dawn to dawn,
Bearing each the other's crosses,
  Wearing each the other's crown.

And from year to year came rolling
  Straight into the parson's door,
That "ein parrel of pesten flour,"
  Always with five dollars more.

They have passed their golden wedding,
  Children's children in their train;
Sweeter grows the wedding music,
  Gentler, tenderer the strain.

Fainter now, and like an echo
  From the bright, the better land,
Restfully they wait and listen
  Full of peace, for heaven's at hand!

Moral : O ye men and brethren
  Who to marry have a mind,
Pay the parson as with trial
  Bliss or misery you find.

———◦◦——

GRANDMOTHER GRAY.

FADED and fair, in her old arm-chair,
  Sunset gilding her thin, white hair,
Silently knitting, sits Grandmother Gray;
While I on my elbows beside her lean,
And tell what wonderful things I mean
To have, and to do, if I can, some day.
You can talk so to Grandmother Gray;
She doesn't laugh, nor send you away.

I see, as I look from the window-seat,
A house there yonder across the street,

With a fine French roof and a frescoed hall ;
The deep bay-windows are full of flowers ;
They've a clock of bronze that chimes the hours,
And a fountain — I hear it tinkle and fall
When the doors are open. "I mean," I say,
"To live in a house like that, some day."
"Money will buy it," says Grandmother Gray.

"There's a low barouche, all green and gold,
    And a pair of horses as black as jet,
I've seen drive by — and before I'm old
    A turnout like that I hope to get.
How they prance and shine in their harness gay!
What fun 'twould be if they ran away !"
"Money will buy them," says Grandmother Gray.

"To-morrow, I know, a great ship sails
    Out of port, and across the sea ;
O, to feel in *my* face the ocean gales,
    And the salt waves dancing under me !
In the old, far lands of legend and lay
I long to roam — and I shall, some day."
"Money will do it," says Grandmother Gray.

"And when, like me, you are old," says she,
    "And getting and going are done with, dear,
What then, do you think, will the one thing be
    You will wish and need, to content you here ?"
"O, when in my chair I have to stay,
Love, you see, will content me," I say.
"That, money *won't* buy," says Grandmother Gray.

"And, sure enough, if there's nothing worth
    All your care, when the years are past,
But love in heaven, and love on earth,
    Why not begin where you'll end at last?
Begin to lay up treasure to-day,
Treasure that nothing can take away.
Bless the Lord !" says Grandmother Gray.

MARY KEELEY BOUTELLE, IN "WIDE AWAKE."

THE SAILOR-BOY'S DREAM.

IN slumbers of midnight the sailor-boy lay;
   His hammock swung loose at the sport of the wind;
But, watch-worn and weary, his cares flew away,
   And visions of happiness danced o'er his mind.

He dreamed of his home, of his dear native bowers,
   And pleasures that waited on life's merry morn;
While Memory each scene gaily covered with flowers,
   And restored every rose, but secreted its thorn.

Then Fancy her magical pinions spread wide,
   And bade the young dreamer in ecstasy rise:
Now far, far behind him the green waters glide,
   And the cot of his forefathers blesses his eyes.

The jessamine clambers in flowers o'er the thatch,
   And the swallow chirps sweet from her nest in the wall;
All trembling with transport, he raises the latch,
   And the voices of loved ones reply to his call.

A father bends o'er him with looks of delight;
   His cheek is impearled with a mother's warm tear;
And the lips of the boy in a love-kiss unite
   With the lips of the sister his bosom holds dear.

The heart of the sleeper beats high in his breast;
   Joy quickens his pulse; all his hardships seem o'er;
And a murmur of happiness steals through his rest:
   "O God, thou hast blessed me; I ask for no more."

Ah! whence is that flame which now glares on his eye?
   Ah! what is that sound which now bursts on his ear?
'Tis the lightning's red glare, painting hell on the sky!
   'Tis the crashing of thunders, the groan of the sphere!

He springs from his hammock, he flies to the deck;
   Amazement confronts him with images dire;
Wild winds and mad waves drive the vessel a wreck;
   The masts fly in splinters, the shrouds are on fire.

Like mountains the billows tremendously swell;
   In vain the lost wretch calls on mercy to save;
Unseen hands of spirits are ringing his knell,
   And the death-angel flaps his broad wing o'er the wave.

O sailor-boy, woe to thy dream of delight!
   In darkness dissolves the gay frost-work of bliss;
Where now is the picture that Fancy touched bright,
   Thy parents' fond pressure, and love's honeyed kiss?

O sailor-boy, sailor-boy, never again
   Shall home, love, or kindred thy wishes repay;
Unblessed and unhonored, down deep in the main,
   Full many a fathom thy frame shall decay.

No tomb shall e'er plead to remembrance for thee,
   Or redeem thy lost form from the merciless surge;
But the white foam of waves shall thy winding-sheet be,
   And winds, in the midnight of winter, thy dirge.

On a bed of green sea-flowers thy limbs shall be laid;
   Around thy white bones the red coral shall grow;
Of thy fair, yellow locks threads of amber be made,
   And every part suit to thy mansion below.

Days, months, years, and ages shall circle away,
   And still the vast waters above thee shall roll;
Earth loses thy pattern for ever and aye:
   O sailor-boy, sailor-boy, peace to thy soul!

DIMOND

NANCY BLYNN'S LOVERS.

WILLIAM TANSLEY, familiarly called Tip, having finished his afternoon's work in Judge Boxton's garden, milked the cows, and given the calves and pigs their supper, — not forgetting to make sure of his own, — stole out of the house with his Sunday jacket, and the secret intention of going a-sparking.

He was creeping behind the garden wall, with one hand steadying his hat and the other his pockets, — stuffed with green corn designed for roasting and eating with the Widow Blynn's pretty daughter, — when a voice called his name.

It was the voice of Cephas Boxton. Now, if there was any one Tip hated, it was "that Cephe;" and this for various reasons, the chief of which was that the Judge's son did, upon occasions, flirt with Miss Nancy Blynn, who, sharing the popular prejudice in favor of fine clothes and riches, preferred, apparently, a passing glance from Cephas to all Tip's gifts and attentions.

"Tip Tansley!" again called the hated voice.

But the proprietor of that euphonious name, not choosing to answer, remained quiet, while young Boxton, to whom glimpses of the aforesaid hat had been visible, stepped noiselessly to the wall and looked over.

"If it isn't Tip, what is it?"

And Cephas struck one side of the distended jacket with his cane. An ear of corn dropped out. He struck the other side, and out dropped another ear. At the same time, Tip, getting up and endeavoring to protect his pockets, let go his hat, which fell off, spilling its contents in the grass.

"Did you call?"

"Do you pretend you didn't hear, with all those ears?"

"I was hunting for a shoestring! I — I got to go over by the back pastur', and I took the corn along to feed the cattle — 'cause they hook."

"I wish you were as innocent of hooking as the cattle are. Go and saddle Pericles."

Tip moved off toward the stable, his pockets dropping corn by the way, and presently called out from the door, "Hoss 's ready!"

But instead of leading Pericles out, he left him in the stall, and climbed up into the hayloft to hide.

From the fact that Pericles was ordered, he suspected that Cephas likewise purposed paying a visit to Nancy Blynn. He lay under the dusky roof, chewing the bitter cud of envy, and now and then a stem of new-mown timothy, till Cephas entered the stall beneath.

"Are you there, Cephas?" presently said another voice — that of the Judge himself, who had followed his son into the barn. "Going to ride, are you?" and the Judge began to polish off Pericles with wisps of straw. "I luf to rub a colt, it does 'em so much good. Tip don't half curry him."

"Darned if I care!" muttered Tip.

"Cephas," — rub, rub, — "if you're going by Squire Stedman's, I'd like to have you call and git that mortgage."

"I don't think I shall ride that way, father."

Rub, rub. "If you're going up on the mountain, I wish you'd stop and tell Colby I'll take those lambs."

"I'm not sure I shall go as far as Colby's."

"Folks say — h'm! — you don't often get further than Widow Blynn's when you travel that road. I've kind o' felt as though I'd ought to have a little talk with you about that matter. They've got up the absurd story that you are going to marry Nancy."

"I must confess, father, the idea has occurred to me that Nancy — would make me — a good wife."

It is impossible to say which was most astonished by this candid avowal, the Judge, or Master Tip Tansley. Tip had never once imagined that Cephe's intentions regarding Nancy were so serious, and now the awful conviction was forced upon him, that if his rival wished to marry her, there was not the ghost of a chance for him.

"Cephas, you stagger me! A young man of your edecation and prospects — "

"Nancy is not without some education, father."

"No doubt, no doubt; and I hain't anything agin Nancy. She's a good girl enough, fur's I know. But reflect on't: you might marry 'most any girl you choose."

"So I thought; and I choose Nancy;" and Cephe started to lead out Pericles.

"I wish the hoss 'u'd fling him and break his blasted neck!" snarled the devil in Tip's heart.

"Don't be hasty; wait a minute, Cephas. You know what I mean: you could marry rich. Take a practical view on't. Get rid of these boyish notions. Jest think how it'll look for a young man of your cloth to go and marry the Widow Blynn's daughter — a girl that takes in sewing!"

"I hear she does her sewing well."

"S'pose she does. She'd make a good enough wife

for some such fellow as Tip, no doubt," — Tip's ears tingled, — "but I thought a son o' mine would a' looked higher. Think of you and Tip after the same girl!"

"The trouble seems to be simply this, father: you don't wish me to marry a poor girl. And I assure you I'd much rather please than displease you."

"That's the way to talk, Cephas! That sounds like."

"Well, what will you give to make it an object?"

"Give? Give you all I've got, of course. What's mine is yours, — or will be, some day."

"That isn't the thing. I want money now, for a particular purpose. Give me five thousand dollars, and it's a bargain."

"Pooh! pooh!" said the Judge.

"Very well; then stand aside, and let me and Pericles pass."

"No, no, you shan't! Let go the bridle. I'd ruther give ten thousand."

"Give me ten, then!"

"I mean — don't go to being wild and headstrong, now! I'll give ye a thousand, if nothing else will satisfy ye."

"I'll divide the difference with you. I'll say three thousand; and that, you must own, is cheap enough."

"It's a bargain." And Tip was thrilled with joy.

"But I wish to ask, Can I, for instance, marry Melissa More? Next to Nancy, she's the prettiest girl in town."

"But she has no position. The bargain is, you are not to marry *any poor girl*, and I mean to have it in writing. So pull off the saddle, and come into the house."

Tip Tansley, in a terrible state of excitement, waited until both had left the barn, then slipped down the stairs, gathered up what he could find of the scattered ears of corn, and set out to run through the orchard and across the fields to the Widow Blynn's cottage.

"Good evening, William," said Mrs. Blynn, opening the door, with her spectacles on her forehead. "Come in; take a chair."

"Guess I can't stop. How's all the folks? Nancy to hum?"

"Nancy's up-stairs; I'll speak to her. *Nancy! Tip is here!* Better take a chair while you stop."

"Wal, may as well; jest as cheap settin' as standin'. Pooty warm night, kind o' — " Tip raised his arm to wipe his face with his sleeve; upon which an ear of that discontented tucket took occasion to tumble upon the floor. "Hullo! what's that? By gracious! if tain't green corn! Got any fire? Guess we'll have a roast."

"Law me! I thought your pockets stuck out amazin'! I hain't had the fust taste of green corn this year. It's real kind o' thoughtful in you, Tip; but the fire's all out, and we can't roast it to-night, as I see."

"Mabby Nancy will. Ain't she comin' down? Any time to-night, Nancy. You do'no' what I brought ye!"   .

Now, sad as the truth may seem, Nancy cared little what he had brought, and experienced no very ardent desire to come down. She sat at her window, looking at the stars, and thinking of somebody who she had hoped would visit her that night. But that somebody was not Tip; and although the first sound of his footsteps had set her heart fluttering, his near approach, breathing fast and loud, had given her a chill of disappointment, and she now much preferred her own thoughts, and the moonrise through the trees in the direction of Judge Boxton's house, to all the green corn, and all the green lovers, in town.

Her mother, however, who believed as much in being civil to neighbors as she did in keeping the Sabbath, called again, and gave her no peace until she had left the window, the moonrise, and her romantic dreams, and descended into the prosaic atmosphere of Tip and his corn.

How lovely she looked to Tip's eyes! Her plain, neat calico gown, enfolding a wonderful little rounded embodiment of grace and beauty, seemed to him an attire fit for any queen. But it was the same old, sad story over again, — although Tip loved Nancy, Nancy loved not Tip.

She discouraged the proposition of roasting corn, and otherwise deeply grieved her visitor by intently working and thinking, instead of being sociable. At length a bright idea occurred to Tip.

"Got a slate and pencil, Nancy?"

The widow furnished the required article. He then found a book, and, using the edge of the cover as a rule, marked out the plan of a game.

"Fox 'n' geese, Nancy. Ye play?"

And, having picked off a sufficient number of kernels from one of the ears of corn, and placed them on the slate for geese, he selected the largest he could find for a fox, stuck it upon a pin, and proceeded to blacken it in the flame of the candle.

"Which 'll ye hev, Nancy? Take your choice, and

gim me the geese, then beat me if you can. Come!
won't ye play?"

" O dear, Tip! what a tease you are! Get mother
to play with you."

" She do' wanter. Come, Nancy; then I'll tell ye
suthin' I heer'd jes' 'fore I come away; suthin' 'bout
yeou."

" About me?"

" Ye'd 'a' thought so! Cephe an' the ol' man
they had the all-firedest row, I tell yeou. Cephe he
was comin' to see ye to-night, but he won't! he·
won't!"

" William Tansley, what do you mean?"

" I guess I know! By jingoes!— Cephe, he was
startin' off, — I'd saddled the hoss for him, — but the
ol' man he stopped him; an' Cephe was goin' to ride
right over him, but the ol' man got his dander riz —
he was tu much for him; he jerked Cephe off 'm that
hoss, and there they had it, rough-an'-tumble, lickety-
switch, hand over fist, heels over head, right on the
barn-floor, while I stood by to see fair play; till
bimeby Cephe he giv in, an' said, ruther'n hev any
words, he'd promise never to come and see ye agin,
if the ol' man 'ud give him three thousan' dollars.
An' the ol' man said 'twas a bargain. Anything to
keep peace in the family."

" Is that true, Tip?"

" True as I live an' breathe, an' dror the breath of
life, an' hev a livin' bein'!"

" Jest as I always told you, Nancy. I know how
'twould be. I felt sartin Cephas couldn't be depended
upon. His father never 'd hear a word to it, I always
said. Now, don't go to feelin' bad, Nancy, an' makin'

yerself sick. It 'll all be for the best, I hope. Now don't, Nancy, don't, I beg an' beseech!"

"What ye think now o' Cephe Boxton, hey?" said Tip, twisting his neck about, and thrusting his nose almost into Nancy's face.

A stinging blow on the ear rewarded his impertinence, and he recoiled so suddenly that his chair went over, and threw him sprawling on the floor.

"Gosh all hemlock! What's that fur, I'd like to know,—knockin' a feller down!"

"Why, Nancy! how could you? Hurt you much, William?"

"Not much; only it made my elbow sing like all Jerusalem! She thinks I'm lyin' tew her. Never mind; she'll find out. Where's my hat?"

"Ye ain't goin', be ye, William? Don't be in a hurry: I wouldn't."

"I guess I ain't wanted here. Ye can keep the green corn: dumbed if I want it. Good night, Mis' Blynn."

Tip fumbled with the latch, and made a show of buttoning his coat, giving Nancy time to relent. But she maintained a cool and dignified silence over her sewing, and, as nobody urged him to stay, he reluctantly departed.

For some minutes Nancy continued to sew intently and fast, her flushed face bowed over her seam: then suddenly her eyes blurred, the needle shot blindly hither and thither, and the quickly drawn thread snapped.

"Nancy, Nancy, don't! I beg of ye, now don't."

"O mother! I am so unhappy! What did I strike poor Tip for? He didn't know any better. I am always doing something so wrong! He couldn't have made up all that story. Cephas would have been here to-night, I know he would."

"Poor child! poor child! why couldn't you hear to me? I always told you to be careful and not like Cephas too well. But maybe he'll come to-morrow, and explain things."

The morrow came, but no Cephas. Day after day of loneliness to poor Nancy, night after night of watching and despair, and still no Cephas.

One evening it was stormy; Nancy and her mother were together in the plain, tidy kitchen, both sewing, and both silent, when, suddenly, amid the sounds of wind and driving rain, came a knock at the door. Nancy started with a wild look; but it was only Tip.

"Good evenin', all the folks. I'd no idee it rained so. Goin' by, thought I'd step in. Ye mad, Nancy?"

Nancy's heart was too much softened to cherish any resentment, and she begged Tip's pardon for the blow.

"Wal! I d'n' know what I'd done to be knocked down for; though I s'pose I dew, tew. But I guess what I told ye turned out about so — didn't it, arter all?"

"Don't, Tip! Don't ye see? ye make her feel awful bad!"

But Tip had come too far through the darkness and rain, with an exciting piece of news, to be easily silenced.

"Hain't brought ye no corn this time, for I didn't know as ye'd roast it, if I did. Say, Nancy! Cephe an' the ol' man had it agin to-day; an' the Judge he

forked over them .three thousan' dollars. I was to
work in the garden, an' seen 'em through the lib'ry
winder. Judge was only waitin' to raise it. Real
mean in Cephe, s'pose ye think. Mabby t'was; but,
linkum-vity! three thousan' dollars is a tarnal slew
o' money."

Hugely satisfied with the effect of this announce-
ment, Tip sprawled in his chair, and chewed a stick.
"Saxafrax,—want some?" He broke off a liberal
piece with his teeth, and offered it to Nancy. " Say!
ye needn't look so thunderin' mad. Cephe has sold
out, I tell ye; an' when I offer ye saxafrax, ye may as
well take some."

He was urging her to accept it,—'twas " re'l
good," 'twas "lickin' good,"—when the sound of
hoofs was heard; a halt at the gate; a voice saying,
" Be still, Pericles!" footsteps, and a rap at the door.

" It's Cephe! If he should ketch me here! I—I
guess I'll go! Confound that Cephe, any way!"

Nancy, all in a flutter, made her escape by the
stairway; observing which, the bewildered Tip—
who had indulged a frantic thought of leaping from
the window, to avoid a meeting with his dread rival—
changed his mind, and rushed after her, scrambling
up the dark stairway just as Mrs. Blynn admitted
Cephas.

Nancy did not immediately perceive what had occurred; but presently, amid the sounds of rain on
the roof and wind about the gables, she heard the
unmistakable, perturbed breathing of her luckless
lover.

" Nancy! where be ye? I 'most broke my head
agin' this blasted beam!"

"What are you here for?"

"Coz I didn't want him to see me. I *did* give my head the all-firedest tunk!"

Cephas, in the mean time, had entered the neat little parlor, to which he was civilly shown by the widow.

"Nancy 'll be down in a minute."

Nancy, having regained her self-possession, appeared mighty dignified before her lover.

Cephas was amazed.

"What is the matter, Nancy? You act as if I was a peddler, and you didn't care to trade."

"You can trade, sir; you can make what bargains you please with *others;* but — "

"Nancy! what's this? What do you mean by bargains?"

"O, nothing! Only I am surprised that you are here to-night. I thought 'twas in the bargain that you were not to come and see me."

"Who under heavens has been telling you anything about that?"

"It is true, then, your father has offered you money?"

"He has, Nancy!"

"To buy you — to hire you — "

"Not to marry a poor girl; that's the bargain."

"And you have accepted!"

"I have; and what I have done is for your happiness as much as my own. He has given me three thousand dollars. I only received it to-day, or I should have come to you before. For this money is for you, Nancy!"

"You dare to offer *me* money, Cephas Boxton?"

"Don't you see? It is your dowry. I promised not to marry a poor girl; but I never promised not to marry you. Accept the dowry, and you are a rich girl, and — my wife, my wife, Nancy!"

What more was said or done I am unable to relate; for about this time there came a dull, reverberating sound overhead, followed by a rapid series of concussions, as of a ponderous body descending in a swift but irregular manner from the top to the bottom of the stairs.

It was Master William Tansley, who, groping about in the dark with intent to find a stove-pipe hole, at which to listen, had lost his latitude and his equilibrium, and tumbled from landing to landing.

Mrs. Blynn flew to open the stairway door; found him helplessly kicking, on his back, with his head in the rag-bag: drew him forth by one arm: ascertained that he had met with no injuries which a little salve would not repair: patched him up almost as good as new; gave him her sympathy, a lantern to go home with, and a kind good-night.

So ended Tip Tansley's unlucky love-affair; and I am pleased to add that his broken heart recovered almost as speedily as his broken head.

A month later, the parish parson was called to administer the vows of wedlock to a pair of happy lovers in the Widow Blynn's cottage: and the next morning there went abroad the report of a marriage which surprised everybody generally, and Judge Boxton more particularly. In the afternoon, Cephas rode home to pay his respects to the old gentleman, and ask him if he would like an introduction to the bride.

"Cephas!" cried the Judge, filled with wrath, smiting their written agreement, "look here. Your promise!"

"Read it, if you please, father."

"'In consideration,' began the Judge, running his eye over the paper, '. . . I do hereby pledge myself never to marry a poor girl.'"

"You will find, sir, that I have acted strictly according to the terms of our contract. And I have the honor to inform you that I have married a person who, with her other attractions, possesses the handsome trifle of three thousand dollars."

The Judge fumed, made use of an oath or two, and talked loudly of disinheritance and cutting off with a shilling.

"I should be very sorry to have you do such a thing," replied Cephas, respectfully; "but, after all, it isn't as though I hadn't received a neat little fortune with my wife."

A retort so happy, that the Judge ended with a hearty invitation for his son to come home and lodge his lovely incumbrance beneath the paternal roof.

Thereupon Cephas took a roll of notes from his pocket.

"All jesting aside, I must square a little matter of business with which my wife has commissioned me. She is more scrupulous than the son of my father, and she refused to have anything to do with me till I had promised to return this money to you."

"Fie, fie!" cried the Judge. "Keep the money. She is a noble girl, after all, — too good for a rogue like you!"

J. T. TROWBRIDGE.